The Color of Hope

The Color of Hope

A Novel by
Diane McBain

BearManor Media

2021

The Color of Hope

© 2021 by Diane McBain

All rights reserved.

Published in the United States of America by:

BearManor Media
1317 Edgewater Dr #110
Orlando FL 32804

bearmanormedia.com

Printed in the United States.

Typesetting and layout by John Teehan

ISBN—978-1-62933-826-2

In loving memory of my mother,
Cleo Ferguson McBain

My father,
Walter George McBain

My grandmother,
Edith McBain

My grandmother,
Katherine Ray

My aunt,
Dorothy McBain Albaugh

And, my dear deceased friend,
Tyran (Ty) Henderson

"They made us into a race and we made
ourselves into a people"

– Ta-Nehisi Coates

WHEN I WAS A YOUNG GIRL, a teacher told our class at school that white was the combination of all the colors in the rainbow and black was the absence of color. She was talking about how light rays behave, but the things she said made me angry and I disagreed with her because I had combined all of the colors in my paint box and they had come out black. So, I thought she was wrong. The color of white is lacking in any other hue or shade. The color of black is full of all the colors. Black is required for all other colors to have depth and variation of hue. That's what I told my teacher and, I remember, she smiled and told me I was right.

One

The extreme heat of the day bleached the landscape and perspiration bathed two men as they faced off. They were clearly at vast odds with each other. One man, Barnette Hester, was a young, outwardly well-off farmer, his station in life signaled by his jacket and crisp fedora. The other was a black laborer, Roger Malcomb, only twenty-four years old. He was tall and skinny, dressed in overalls with a stained-dirty shirt. He wore a cap on his head. Malcomb was drunk with rage.

The distinctions of class separated these two former playmates like a machete separates a stalk from its roots.

A hawk flew overhead cawing as if in warning of an impending disaster. Fields of white cotton loomed in the background crackling with the deep heat of the summer day.

"Goddam nigger! Come 'n git it, you black-ass no good." Hester owned the farm on which the two men stood and where they played as children only a few years before.

"There were a day when we played here as kids, but we've come a fer way from then," Roger Malcolm angrily replied. He held a knife, but Hester had his ace-in-the-hole, a pistol in his pocket. Both men were aware of the odds. They knew one would die today or would be badly wounded. Equal in age and strength, the two men dripped in perspiration from the hot sun and the enormous tension created between them.

"What yew done's unforgivable, Hester. M' wife belong to me. Yew soiled her," Malcomb accused.

"Yo woman is yew common-law wife and she free to do whatever she wants!"

"She didn't want yew!" The words spat out of Malcomb's mouth like fire. "Yew took her and raped her."

The entire Hester family stood near the door on the wrap-around porch. Ida, Hester's wife, came to the door, terrified for both men. The hatred that flamed between them was palpable to the dismayed family who watched.

Hester lunged at the legs of Malcolm which took him off-balance and decked him. They scuffled in the dirt road that fronted the house, each overcoming the other as they fought it out. The dust choked each man making the confrontation all the more vexing.

At last, the knife held by Malcomb rose in the sky as Hester reached for his pistol. The knife plunged into Hester's stomach and the force of it drove the blade into his intestines, taking the strength from him. His gun flew. Blood poured, covering the dirt beneath him, staining it a dark crimson and causing him to wretch.

The wife's screams were heard over the whole valley and reached the ears of the entire farm. Farm hands, their wives and children ran from their cottages, leaving noonday meals to discover where the scream came from.

"I'll kill 'em," shrieked Hester's brother as he moved after Malcomb, his arm caught by Ida.

"No, yew won't," she ordered decisively.

"No! No!" The others objected. "He has to pay! He's a damned nigga' and he has ta die!"

"No. Yew let the law take care of it," she continued. "We need yah here, not in a jail cell."

Soon, the Sherriff drove up and gathered Malcomb into the patrol car, his hands cuffed behind his back as the others, accompanied by the farm hands, angrily looked on.

July 23, 1946

It was several days later and the entire valley had heard the news. Hester was in a local Georgia hospital tenuously clinging to life while Malcomb sat in a jail cell. Rumors abounded in the valley located in Monroe, a major cotton-farming town some forty miles east of Atlanta.

Dorothy, Roger's woman, was at the cottage of her friends Mae Murry Dorsey and her husband, George, also a dirt-poor black laborer working the farm of Loy Harrison, another white Monroe farmer who needed workers for cotton harvesting. "We got 'ta git Roger out 'ta jail," Dorothy cried. "He was only defendin' m' honor! Yew know dat!" she demanded.

The summer air still bristled with a powerful heat as all three trudged to the main house on the property to confront Harrison.

"We come to git Malcomb outta jail, Dorothy pleaded. "Ya know yer short of hands and harvest time's right around tha corner." Dorothy's face prickled with perspiration as she pled her case to Harrison. "My husband's a good worker 'n yew know it."

Soon Harrison drove his yellow Chevy downtown to secure Malcolm's release with Dorothy, Mae and George in the car, all steaming with desperation. Harrison had agreed to make a deal with the sheriff, a common practice with cotton farmers allowing inmates to work off the amount of bail in the fields rather than rot in jail awaiting trial. The sheriff reluctantly agreed to the deal warning Harrison to make sure Malcomb was returned as soon as the harvest was done.

"Yew be sure he don't git away now, y' hear? Or, my ass will be in BIG trouble!" the sheriff asserted with all the certainty he felt in his gut. The townspeople would surely destroy him.

The day was getting late but the heat from the unremitting sun didn't abate as Harrison, with the two black couples in tow, drove out of the Monroe town on the way back to the Harrison farm. They approached a wood slat crossing called Moore's Ford Bridge, spanning the Apalachhee River. Its vapor hung in the air like a heavy shroud.

On the other side of the bridge stood a cadre of angry and armed white men, their fedoras crunched atop their heads, dressed in rolled-up shirts, some coldly chewing tobacco. The leader was an older man about sixty with a pot belly and white hair. He gnawed angrily on a cigar.

Squinting in the hot sun from inside his Chevy, Harrison drew a labored breath. "Oh Lord, here we go."

The men were menacing as they confronted the yellow Chevy, stopping it in its tracks. With nowhere to go, the group in the car was enveloped with terror as they found themselves surrounded by the armed whites.

"Where's that nigger boy that tried to kill my neighbor, Barnette Hester?" The leader howled into the Chevy.

"Yew can't take 'im. I just paid money fer 'is release. He gotta pay me back with 'is labor." Harrison's voice was shrill with fear.

"Yew a nigger lover, white boy?" Asked the leader.

"No, jist a farmer who needs hands," Harrison pleaded. "I paid good money."

"Too bad. No colored ass's gonna git away with stabbin' my friend and neighbor."

The men forced the car doors open and brutally dragged the Negros, both men and both women, from the car, throwing them onto the farm road. The dirt choked the air and strangled their nostrils.

"Git the rope and string 'im up," the leader demanded.

"My husban' was defendin' my honor!" Dorothy screamed.

He raised his hand against Dorothy and knocked her to the ground. The men sniggered at her bold insolence. "In fact, as long as we got 'um, why don't we just hang 'em all up.

"We don't got enough rope fer that," a short white man with the rope yelled as he tried to get the twine around Malcomb's neck. Malcomb was much taller and the man's effort was comical. The men roared with laughter at the sight.

"Tie 'em up then," ordered the leader.

"I know who yew are," Mae Murry yelled, "I've seen yew b'for. Yer Bar ..."

"No! No!" hissed Dorothy. "Shut up yer mouth," she urged her friend.

With help from the others, the man tied the group together as they screamed and whimpered in their terror, knowing what would come next.

Thunderous shots rang out in the searing hot summer afternoon leaving all four dying in pools of their own blood.

It wasn't long after the white murderers fled that townspeople, who knew a lynching was coming down, and some who had witnessed the carnage, came around to ogle the dead black laborers and their wives. One woman proudly held a tooth her boyfriend gave her and gleefully vowed to wear it on her charm bracelet.

Another young man, dressed in an Army uniform fresh from basic training, was fascinated. He had witnessed the whole event from a hiding place in a nearby grove of trees. Feeling as if he had been reborn on this gruesome day, he severed the finger of Malcomb, the man whose fate the other three had fallen heir to, palmed it so no one could see what he had done, and walked away whistling. His name was Zackary Hughes.

Two

The trip from Cleo Henderson's neighborhood in Watts to the address in Glendale, California, would take an hour and a half by rail and bus plus walking time. It would be another hour and a half back, not counting the problems of traffic. Cleo would board the Blue train at the Rosa Parks station at 103rd Street, where the old Pacific Electric used to be. Her mom told her that. The train passed by the projects. Along the way Cleo noticed block-long sections of homeless encampments. She got off at 7th and Flower in downtown Los Angeles, and then walked to Olive to catch the bus to Glendale.

On her walk, she noticed a lot of homeless people. One woman caught her eye. The woman, dressed in white shirt and slacks, carried a white sack, maybe a pillowcase, apparently filled with her life possessions. A shaggy dog, likely a Shiatsu, trotted behind her on a leash, his white whiskers and withers stained with dirt and oil.

There was so much strife in the world and Cleo knew she would always have to struggle. That was a part of her culture, the culture of being black in a white world. She only hoped she would not have to strive as the white woman with the little dog. She wondered how the woman had gotten there. She apparently enjoyed a much better lifestyle than the one she had now, and Cleo felt bad for her.

The long commute was a huge problem because it took Cleo away from her favorite job of rearing her young son, Jamal, now a six-year-old child. She knew her mom would do her best to keep an eye on him after school, but Edith was aging in ways she hadn't expected and Cleo worried the job of looking after Jamal would be too much for her. More than anything she wanted to afford to stay at home, to be the mom she dreamed of being. There was no way to make a living and be with her son.

Cleo's young age was the obstacle she faced as she awaited the public transportation that would take her to this new assignment. Men, young enough to be in Junior High and old enough to be her grandfather, plus everything in between, ogled her and her breasts as she walked toward the train station, making her feel conspicuous. She wished they wouldn't stare. A cop joined the chorus of onlookers and the fear made her want to flee. She just wanted to be seen and treated as human, not as a sexual object, not as a black person, not as a whore or whatever objectified symbol men came up with.

Cleo remembered when, as a teen, one of her friends came to school one day dressed like she wanted attention, notice from the boys. She and her high school friends had made a pact early on to marry as virgins, to stay away from sex. It had been hard to do as they grew older and their boyfriends would dump them for not putting out. When she fell for her future husband, Jesse Henderson, it had become impossible and when she got pregnant just before graduating, they did marry. But she had not kept her promise, not that any of the other girls did either. She found the temptations too great. Since, she had done better especially when it became obvious Jesse was playing around with other women. Her son, Jamal, depended on her and she was determined to be a good mom, no running around like some of her friends did, often getting stoned or drunk and landing in bed with some dude she'd never want to see again.

She knew very little about the man she was assigned to. Was his name Zackary Hughes? He was 94 years old and had suffered a stroke which made him unable to take care of himself. She wondered just how feeble he would be. Would she have to take him to the bathroom every time and maybe even wipe his butt? Probably this would be the case. She knew he was a white man, but that was all. White and ancient. What else would await her as she took on this task? She couldn't imagine it would be easy. Not everyone was openly prejudiced against black people, but at his age, it was unlikely he would have a good attitude about their differences.

She wondered if Zackary had been born in California or if, like most people, he had come from some other part of the country. If he came from the South, he could be trouble. She hoped not. She desperately needed this job and the ability to get along with Zackary was essential. If only she'd had time to finish her nursing degree, things would have been different. She could have gotten a job in a doctor's office or in a hospital, both positions preferable to the one she was taking now.

Marrying her high school boyfriend when they were barely out of school was a big mistake. Her son was born eight months later. Now she couldn't imagine aborting her baby; then it was a difficult decision.

Marrying Jesse Henderson, the father, was the only option. It hadn't been easy but she managed to make her way into nursing school when Jamal was three. Before she had a chance to graduate, the marriage was over and now she had to work. Jesse had never been much of a wage earner and the divorce netted her nothing in the way of alimony or child support.

Jesse had been her first love. They had met in high school and she had fallen in love immediately without any thought about what she might be in for. He was hard to resist. He was handsome, tall and slender, wore dreadlocks, and instead of dressing like the other kids, he wore clothes more suitable to an ethnic culture—long white cotton pants tied by drawstrings, and a long-sleeve white cotton Nehru shirt. He had studied stuff on the Internet and wanted to be more like his ethnic ancestors. Cleo thought that was really hot. He even wore beads around his neck and leather bracelets. Everyone in her class thought he was killer hot. All the girls thought he was the best catch around and most campaigned for his attention. When he went for her, she felt truly special like an African princess. She didn't know that he kept a lot of the girls around, and women later when they were married. He'd never given them up. Jesse once told her that his African ancestors were more real about sex; they kept harems, had many marriages at once. Of course, the women didn't do such things. That was entirely reserved for the men. It was sexist in its soul. Jesse said he had a strong libido and had to satisfy his need, that one woman could never be enough for him.

He left her with few choices. She had to divorce him; he wasn't spending any time on supporting her and Jamal, always chasing after some dream or other. Quitting school and going to work was her best option, so she took it and now it was taking her to Glendale, a sleepy municipality near downtown LA.

Finally reaching the bus at Olive Street, she found it was unimaginably crowded. People were practically hanging out the windows like she'd heard folks did in other overcrowded countries. Cleo hoped the transit home would be less congested than this one. It was stuffy and uncomfortable. The heat was oppressive, the air conditioning apparently not working.

She struggled to find an empty seat when suddenly a young man rose to get off at the next stop. Grabbing the plastic bench, she sat down hard noticing a sharp pain as it travelled down her leg. The sweat trickled down the side of her face. Thankfully, she had worn her hair in a tight bun at the back of her neck and her work clothes were a light cotton. Nevertheless, she perspired profusely hoping her uniform would not show unsightly stains under the arms. Phyllis at the agency had stressed Hughes was fussy about cleanliness. She also wished she had brought along a book to read or a puzzle to absorb the enormous amount of time it would take to get there. Another nagging thought— she hoped her large breasts that hung down nudging themselves out from under the bra, would stop sweating and making her uncomfortable; she could feel little trickles of perspiration. The summer air was too hot and there was little she could do about it. She wondered if those panty liners she'd seen at the grocery store, the ones her mom wore to absorb light bladder leaks, might be a solution to the perspiration under her breasts. It was a possibility and she decided to borrow some from Edith to see if they worked.

At long last, the bus arrived at her destination and she was able to wrestle herself from its innards, pushing forward through the mass of bodies now beginning to thin out with each stop.

Her memory of Glendale was its alleged whiteness. It had been overwhelmingly white and middle class in the past, even had "sunset laws" which meant people of color, like her, had to leave Glendale before the sun set, but now sported a mixed population of white folks and Armenians. The Armenians had moved in as they migrated from their torn country to the United States. Why they had chosen Glendale as a preferred destination was a mystery, although the town was very appealing with its tree-lined streets and abundant neighborhoods.

Glendale was nestled up against mountainous hills that rose at the end of the main street called Brand Boulevard, protecting the town like a baby's blanket. Tall buildings rose along the boulevard competing with the mountainous background. Old lamp posts lined the thoroughfare which oddly gave the modern city a quaint feeling.

Actually, Cleo found Glendale to be much more pleasing than Watts could ever be, even with its famous Watts towers, seventeen spires that reached for the sky, an impressive construction that became a monument to the African American community that grew there.

Glendale was bustling and bursting with Armenians everywhere. There were a lot of white folks, too, but they seemed to be the older population, the ones left behind when people moved away making room for the newcomers. Watts was Watts and Glendale was Glendale. They were very different in their populations, even now that Armenians had moved into Glendale and Hispanics were moving in to south central LA.

Watts was so over-crowded with homes squeezed together, leaving very little air in between; Cleo found it was hard to breathe there. Here the houses were huge and the lots spread out, leaving a good space between the homes providing privacy. Unlike in her neighborhood, the telephone cords were hidden among trees or placed underground where they couldn't be seen. In Watts, entire districts looked like they were strung together with lines woven everywhere like random spider webs. Here, there were few fences, nice ones more like the proverbial picket-fences in old-fashioned movies and American lore. In Watts, every house had a fence, usually barbed-wire, chain-link or tall metal bars. They made the place look like little individual fortresses stuffed together like asparagus spears in a can.

Finally, after getting lost, she found the street she wanted and made her way to the house on yet another tree-lined avenue. It was a large and charming two-story Spanish-style with white stucco and red tile roofing plus a tall bay window in the front. The lot looked to be at least a half-acre. A giant oak tree, ancient and gnarled, sat in front of the residence providing shade. The walkway to the house was cement slabs surrounded by red brick. Here, she felt like she could breathe.

She approached the giant front door and rang the bell. A young blond man answered, a boy really, about eighteen with hair that spiked on top of his head. The sides of the haircut were very short, almost shaved away and he had tattoos peeking out from under his shirt. It was a clean white button-down with the sleeves rolled up revealing images of snakes. He wore Levis, even with the hot weather. She guessed the place he worked for required he dress in something other than Tee-shirts and shorts. He was tall and lanky with a menacing stare.

"Oh, hello," he said with that edge of disrespect she had come to associate with white folk. She decided to overlook it.

"Hello, I'm Cleo Henderson. Does Zackary Hughes live here? I'm his new caretaker. The agency sent me...."

"Yeah," he interrupted. "I know who you are. You're late. We were expecting you fifteen minutes ago."

"I had a hard time finding the house from the bus stop. Sorry, I didn't mean to be late. It won't happen again. You can't be Zackary. You aren't old enough."

" 'Course not," he said with a tone of derision. "He's in the family room in the back. I'm late for my job. So, later." With that he pushed past her out the door grabbing a bicycle that leaned against the porch wall. She hadn't noticed it before, but wasn't surprised it was his transportation.

Moving to the family room down the hall from the foyer, Cleo could smell the scent of fresh coffee as she found Zackary Hughes, old and withered like the ancient Oak tree that stood in front of the house. He sat watching the flat-screen television from his recliner, covered in a blanket from his chin to his toes, the cup of steaming coffee on a small table next to his chair. His hair was thin, almost non-existent and his skin wrinkled like—well, the bark on the old Oak tree.

He looked up at her, surprised. "I didn't expect a nigger." His gravelly speech had a latent southern accent.

"I beg your pardon," she responded with pique. "I may be a Negro, but I am no 'nigger,' as you put it."

"I'll put it however I want," he groused. "I didn't expect a nigger. I asked for a white woman. I don't care what she looks like, I just want someone of the same skin color and species that I am."

"Well, Mr. Hughes, I'll leave then," she responded with pique.

"No, you can't do that. I'll be alone and I can't be alone."

"I was told you are ninety-four years old and infirm. It appears you can't walk either judging from the wheelchair propped next to you." The chair was folded and leaned against a wood-paneled wall. It looked well-worn, the chair *and* the wall.

"No, I can't walk without help either." His tone was patience with an edge to it. "You will have to take me to the bathroom when I need to go. You'll have to wipe my butt, too. I hope that isn't too much for you."

"Of course not. I've wiped many butts," she lied. "In my business it is often a requirement."

"Well, that's good. You can have a trial period and if you work out, I will keep you."

Cleo felt put out by his blatant racism. "Yes, Mr. Hughes. I have a trial period, too, and I will remain in your employ if I feel comfortable doing so." Her response elicited scorn. She was uncertain she could refuse to work for him, but she meant what she said. This man would be a challenge, that was certain.

"The kitchen is through that door." He indicated with his right hand where she was to go. "I want some breakfast. The kid doesn't know how to cook anything. I hope you do."

"Of course, I do. I have a six-year-old at home and a mother. I cook for them both."

"Your mother lives with you?" He asked.

"Yes, and she takes care of my boy while I work. My father died a couple of years ago and she has been invaluable to me as I have been going to nursing school. I couldn't do what I do without her."

"Oh," he responded curtly. "So, there's no boyfriend, I take it."

"I haven't had time for dating for some years, since my husband left me soon after our son was born." She wasn't sure she should have offered so much information.

"I will need you full time without poor concentration. Men take up too much of a woman's attention."

"You will receive my full care and consideration." She moved toward him with her hand extended. "My name is Cleo Henderson. Do you suppose we can forge a working relationship?"

He refused the gesture, reached for the remote control and pushed the button for the TV, again with his right hand.

Feeling uncomfortable with his refusal to shake hands, she left him sitting there while she went into the kitchen.

The kitchen was efficient. It had all of the necessary implements and appliances which were dated from the 1970s or 80s. She would learn that they all worked fine. She wondered if some woman, a wife perhaps, had been involved before. She'd been told that all the relatives this man had were gone now and he was desperate for the help. Good, she thought. She was desperate, too, needing the work.

When she was finished cooking his breakfast—scrambled eggs, bacon and toast—she returned to the family room where he sat unmoved and asleep. She assumed he couldn't move without her and wondered how long it had been since he had been to the bathroom. That thought brought up another question—did he wear diapers? She figured he must. Oh boy, changing diapers on a grown man was something she didn't relish. She wondered how cooperative he would be and who had been attending to him before she arrived. The boy didn't look like the type to be changing diapers.

He startled awake. "You're back. I need to pee."

She placed the plate of food on the coffee table. He was heavy and not very co-operative. He'd had a stroke the year before, he said, and was paralyzed on the left side. Cleo wondered if she would be able to handle him on a regular basis. Her workout routine had suffered while she was in nursing school. This would be difficult, but she was sure she would be able to cope with him, even with his foul personality.

When they returned from the bathroom, she placed him back in his recliner and took up the food. "Can you feed yourself or will I have to do that too?"

"Of course, I can feed myself. I'm not totally helpless." Again, with his right hand, his left tucked neatly by his side under the blanket, he took up his fork and dug in.

"These eggs are cold now. You'll have to warm them up. I can't stand cold food." The fork clanked on the tray when he slammed it down.

"I didn't see a microwave in the kitchen. Do you have one?"

"No, of course not. I don't eat food that has been warmed or cooked in one of those damnable machines. They give you cancer, you know."

"No, I didn't know that. It must be an 'old wife's' tale you heard."

"I don't engage in fantasies. I know what I'm talking about. You will have to cook this over again."

He was obviously a stubborn old coot. She returned to the kitchen and began the cooking process, saving the food he wouldn't eat for her lunch.

During the latter part of the day when Zackary was napping, she had a little time to explore the house beyond the family room, dining area, kitchen and his bedroom which were all located on the first floor. Apparently, other bedrooms were upstairs, but no one seemed to venture up there anymore. At least, that was what Zackary had said about it. She wasn't about to go up there just yet. It looked dark and foreboding. But the living room in the front of the house, and quite separate from everything else, was a mystery, too. She wanted to see what it was like.

The area was quite lovely. It was obvious a woman had dominated this part of the house at one time. It was kept clean, but abandoned. The furniture was French-provincial, the wood framing creamy-white and ornate. The walls were covered with a pretty white and silver brocade wallpaper. Large original oil-paintings dominated. A large fireplace, surrounded by brick with an ornate white mantle, was in the center of the room. There had been no updating for some time.

Cleo had never been in a room like it before and she felt truly overwhelmed by its beauty. There were lovely porcelain vases and other items, such as ivory statues from Asian countries, French figurines and Italian sculptures. She wondered if these were treasures that had been brought back from these destinations. It was truly impressive. She felt incredulous and awe-struck. There had been such places depicted on television, but this was the first time she had seen these things in reality. The size and spaciousness of the room, too, made her feel small and insignificant.

On the front table near the window, all of the family photos were displayed. She noticed the people were very light; their hair was either silver-blond or a light brown. Of course, the older members, now long in the grave, had gone white or were quite bald while the children had blonde curls all over their heads. They were a handsome group of people. She guessed which ones were pictures of Zackary as a young man. He was good-looking, tall, slender and had spent some time in the military. Then as time went on, his features grew older and finally he was a very old man. The last photo of him and his wife, now deceased, showed two old people who were obviously very proud standing in front of the house Zackary now occupied. He had told her his youngest son was the last to die and leave him 'the last one standing', as he put it. The son had done a lot to make his father's life bearable in his old age. It was hard to know, out of the myriad of photos of his sons, nephews, cousins, etc., which were the most direct relatives, the children of Zackary and his wife. It had at one time been a huge clan of people, but they all had died. It was no wonder the man needed full time care from strangers.

When she turned around to view the rest of the space, Cleo was surprised by the baby grand piano, a Steinway, tucked in the corner of the room. It was beautiful, shiny and kept in the best condition. She opened the lid and ran her fingers lightly across the keys. Memories of piano lessons and practicing until her hands felt they would fall off, flooded her mind. She remembered her fingers and hands aching afterwards as if she had been climbing a sheer mountain face. Her dreams were filled with her instructor chasing her through long hallways and cornering her up against a piano. The teacher had been her father's sister, Aunt Dorothy, and she loved her, but felt trepidation when she heard the doorbell ring knowing the time had come for another lesson.

The woman put her through her paces, day after day, until the notes and sounds were hammered into her head. She had forced Cleo to reach beyond each level as she achieved it, giving her classical pieces to play and master. She was not allowed to play current, more jazzy pieces or rock 'n roll, heavy metal, hip hop and certainly not rap, the music she thought her friends would like; rap, the poetry of the Negro heart. Aunt Dorothy thought that kind of music was disrespectful. She simply didn't understand. Cleo didn't think it was her fault; she was only a product of her time and culture. And, Cleo had her own ideas.

It had been a rigorous program and Cleo stuck with it until finally she begged her mother to stop the lessons. Aunt Dorothy was furious with her. She thought Cleo had real talent and would be a fine piano player if she kept it up. But at that point, Cleo was entering teenhood and was only interested in her friends, and she was beginning to take an interest in boys. Classical music just didn't fit in. Cleo always thought she would have continued the lessons if her aunt hadn't been so strict about the style of music. It was a big disappointment for both of them.

At six in the evening, after Zackary had his evening meal, an older woman, small and plump with white hair, a mouthful of crooked teeth and dressed in nursing attire, arrived at the door to relieve Cleo from her duties. It took another 45 minutes for the two of them to get Zack cleaned up and into his chair to watch his evening TV.

The night-nurse's name was Elsie Larson. The name Elsie suited her perfectly. Cleo thought she was a lovely person and had the patience of a saint. Elsie wore a crucifix on a chain around her neck and told her she was Catholic. Cleo thought she looked like a nun with her short-cropped white hair framing a full face.

Cleo ran to the bus stop hoping to catch the last bus scheduled to go downtown so she could catch the train to her neighborhood. By the time she boarded the transportation back to Watts it was well past 7:00 p.m.

The day had been as hard as she thought it would be. Mr. Zackary Hughes was impossible to get along with. The old man had an offensive way of thinking and it would be hard for her to absorb his attitude without wanting to correct him. He thought all kinds of things that simply were not true, negative things against all ethnic folk and especially against black people. He would be a major challenge to her love of mankind, the kind of love her mom tried to instill in her even though there was much evidence that love was meaningless to many. It certainly was meaningless to the old man.

There were few in the world who could 'hold a candle', as he put it, to his now deceased wife who apparently was an angel with no faults. She must have been awesome to have put up with Zackary Hughes for a lifetime.

With another hour to kill, Cleo ruminated about the day. She had to change Zackary's diaper after his nap and he complained, "I can't believe I am allowing a nigger's dirty hands to touch me."

"These hands have been freshly washed, sir, so you won't have to worry about that," she'd replied defiantly and with a great deal of patience.

Cleo had to turn her mind away from Zackary just so the anger arising in her would not take hold and make her want to refuse to work for him. She had to work and she couldn't become known at the agency as one who was unwilling to take on a white client. She had to find a way to feel differently, as least temporarily.

She chose to focus on the piano at the Hughes' residence. It was a beautiful instrument. It was doubtful Zackary had been the one to play. His wife must have been a good player to have such a lovely Steinway in the house, and she wondered if her children had learned as Cleo had. They might have had a teacher come in to teach them, maybe an aunt like her Aunt Dorothy. Or, maybe the mother taught them herself. It wasn't likely all the children had taken to the art; her brother, Whitey Walter, as she like to call him because of his lighter skin, didn't like the lessons and had quit early in the process. Cleo was curious, though, and wanted to ask Zackary about his wife and children and whether they played the piano. Cleo felt a kind of kinship with his wife even though she had no idea how the woman felt about race.

Three

AFTER CLEO LEFT, Angus Dunne, the grocery boy, stood at the front door of the Hughes' house. Viewing the huge knob at the center of the oak door, he knocked hesitantly not sure if he should be there. It was the first time he had taken Zackary up on an invitation to 'come by anytime.' Any time could mean earlier in the day and he wondered if Zackary was in bed yet. Remembering his grandfather when he lived with his family before he died, Angus thought the elderly man went to bed too early. He was usually put to bed around seven in the evening, even after having a long nap in the afternoon.

Angus rang the bell when there was no answer to his knock. Elsie finally came to answer his ring.

"What are you doing here, Angus? Isn't this a little late for you? You don't have any groceries to deliver, do you?"

"No ma'am. Zack… That is, Mr. Hughes told me to come by anytime. I think he wants some male company."

"Oh. Sure. I suppose that might be a good idea. He's in the family room watching TV. Go on in. I'm busy with his nighttime medications." She waved him in and moved through the dining room toward the kitchen.

"Hello, Mr. Hughes. It's just me, Angus."

Zackary looked up, startled. He sometimes became disoriented and Angus' presence at this late hour confused him. "Oh, oh… Oh Sure, Angus. This is a surprise. What brings you here at this hour?"

"You mentioned you'd like to hang out with me some time, so I thought I'd come by tonight. I hope that's okay."

"Sure, sure. Come on in and sit on the couch here next to me. I was just watching Fox News. You know, they are the only news people you can count on these days."

"I don't watch the news much. I rely more on my Smart-phone. I can get the Internet and find the kind of stuff I like to watch." He sat down on the couch near Zack so he could hear him better, again thinking about his granddad who couldn't hear well.

"That right? Well, I suppose those new-fangled gadgets must be helpful since everyone uses them now."

"Yeah, I find it to be better than watching all that stuff on TV I don't care much about."

"You have to know where to look, that's all. And, I know where to look."

"I'm sure you do, sir."

"You know, you're a little different than most of the kids today. I don't get to see much about them, but most of what I do see, well, it's hard to watch. They seem to focus too much on niggers. You know what I mean?"

"Yeah, it's like they're the most important when they're not," Angus said with a definitive tone.

"I see you have some tattoos there, boy."

Angus was dressed in his casual clothes since he wasn't working. It was a hot summer evening; he wore a tank top and long khaki shorts. His arms and chest were covered with all kinds of images. He was proud to wear them, but his boss didn't like them, so he had to cover them up when he worked. "Yeah, I guess they pretty much sum up my life so far."

"So far? Where the hell do you suppose you'll put the rest of your life? It looks to me you're all filled up now."

"Yeah, I suppose so," Angus laughed. "There's room though. I have my back and legs, my butt too." He snorted.

"The snakes twisting around your arms, they're snazzy. Quite a touch."

"Oh yeah, I don't like some of the other choices for arms. I thought snakes slithering up and down would look hot. I had a snake I found up at the Kern River one summer when my family visited there. I caught him and took him home. He lived in a fish tank and I fed him live mice, which is the only thing he seemed to like. They couldn't be dead or he'd ignore them. His name was Kern, like the river. Mom made me get rid of him one day when Kern had escaped his enclosure and reappeared on the kitchen counter when mom was preparing something for dinner. Freaked her out. She screamed all the way to hell and back." They laughed.

"Do I see a Swastika, there boy?"

It was small and couched in the middle of the hair of a Raven-clad maiden. Her mane covered most of his upper body and the Swastika meshed in effectively. His dad had coached him not to be too obvious or he wouldn't be able to go some places with stuff like that showing.

"You noticed?"

"Well, sure. Who wouldn't?"

"If you could see under my shirt, you would see a tattoo etching of the president on my chest."

"How come you hide it?"

"Hoping to be careful. My dad cautioned me about it."

"I suppose the swastika isn't too noticeable. I noticed because that kind of thing interests me."

"Yeah, I was surprised to see you had a colored healthcare lady here today."

"She wasn't what I requested. I asked for a white woman, but they didn't have anyone like that available. These days, you have to take what you can get."

"I wouldn't put up with it if I was you, sir. You have a right to what you want."

"Healthcare workers are hard to find. I called several agencies and asked for white only. Most of them hung up on me. At least, the one I went with tried to work with me on it. They said they didn't have any whites available now and to try this one out. If she didn't work out, maybe they would have a better choice for me later."

"Yeah, I guess."

"Trouble is, they're taking over. You can't find white help much anymore. They're either niggers or Mexicans."

"Yeah, my dad says the white race is losing ground. He thinks by the end of this century, there won't be any white left."

"I think it could happen sooner than that!" Zackary's gravelly voice took on a note of grave concern and alarm. "I think it could happen as soon as mid-century. There may be whites but the colored people will be in control. Not good for us.

"We have to do something about it now, don't you think, Mr. Hughes?"

"I won't be alive to see it, so what happens after I'm gone doesn't matter to me much. But my grand-kids 'll have to deal with it and I'm worried. They say the change in the weather is more important, but I think it's the nigger problem that's going to ruin us—never mind a little hot weather."

"You sure could be right. My mom is terrified. She thinks they might come to live right here in our part of Glendale. Already some neighborhoods have 'em. There's nothing to keep 'em out any longer with the laws the way they are."

"You're right. Did you even hear about Tom Metzger? He's old now, but in his day, he did a lot for us. He came here to California just about the same time I did, after he got out of the Army. Probably for the same reasons, too."

"Oh yeah, I've heard of him. He was responsible for the White Aryan Resistance, the skin-head movement."

"Where're you from Angus?"

"I was born here at Glendale Memorial. But, my folks hail from Baltimore. They left because business was bad and there were always a lot of coloreds."

"Yep, they sure do got 'em there, alright. You hear about it all the time."

"What do you suppose it'll be like? I try to imagine what things will be like when I'm older. I want to get married and have kids, but it scares me to know they might have a tough time when they get big. I mean, there're places I won't go to now because of the niggers, and the Mexicans too. They let those bastards in all the time and it's hard to find any real estate without Mexicans."

"You plan to stay here in Glendale, don't you?"

"Oh sure. My folks will give me the house when they go. They've got money so I'm not too worried. My dad says he'll help me get a car of my own pretty soon, too. He lets me use his car sometimes, but I want one of my own so I don't have to depend on his. He wants me to go to a college close by, though. I guess I'll go to North Valley instead of Glendale College. I mean I want to get away from my folks so I can decide for myself what to do 'n stuff. You know, I mean about girls."

"Oh yeah! I remember those days. You got to sow your oats, boy." Zackary laughed heartily until he began to choke and hack.

"Are you okay, Mr. Hughes?" Angus asked, alarmed.

Elsie came in from the kitchen. "Aren't you through with the news yet, Mr. Hughes? You got 'a get to bed pretty soon."

"Ah, Elsie, leave me and Angus alone. We're having a good time," he grumbled. His chin dribbled with some spittle and she took a tissue to wipe it off.

"I guess it's okay. You have to deal with the lack of sleep if you don't get enough."

"God, I get plenty of sleep. What I don't get enough of is a good chat with someone more like me. We're boys, ya know, and we've got things to discuss."

"I'll leave you two alone then. Just let me know when." Elsie grabbed a book she'd been reading and headed for the living room.

Four

WHEN SHE FINALLY GOT HOME, Cleo barely had a moment with her son, Jamal. He was a lively six-year-old as curious as he was rambunctious with a full head of afro curls and an adorable turned-up nose, sparkling eyes, the whole works. The only issues were his two front teeth. The missing teeth were as much fun as a laughing baby. He was filled with questions she really couldn't answer comfortably about the old man. She covered her true feelings and told him Zackary was okay, which was barely true.

After she put Jamal to bed, read him a story and kissed his forehead good night, she wondered if Zackary Hughes was really okay at all. He was timeworn and that counted for a lot. His face was pinched and the lines that pleated his face were deep; his expression was one of great and enduring pain. One couldn't expect a person who had suffered so much loss to look happy or to be cheerful.

She headed down the stairs to visit with her mom, Edith. The woman who was thirty years older than Cleo, had grayed prematurely some years ago. Cleo thought a visit to the beauty shop was in order, not just a dye job and a new hairdo, but also a facial and maybe a makeup session so she could see how beautiful she is. Mom deserved to look her best and now that Cleo had work, she could fit such a visit into the budget. All she had to do was keep the job with the irascible old man.

The living room, though usually orderly, was bursting with toys and the rambunctious spirit of Jamal. Her mom had waited dinner to eat with Cleo and she was busy in the kitchen getting it prepared at table. The only table to eat at in the small house was in the kitchen. There was no dining room. Cleo threw most of the toys into the toy box and joined Edith. This was the time she most cherished, to sit with a glass of wine, the cheap variety, and visit with Edith while eating a meal she hadn't cooked herself.

After dinner, over a hot cup of tea they chatted. "Are you sure Jamal isn't too much for you, Mom?"

"Now honey, why would you ask such a question?" Edith countered, her pretty face broadening out into a wide unrepentant smile.

"You aren't as young as you used to be. I know you think you can take on an Army, but I can see you're tired."

"You are tired, too, Cleo. I can see it in your eyes."

"I did have a difficult day." She continued with her story about Zackary, the house, the grocery delivery boy and the nurse. She finished with the rides on the train and bus to and from. As she recounted all the details, she allowed a release of anxiety, letting out a big sigh at the end letting Edith know how tension ridden the whole experience had been.

"Of course, it was, honey," Edith replied. "The first day of any job is filled with tensions we never expect. I'm not surprised."

"But I haven't told you about Zackary's attitude toward black folks."

"Oh! He's an old white man who lives in Glendale, and you expect him to love people of color?"

"Well, no, I suppose not. I just found it to be so insulting. In this day and age, can't people at least be more civil?"

"No," Edith replied derisively. "I know men like that never get over their hatreds no matter what society tells them. And, by the way, who said racism has been wiped from the earth?"

"No one, of course," Cleo lamented chuckling. "But I was hopeful going in. The nurse, Elsie, I told you about, she didn't have anything prejudicial about her. *She's* white and old."

"Your expectations are a little overblown, wouldn't you say?"

"You're right, Mom. I just have a lot of hope."

"It's good to have hope, honey, but your expectations must be realistic or people will take advantage of you; ya hear?"

"Mom, you're being negative again and I wish you'd stop." Cleo's mind was racing with the stereotypes she hoped would be a part of the past by this time. As a teen, she had worked hard in civil rights causes that had become a feature of the confidence she had that things would change.

Cleo had spent a lot of time studying and thinking about African-American history during her high school days. It was appalling to realize how horrific it must have been to be thrust into the bowels of a slave ship with a lot of folks they didn't know. In Africa where her people came from, there had been tribes who were as different from one another as Saturn and Jupiter. None of them spoke the same language, had the same customs or even the same God. They were complete strangers to each other. Shackled and chained to people they couldn't talk to or relate to, must have been abysmal. The filth, vermin and untenable conditions of a slave ship was more than she had the resources to understand. Just the stench would be unbearable. She'd read there was no place to go to the bathroom. You just had to pee and shit where you were. People got sick and puked where they lay. There was no getting away from the person next to you no matter how you felt about it. People died in the middle of the night only to be discovered the next morning and left to rot there for another day or two before someone came and got them. Then, they were thrown into the ocean like a bag of garbage without any thought or respect for the dead. She had read about the moans as people struggled against their chains trying to put some space between them and the abhorrent conditions they found themselves in. The moaning was all that could be heard in the bowels of the ships.

The whole thing was unimaginable and Cleo wanted to do something in her life that would make a difference, in some way make it up to those poor folks who had to endure the crossings, and the treatment they got when they arrived on American shores. There was no Statue of Liberty for them, only being sold into slavery and working their lives away for some white guy and his family, suffering rape and flagellation that was unbearable for doing nothing but trying their best. There was nothing to look forward to, nothing to hope for. And, Cleo wanted hope to rule her life if at all possible.

The old spirituals often echoed through her head. "Ooh Lord, remember me."

"Speaking of hopefulness," Cleo was anxious to change the conversation, "How was life with Jamal, today?"

"I got him ready for day camp just in time for Willie when he came by," Edith replied, relieved she had accomplished her morning goal. Willie was the kid down the street who was older than Jamal. Willie was in his late teens and had agreed to walk him to the summer day camp they both attended at a park nearby.

"Good."

"Honey, you bet it was. Getting that child corralled enough to get his breakfast down is a huge chore. Keeping up with him when he got home, was equally challenging," Edith replied. "But I did it."

"After he changed his clothes, I let him go out to play with instructions not to wander very far from home."

"He followed your instructions?"

"Well, yes, he did, sort of."

"What is that supposed to mean?"

"Well, Mr. Hayes down the street brought him home after taking Kisha home first."

"Jamal was playing with Kisha next door? How did they end up down the street at the Hayes' residence?"

"Apparently, they had a little fun down there. Now don't freak out."

"Freak out? Why am I going to freak out?"

Edith measured her words. "Because honey, with your history, you may."

"Come on, Mom. Tell me the whole story."

"I'm getting around to it," Edith replied as she headed for the stove to pour more hot water into the pot for another cup of tea. "Patience is a virtue," she added. "Do you want more tea?"

"For heaven's sake, what happened?"

"I'll take that as a 'no,'" Edith responded. As she headed to her chair she continued. "Well, Mr. Hayes came to tell me Jamal had Kisha behind the garage, hidden so no one could see what they were doing." She sat down with a thud. "Kisha had all of her clothes off."

"What on earth?"

"Now, don't assume anything here. They are both young and you know they are both *only* children. They don't have sisters or brothers and curiosity apparently overwhelmed both of 'em."

"Curiosity? My son may be developing some horrible tendencies and you're attributing his actions to curiosity?"

"Yes, Cleo. I am sure it was all very innocent."

"I'm going to have a word with him first thing in the morning."

"Honey, now, don't do that. Your history makes you vulnerable to assuming the worst about this kind of activity."

"Rape does have such an effect, Mom."

"I'm just sayin', think before you speak. Don't go blaming him for things that have nothing to do with 'bad tendencies'. He is curious and he probably had all of Kisha's curiosity going for him as well."

"I dunno, Mom. He has to be warned not to do that kind of thing again. I can't have him going around the neighborhood taking girls' clothes off. The parents won't be so understanding."

Edith wiped her eyes with a tissue. "I suppose he needs to be stopped, of course."

"Did you say anything to him?"

"I only told him his mother would hear about it."

"How did he react to that?"

"He just got real quiet and went to his room. He's been in there ever since. Played his hip hop music and ate his dinner in there, too."

"I put him to bed, so I assume he's asleep by now," Cleo replied. "Maybe I should check to make sure."

"Check if you like, but I wouldn't bring this up tonight. And I sure wouldn't wake him up to confront him."

"No, Mom, I won't wake him up. In fact, 'I'll leave sleeping dogs lie,' she said pointedly.

"That's an odd way to put it."

"Maybe I'm not in a mood to talk to Jamal tonight," she sighed. "The old man has me wondering if I'll be able to deal with him over a long period of time."

"He sounds like a handful. I hope you can manage okay. Would you like some more tea to take to bed with you?"

"No, thanks. I'm swimming in too much now. Good night."

Five

CLEO DIDN'T SLEEP. She worried. She worried about her son, Jamal; she worried about her new job. She worried about the old man's attitude toward her and her race. She worried about Kisha and how she would grow up knowing she had taken her clothes off for Jamal. Was this some form of sexual abuse, as innocent as it may seem? How would the girl frame this event in her life as an adult? How would her son come to think of himself? Would he continue to be curious about what little girls look like without their clothes? Would that curiosity inform his decisions in adulthood? He was a bright boy and she was proud of that. But she worried about how he would grow up and become a man.

Before going to sleep, she thought about that horrible night when she was raped. He had been a white man, had cornered her behind the nursing school and without any concern for her protestations, raped her, thrown her to the ground, ripped her tights and thrust himself inside her. The painful recollections which always brought tears to her eyes never stopped and she wondered if they ever would. She wanted to report the incident but couldn't knowing she would be blamed. It was regretful and she did grieve it deeply, but couldn't bring herself to overcome her fear of the police and what they would do to her or if they would believe her. Nor did she feel secure going to the hospital even if she could get the evidence. How would they ever find her assailant even if they did take her seriously? She supposed the semen would be in their database, but what good would it do? She wasn't up to the repercussions and wanted to hide rather than tell anyone. The best she could do was tell Edith who was able to hear her words of assault with unimaginable calm and intelligent advice. She, too, thought it would be fruitless to call the authorities or go to the hospital.

After hours of pondering the untenable situation, Cleo finally fell off to sleep.

She woke up often with worries about money, about her mom, mostly about Jamal and about Zackary Hughes. Her endless reflections kept her from getting enough sleep all night.

When the alarm awoke her early the next morning, she was exhausted. Cleo didn't know how she would survive the whole day with the old man. She didn't even know how she would approach Jamal. The lively boy was up already and pulling her out of bed.

"Mom, come on! I loved summer camp and I want to get ready."

"That's exciting news, Jamal," she said as she tried to wipe the sleep from her face. Grammy didn't tell me about how you like camp so much."

"Gammy didn't like me much yesterday." His lower lip told her how he felt.

"So, she did tell me about you and Kisha behind the Hayes' garage. Why were you hiding like that?"

"I wasn't hiding. Kisha was."

"Did you ask her to take her clothes off?"

"She said she wanted to."

"Grammy told me about it and I am a little worried," Cleo admitted.

"Kisha did it." Jamal was agitated and defensive.

"Oaky. So, you had nothing to do with it? You know, it isn't okay to take your clothes off."

"I didn't do it," Jamal insisted.

"Did you tell Kisha not to?"

"No," he admitted. "I wanted to see what a girl looks like without her clothes on."

"Well, I'm glad you're being honest. But I don't want to hear that you have done this with any other girl. Do you understand me?"

He lowered his head. "Yeah. I understand."

"Good. Now let me get dressed and we'll have breakfast."

Cleo wasn't sure she would have the time to sit down to breakfast, but she wanted to spend more time with her son. She felt better now that the subject had been put to rest. At least, she could concentrate of the other problem of Zackary Hughes.

Having showered and dressed, Cleo headed downstairs to the kitchen where she found Jamal still in his pajamas playing with a toy car. Edith was admonishing him to finish eating his breakfast. "You won't be able to go to summer camp if you don't finish your cereal."

"I'll have a cup of coffee, Mom." Cleo sat down next to Jamal and picked up his spoon which sat next to the bowl. "Come on, Jamal, finish up so you can meet Willie and go to the park."

She dug the spoon into his cereal and held it up to his mouth.

"I can do it myself," Jamal said defiantly.

"Of course, you can, but will you?"

"Oaky, I'll finish it myself."

Her son was headstrong and she wondered how Edith would manage. She had done a good job with Jamal when Cleo was going to nursing school but he was older now and quite obstinate. Edith was older too, so time wasn't on Cleo's side. She hoped after a while she would be able to hire someone to come in for the afternoon hours to give Edith a break and maybe a time for napping.

Six

THE RIDE BACK to Glendale was just as harrowing as it had been the first morning so she expected it to always be difficult. But she managed to get to the house on time and the young man was waiting as she expected him to do every morning. He apparently was the fill-in between Elsie's nighttime attendance and her daytime arrival.

Soon she learned that Zackary liked to read the *Los Angeles Times* and the *Glendale_News Press* right after breakfast and it was her job to collect the papers from the front walkway and deliver them to him without the plastic outer coverings.

"I read this morning they're going to bring that abominable Black Lives Matter movement into the Glendale schools!" Zackary said with his usual uppity irascibility intact. "Can you imagine the trouble that's gonna cause?"

"Frankly, I think it's a good idea."

"Of course, you would." It didn't seem he could say anything about blacks without sounding angry or dismissive.

"I suppose there are plenty of prejudiced folks here in Glendale. I've always heard that," she replied.

"The Armenians have taken up the same ideas which is to their credit. I know a lot of people who moved out of Glendale because of the Armenians. But that group is fitting in quite nicely as it turns out."

"I think it is a good thing the Glendale School District wants to eradicate racism in the schools. It'll make things better for everyone."

"Don't count on it. There's plenty of people here who think the way I do. They aren't likely to put up with this new thing they have with Black Lives Matter." He brought up the fact that California had a slave law that allowed white folks to own Native Americans, especially children, up until 1937 when the law was abolished. "I was just a kid then." He spoke about white privilege, as if it was the nation's saving grace, with awe, and the Black Lives Matter movement with nothing but vitriol in his voice. Cleo wondered how easily she would be able to handle him.

"You know, the only reason I am able to tolerate you is that I need you." Zackary changed the subject. "I called the agency yesterday to ask if they had someone else they could send over and they didn't. That's the only reason you're here. Understand?"

Cleo swallowed her pride. "Yes, Mr. Hughes. I understand perfectly."

"We did have Negro servants when I was a child. I guess I can tolerate it again."

After reading his newspapers, he dozed off in the recliner. This gave Cleo time to clean up the room and get the morning dishes done before he woke up.

Seven

THE NEXT MORNING, Cleo didn't have time to eat or to get Jamal dressed. Leaving the chore to her mom, she ran to the train stop. For some incomprehensible reason the train was late. It was late to the stop in downtown, too, and Cleo had to run down Flower to Olive, but found the bus awaiting her. "Thank you," she said to the bus driver, surprised he had delayed leaving.

"You're welcome. I saw you running and I try to pick up my regulars so they can get to work on time."

"How do you know I'm a regular?" She asked.

"I've seen you before and you were running for my bus yesterday. Folks don't usually run unless it's important, like getting to work."

"That's insightful of you."

"I am working on being the best bus driver. It makes the job more interesting."

She laughed. "You are hoping for some accolades from your boss?"

"No. I just like to challenge myself in whatever I'm doing."

He had a Hispanic accent and she appreciated his attitude. "I think that's wise," she added as she paid the fair. "What's your name?" She asked before heading to a seat so he could get moving. Time was of the essence.

"Carlos. How nice that you asked."

"I'm Cleo. I noticed you're driving this bus in the morning and at night. Do you work that entire time?"

"No. I report in the morning at five and go home for a rest at eleven, just before lunch hour. Then, I report again at 4:00 p.m., until nine at night."

She heard and felt the swoosh of the bus doors as they closed behind her.

"Wow, that's quite a schedule. My dad was a bus driver for most of his working life. Finally, he was promoted to supervisor. He died a couple of years back."

"I'm sorry for your loss."

"I'll get to a seat so you can get going."

"Muchas gracias," he answered.

"De nada." Cleo didn't know much Spanish, but she was willing to speak what she knew.

When she arrived at the Hughes' residence, again, she was thankfully on time. The boy, as before—his name turned out to be Angus Dunne—answered the door and let her in. He didn't say anything, just grabbed his bike and headed down the street.

When she saw Zackary, she said: "He is a boy of few words," referring to the young man.

"He doesn't have much to say—to you." Already, he had his breakfast. Apparently, Angus had brought it to him.

"Does he cook your breakfast for you?"

"No, Elsie, the night nurse, does, usually."

"Good. That'll save me the chore."

"Sometimes, I don't get it when it's warm and I like my food warm, not cold."

"Understood," she acknowledged. "Um, I was wondering. I noticed there's a Baby Grand in the living room."

"So, you took a tour of the house when I was asleep?"

"Yes, I did. I hope that's alright."

"As long as you don't steal anything, I guess it's okay," he said reluctantly.

"Do you have a housekeeper come in to clean?"

"She comes in once a week, usually on Fridays."

"Good. That means it isn't a part of my job to clean."

"It is a part of your job to keep the house picked up and orderly. I dislike anything that is disorderly."

"Okay, I'll take that under advisement. No problem for me. I don't like messes either."

"I'm glad we can agree on something."

"Of course. I hope we can agree on many things. Which brings me to my next question. Would it be okay for me to play the piano if I don't disturb you in any way?"

"You play the piano?"

"I was taught by my aunt. She was a brilliant pianist and she wanted me to learn the art."

"My goodness. I would never have thought a colored could be brilliant at anything."

Offended, Cleo managed to answer him evenly. "I suppose you would be surprised by my ability, too."

"I am astonished you play at all." With that he stuffed his mouth with some bacon.

"Would you like a demonstration? I'd be happy to play for you."

"What do you play?"

"I can play Scott Joplin, Beethoven and Chopin, among other composers. Joplin is my favorite. You know, he created Ragtime."

"No, I didn't know that. So, you say you can play those fancy composers. Prove it."

"Okay," she said defiantly. With that she rolled him into the living room in his chair with the tray of food on his lap.

He continued eating without pause.

Once he was situated, she sat on the piano bench and began a Joplin piece. It was naturally a piece of Ragtime and she did it from memory. Joplin's music always lifted her spirits and she was excited she could play it for her employer and do it well in spite of the fact that she had not practiced. It had been quite a while since she had played anything and the experience was amazing, bringing fond thoughts of her aunt, who had moved away some time ago right after her brother, Cleo's dad, passed away. She missed Aunt Dorothy and wondered if she would ever get to see her again.

Then, she switched to Handel, *Suite No 1, Gigue*. It was the most cheerful she could think of. She remembered when she learned it, practicing hours and hours to get it right. The keys worked perfectly as she expected. She wondered who the person was that tuned the instrument and how often it was done. The Steinway's sound was superb. It was full and rich unlike her piano at home, an upright. Its sound was why she spent so little time playing it. This piano she could play all day and never tire of it. Finishing with a flourish, she looked to see if Zackary Hughes liked the music.

"That was amazing!" Zack commented rather sincerely. "I would never expect anyone of your species to do that well."

"Thank you. Humans usually do quite well when they practice the way I have. I hope to prove to you over time that I can do a lot of things well. Maybe you'll change your mind about people of color."

"That would be a miracle. I've seen too many niggers and they all seem pretty stupid to me."

"You may have assumed more than you should have."

"I didn't assume anything, as you put it. I am always right."

"Really? Okay, I hope you will be right about me, too." Cleo knew she sounded defiant. Not wanting to leave things as they were, she began playing *Moonlight Sonata,* her favorite. The music reflected perfectly the moon shimmering on the sea as it slowly rose to its imperial place in the sky. It always made her heart ache with its beauty.

When she finished, she found Zackary in tears. "Oh my, I didn't mean to make you cry."

"You didn't. It's a memory of the first time my wife played that for me, before we were married. She was seducing me that night which surprised me, but delighted me nevertheless."

"She must have loved you very much."

"I believe she did. I miss her desperately. She was the love of my life."

"You were very fortunate to have her with you for so long."

"It wasn't long enough. I need her now. You know, I am the last person in my entire family who is left standing," he said for the second time.

Cleo figured his memory was failing. If nothing else, he was consistent.

"Well, I guess I'm not exactly *standing*." He smiled ruefully. "I think God wanted me to suffer, made to grow so old and left behind as punishment for my sins."

It was an astonishing thing to say. Not knowing how to respond, she asked, "You had children?" She knew the answer but didn't want to let on.

"Four sons. They're all gone, too. Imagine. Everyone, no cousins, no aunts, no uncles. I have grandchildren but they've all scattered to the wind. I never hear from any of them. No children, no wife. Just me."

"I'm sorry." Hoping to change the subject, she asked: "Where do you come from?"

"I was born in Georgia; had a good family. They're all gone, too."

"When did you come to California?"

"I was deployed here early in 1947."

"Did you serve in the war?"

"World War II? No, no." He answered. "I was too young for that. My older brother died in that war. He didn't have a chance. Got caught in an ambush by the Germans. It was close to the end and he never made it home. Killed my father who loved him more than life itself. As soon as I was old enough, I signed up and they sent me to Colorado to train and then here. I was hoping to fight in something, but my timing was bad. I was out by the time the Korean War started, so my dad had twice as many reasons to hate me; said I was a two-time loser. I was trying to take my brother's place in his heart." He laughed dryly, "Didn't work."

He passed it off like it was nothing, but Cleo knew it hurt him a lot. "Life can be like that. Disappointing."

"You can't imagine."

Then she said, "You said you had servants in your home when you were young."

"Yep. My father was very rich. He was self-made. Had his own farm growing cotton."

"Were all your servants black people?"

"Only one white woman worked for us. She was my nanny. She was hired after my father discovered the black nanny was coddling me and making me fall in love with her. She was young and beautiful, so he hired an ugly old white woman to care for me. At least, that's what he told me when I asked why he had hired the woman. I didn't like her at all. She was mean."

"Did she make you study when you went to school?"

"Sure did. She was a taskmaster. I don't remember much about the nigger nanny. I was too young, but I do remember she held me in her lap and made me feel secure. I guess that's why I fell for her." He passed it off with a wave of his hand. "I was too young to know better."

It was obvious that Zackary was hurt beyond repair by his father's disinterest in him. She was beginning to learn why his face disclosed such pain and defeat. She was also learning why black folks were on his hate list. Coming from the deep south, as he did, influenced his attitudes about race. She couldn't help but feel bad for him even though she was hurt and put off by his racist attitudes.

But it was hard for Cleo to understand why he hated black people with such a passion when there had been such a kind woman of color in his past. Maybe he somehow conflated his father's lack of love for him and that experience with her. Sometimes people made weird associations that had nothing to do with their true feelings at an earlier time. It was something to ponder, though. Zackary was turning out to be something of an enigma. That such a mixture of love and hate could exist together in one person was confusing.

It would be quite a few months of getting to know him before she could come to any real conclusions. One of her favorite pastimes was figuring people out; why they felt the way they did, and how they had grown up, was interesting. She considered doing classwork in psychology when she got a chance to go back to school.

Eight

AFTER CLEO LEFT for the evening and Elsie arrived, Zackary had his dinner, then excusing himself, he asked Elsie to help him to bed. "I'm tired, too tired to stay up for my usual shows." She kindly obliged as Elsie always did and took him to his room, changed him and got him into bed. She turned off the lights, yet there was still light coming through the window. It was early, but he was weary with all the things that had happened. The day had taken a lot out of him and made him think about things he had long forgotten. His family, especially his father, were best left in the past.

His father had been a very successful man and because of that everyone admired him more than he deserved. Zackary remembered him as an angry man with a short temper. There was a thick black strap that hung in the hall closet and every time it was opened, there the strap was as a reminder of the wounds it could cause at the hands of the man. For no reason that Zack could understand, his father had picked on him more than his older brother, the first son of the family. Zackary was the second and last even though his mother wanted more and tried for more. Somehow Zack couldn't measure up to Harold, the image of that firstborn son.

Of course, when they gained maturity and the war started, Harold had enlisted immediately, unwilling to wait for the draft to take him. He was a true American in the best tradition of the men who marched off to war and his father was immensely proud of him. Zackary would have signed up immediately, too, if he'd been old enough, but he was two years behind Harold. He was slight of build then, and never gained the heft his brother had.

But most of all, he remembered how beaten down he was by his father's rage. It had been mostly a rage of his own making. Zack had done everything he could to make the old man happy. Nevertheless, that goal had been impossible to achieve.

He wondered, as he thought about the nigger nanny whose care had caused him to need her more than he needed his father, if that had something to do with it. He came to know why, of course. But only later. The woman was no more than an animal not worthy of human care or affection. He knew that now and had known it as soon as he was old enough.

It was odd how he, his brother and some neighborhood children were allowed to play with niggers. Those kids were fun to play with. They were there because their parents worked at the family home and had no one to care for them at their place. As soon as they reached a certain age, that practice was stopped. He surmised now it was because they had become teens with teenage hormones exploding through their bodies. The nigger boys were known to rape girls, and they started fights with the boys, so it was logical to Zackary they would not be allowed to play together any longer. It just didn't seem obvious at the time.

Zackary was a good student, however, and he learned well the lessons of the South. He completely agreed with them once all had become clear. And, when returning from boot camp, all fresh to serve his country, he'd had an opportunity to witness a real lynching, an activity he had only heard about. He was thrilled to be, in his own way, a part of it. It was a kind of vindication. When his father saw the finger Zack had severed, he felt honored he had a boy who could do the right thing after all. Zack remembered how his father had slapped him on the back and welcomed him home as the son he had been waiting for.

That had been a brief lapse in his father's rage. After Zack's two years in the service, he got out and went home. Life was good at home for a while. Then, the Korean War broke out. Now that there was a war to fight, Zack regretted leaving the military. His dad was displeased and soon the man was throwing Zack out to make do on his own. If only he had been more like his older brother, he was sure he could have gained acceptance from the only man who mattered to him.

The only good that had come out of that time was his trip to California. He'd served here in the Army and returned knowing how good the weather was. He was also aware that Eugenics, the principle of ethnic cleansing Hitler adopted had originated in the state. He figured he'd find many folks who believed the same as he did.

Maybe he should have been glad that his father kicked him out because this is where he had met Miriam, the woman who would become his beloved wife. They made a terrific match. He'd met her at work. She was a secretary for his boss. They had been attracted to each other immediately, so life was good from that point on.

When Zack finally felt sleep coming, the light in the window had turned to dark night very much like his life had turned dark that day his father threw him out and later when Miriam died. He continued even to this late date to have nightmares about those times. And so, he fell off to sleep and dream.

Nine

ANGUS DUNNE WORKED his job as the grocery boy before and after school hours. He felt proud that he did as much as he managed to do with his days. He was a senior at Glendale High. He liked his classes well enough and was a pretty good student, but not a stellar one like some of the smarter kids. Those guys were the nerds who were never popular. Angus wasn't either, although he didn't think he was nerdish. He was tall and slender with fairly good looks. His blond hair was cut in a style that made him look like he was bad, and he sported those tattoos his dad didn't want him to show off. In Glendale, he didn't think it would matter, but he didn't display the most controversial ones just to avoid any conflict with teachers or classmates.

Angus was not popular in the least. He wasn't sure why, but the guys at school didn't like him much. They called him the pejorative, Angus 'Dung', which had been going on since early grade school when the kids were just old enough to know about the breed of cattle known by the same name. He hated his parents for giving him such a lousy name, one which they could have assumed wouldn't wear well with the other kids. He wondered if they'd done it on purpose and he asked his mom once if it was. She was shocked that the other boys had come up with that name for him, so he refrained from asking his dad; but it stuck in his craw like a thorny cactus.

Angus felt like the only friend he had in the world was Zackary Hughes. They were enjoying occasional evenings just shooting hot air with each other. They shared a lot of the same views which, in this time, was satisfying like none of his other conversations with his parents, his teachers or the occasional dude who would deign to speak to him at school. Most of those kids were kind of stupid and never said anything he could relate to.

When Angus was just entering his teen-hood and his folks got him his own computer, he became fascinated with the Internet and followed some stuff that absolved Hitler of any wrong-doing. He'd seen some old war movies and thought, like most other people, that Hitler was a rogue killer with the deaths of six million Jews on his hands. But his parents were against Jews and other ethnic groups, especially niggers. So, the news about Hitler was welcome in his household. His dad had said he thought it must be true, that the Americans had demonized the man because they could. He was supposed to be dead, so they could say anything they wanted to justify the war.

From there, Angus explored some more Internet conspiracy theories and found them to be fascinating. He wasn't sure what to believe, but they sure did get his attention. When he mentioned to some classmates about what he was watching, they scoffed at him and pretty much avoided him after that. He thought that was unfair—free speech was supposed to be allowed, but he learned that people were free to avoid hearing anything they didn't want to hear. He felt caught between two worlds like comparing Mercury and Jupiter. The two seemed completely different.

So, when he discovered that Zackary believed a lot like he did, he latched onto him like a baby duck to its mother. He wanted to spend more time with the old man, but had a tough schedule that didn't allow for much socializing.

Ten

ONE AFTERNOON AFTER LUNCH, Cleo and Zackary were sitting in the den. The television was on tuned to Fox News, not Cleo's favorite station. But she was trying to be tolerant with Zack, practicing the kind of love her mom had tried to teach her. She concentrated on the commercials which were sometimes interesting and sometimes not. Sometimes they were just silly and often they focused on something that had little to do with the product itself.

"I can't stand 'chesty,'" she said during a commercial break.

"Who's chesty?"

"Haven't you notice? She's that girl who thrusts her breasts out like she is very proud of them."

"What's wrong with that? She might have a reason to be proud," he said absently.

Surely, he had noticed. It was hard not to. "Well, they're okay, I guess. But they have absolutely nothing to do with what she's advertising."

"What is she advertising?"

She had his attention now. "Frankly, I don't remember. I can't imagine anyone would remember what that commercial is about."

"You might be surprised." When she didn't respond, he asked, "Why do you think she is thrusting her chest out that way?"

"To get your attention, obviously."

"My attention?"

"Well, yeah, you're a man after all. Don't tell me you don't care about those things anymore."

"Oh, I do."

"See?"

"I wish I knew which commercial you're talking about."

"It was on just a few minutes ago. Don't you remember?"

"Uh, no. I guess not. You know, my short-term memory is … short."

"Well, she's walking along a path talking about the product, or something like that. And, she tosses her breasts out and sashays down the walk. It's very distracting that she throws those things around like that."

"Obviously, you were distracted. Makes me wonder why. Are you jealous or is there some other reason she tics you off the way she does?"

"What other reason would there be?"

"Oh, I don't know. Maybe you're interested in women."

"Good heavens, no." She laughed. "That kind of thing doesn't interest me." She wanted to say there was nothing wrong with it, but she thought it better not to stir that cauldron. Then, "No, I'm not jealous either. I have enough going for me that I don't need to be envious."

"What is it then?"

"She distracts me from the object of the commercial. She's advertising something important to the advertiser."

"Do you have to know what it is?"

"No, not me. But someone. Knowing the reason for the commercial is what they're paying for."

"I suppose so."

"There is one commercial in which I do remember the product. It's that one where they suddenly cut to the woman knocking over a glass of red wine onto a white carpet. Every time, I want to catch the glass before it breaks on the rug. I jump trying to catch it. The product is supposed to clean up the red wine, but why spend a lot of money on such a product when plain soda water can do the same thing?"

"I had no idea soda water was so effective."

"My mother has used it for years. It cleans up red wine and blood, as long as the blood hasn't coagulated yet."

"Do you have a lot of blood flowing at your house?" His question was serious.

"Heaven's no! Why would you ask such question?"

"I dunno. You brought it up." To deflect he asked, "What other commercials bother you? I'm fascinated."

"Well, don't get me started on how black people are depicted in commercials *and* entertainment television. There are times when it's very demeaning."

"Don't worry, I won't let you get started. Tell me something else."

"Okay. There is that commercial about some toilet paper. It's supposed to be so soft it can clean a peach. Now, who the heck needs to clean a peach with toilette paper?"

"Toilet paper cleans you know where."

"Yes, exactly. They say 'down there,' to describe what it's supposed to keep clean."

"What kind of toilette paper is it? Maybe we should get some. I'll tell Angus to put it on the list."

"I couldn't tell you. That peach is so distracting and, I might add, disgusting. So, I don't remember."

"The peach is supposed to remind you of something."

"Right! It reminds me of what is 'down there'!" She laughed. "It doesn't remind me of the merchandise which I suppose is what it should do. I'll try to pay better attention to the product next time."

"Cleo, you are a very strange woman."

"Stranger yet, is the commercial about a toilet paper that invokes a kind of obscene love affair with the product. It's supposed to be cute because it's a cartoon with a bunch of bears in it. They wiggle their little bottoms around displaying how 'clean' they are. Good God!"

"Now, I'm sure I would remember that one. But frankly, I don't catch many of the commercials. I kind of snooze during most of them."

"You're not missing much; it's all pretty silly." Cleo thought again, "Well, some are clever. Then, they play them endlessly and they become tedious and boring. It's a wonder they are able to sell anything at all."

Just then, the program they had been watching returned. "One thing I can agree on," he said, "there are far too many commercials. I'm lucky I don't fall dead asleep; they take so much time."

Cleo was actually beginning to like him.

Eleven

THINGS WERE WORKING OUT okay at home. Edith was handling Jamal and all of his issues pretty well. Her mom was an intelligent woman and she had reared her and her brother, Walter. Cleo was sure she would be fine with Jamal. Of course, life in the 'hood' was a bit different now than it had been back then. Problems awaited her son as he grew.

The neighborhood they lived in had grown more problematic during that time with gangs roaming the streets. The teenage boys were known to recruit younger kids to their way of life. The kids who went that way usually were lonely with divorced parents and no one at home to care for them, and sometimes, regrettably, drugs and alcohol were involved. For those families, there was never enough money; the jobs they were able to get were inadequate. As a result, kids were vulnerable to gang activity and selling drugs gave them the money they desired. There were black gangs and Hispanic gangs. Even some Asian kids got together. They fought each other like dogs. And some got killed. The young ones were easily influenced by the 'family' the gangs provided. Cleo didn't think Jamal would fall for that come-on. She would make sure he was aware enough when the time came.

Edith would too. Her mom was quiet about some things, but she became very vocal when it came to the safety of her family and how Congress, State and Federal, was handling, or not handling, the problems that arose far too often in the neighborhoods. Civil rights leaders of the earlier era, her mother's era, had done a lot to raise the consciousness of many Americans. But Edith would gladly tell you they had failed to go beyond the limits of their collective imaginations, their narrow expectations. They were thrilled to see black American athletes, some wonderful actors, musicians, highly qualified professors, politicians, doctors, attorneys and other professionals reach the pinnacles of their professions. There was some school integration here and there when red-lining stayed out of the way of neighborhood integration. There was a lot to be proud of. But Edith would point out the neighborhoods, where the brothers were languishing unable to get enough work or pay to get by. She would point out the homeless problem which had grown by leaps and bounds as the rich got richer and the poor … well. The violence within the African-American communities had only grown worse as time wore on. And, police violence against pissed off black men was clearly out of control seemingly without consequence. Why did black parents have to subject their children to 'The Talk', warning their boys to be careful while white parents could pretty much sit back and figure their teens would be okay?

Cleo did not want her son to drug himself up to bear the fear of his ancestors. She did not want him to twist himself inside out to achieve the freedom that should belong to him as his right. Cleo thought about her own brother, Wally, who couldn't concentrate long enough to finish a math problem or read a paragraph. He was a young man who needed to run away from his family to feel okay or to find whatever would make him whole. Martin Luther King, John Lewis and others had been great Civil Rights leaders in their own era, but there was little proof that more great black leaders had taken their place or were on the horizon.

The job with Zackary took up a good deal of Cleo's schedule, but she made sure she spent the weekends with her son taking him swimming down at the community pool during the hot months and often to a skating rink during the winter months. They had to take a bus to that venue, but it was worth the trip. Jamal liked ice skating and he was good at roller skating and skate boarding, too. There were plenty of activities. It was a shame that many broken families couldn't manage the time to do them with their children. She was determined to make life good for her boy no matter what it took to make that happen. Cleo didn't want Jamal to have to live in fear.

Twelve

BACK AT THE JOB, Zack asked her to do him a favor. "I know this isn't a part of your job, but the medicine I take is running out and Elsie said she couldn't figure out how to order them on the computer. Do you know how to use a computer?"

"Sure. There's one down at the library and I use that sometimes. I used to do my homework on it when I was going to school."

"You went to school?"

"How do you think I learned to care for people like you without an education? Of course, I went to school. I took college courses and nursing. In fact, I told you some time ago that I went to college. I planned to be an RN."

"I don't remember. You surprise me all of the time. I didn't know niggers could go to college."

"Oh, come on, Zack. People of color can become doctors, lawyers, even presidents. Obama is a black man after all."

"Oh yeah. I almost forgot about him. At least, I tried to."

"You surprise me all the time, too, Zackary Hughes. You are a mixture of hope and loathing."

"Why would you say that?"

"Because that's what I see in you. So, do you have a computer?"

"Yeah. I do. I don't know how to use it. My youngest son bought me one just before he passed away."

"I've never seen it. Where is it?"

"It's in my closet. It's a—what do they call it?—It's a Lap Top."

"May I go and look for it?"

"Don't know how else you'd find it."

"Okay, I'll be back." With that, she left him in the den and went to his bedroom closet. She rummaged around in his messy wardrobe thinking she would clean it up soon. Looking around, she could see clothing and shoes Zack had used when he was mobile. No one had ever cleaned the closet out. She wondered if there were clothes in some closet that belong to Mrs. Hughes when she was alive. When she looked up, she found the computer right there on a shelf. If it had been a snake …

Returning to the den, she asked, "Do you happen to know what company you order your medication from?"

"Uh, it's a, let me see." He searched his mind for a minute as she waited patiently. Running through the alphabet he got to 'O', and said, "Oh, I remember now. It's a company called 'Optimum-Care'."

"Good, I'll look it up. I assume you have Wi Fi here."

"A-course. It should work just fine. Elsie uses it all the time."

Cleo sat down and found Google easily as she hoped. Typing in Optimum-Care, she accessed it without a problem. Elsie probably pulled it up the night before.

"Okay, what are the medications you're running out of?"

He gave her a list he had written in his shaking script and she typed it in along with his information. But there was no place to check an enter box, nor any way to finalize the order.

"That's odd. Thought this would be easy, but…." She stopped herself knowing he wouldn't know what she was talking about. "I'd better call. This is silly. They don't have a space to finalize the order."

Making the call, Cleo was put on hold for a more than an hour before the person came on the phone to help her. By that time, she was furious. Zack had fallen asleep and she went into the living room so she wouldn't wake him.

"Good morning. Can I help you?" The honeyed voice of a black man answered the phone.

Still piqued after the long wait, she barked, "Well, I certainly hope so. I've waited long enough to talk to someone."

"What can I do for you?" The man on the other end was patient.

"Well, you can help me finalize my order on the computer," she snarled. "I don't know what you people expect if a person can't easily make an order. And, I don't know what you can expect when you make people wait a whole morning on the phone!"

"It does take a long time, doesn't it?"

"Ya think? My boss fell asleep a half hour ago while we waited for you to answer."

"I am very sorry, ma'am. But we don't have nearly enough operators for all of the customers."

"You bet you don't. I don't have all day, ya know. Why can't your bosses make it easier for us?"

"Well, I have asked. And, you are so right. I don't know what it will take to get them to do something about it."

Cleo was softening. "But, it's impossible to finalize my order on your site. What about that?"

His voice was deep, soft and pleasing. "Well, let's see. You put all of the information in, right?"

"Of course. I'm not stupid." Cleo's attitude hardened when she thought this man might be like Zack and would think she didn't have enough smarts.

"Ma'am. I would never imply such a thing. Of course, you are as smart as anyone. I am sorry if I upset you." He wasn't being obsequious, just nice.

Unable to keep up her earlier displeasure, she quieted. "I'm sorry if I sound impatient."

"I'm sure you have your reasons, ma'am." His voice was actually sexy.

"Well, I would never say this if you didn't sound like a very nice man, but my boss thinks all black people are stupid. He makes sure I know how he feels about people of color all the time."

"I sure know how that feels." He confirmed his race with that simple sentence.

"Thank you." She responded, feeling grateful she had found a fellow traveler. "Now, what about your Internet site? Why can't I finalize my order?"

"If you put in all of the information, then it is finalized. May I ask the name of the person for whom you are ordering?"

He sounded intelligent. "Yes, Zackary Hughes." Cleo wasn't angry anymore. She was charmed.

"Okay, I've got it. Looks like he is running out of just about everything."

"Apparently. That's why he asked me to do this for him. He doesn't use the computer and the night nurse was unable to complete the order, too."

"No problem. I've found your input and I will make sure the order goes in immediately."

"Gosh, thank you. You've made this so easy."

"I try. It should be delivered to your boss's home by tomorrow."

"That's fast. What's your name?" She asked, suddenly wanting to speak to him as a person and not just an order clerk.

"It's Clarence."

"That is a very nice name. Where do you live, Clarence?"

Suddenly, she was embarrassed. "Oh gosh. I don't mean to pry, to be too personal."

"Not at all. I live in Compton."

"Compton?" She asked incredulous. "I used to know someone from there. Sadly, he died recently and I miss him terribly."

"I'm very sorry for your loss."

Tyran Ferguson had been a dear friend. He'd lived near Wilshire Boulevard and she had been to his apartment several times with her mom. They had gone to the same church for a while and had become very close. Ty was a pianist too and they took turns playing for the congregation.

"Where was he born?" He asked. "I hope I am not being too personal."

"No, of course not. Ty actually hailed from Beverly Hills. Although his mom was from Compton, she was also a maid for a family who lived in Beverly Hills and he was born and raised up just like a white boy in that glitzy place. That was before there were any black folk there. He went to Beverly Hills schools all his life and mastered the violin and piano. My aunt knew him first because she taught him how to play. We all became good friends through our mutual love of classical music. We even went to church together."

"Wow! He sounds like quite a character."

"Oh, he was. I loved him like an uncle even though he was younger than my aunt and my mom. The reason I thought about him is that his brother lived in Compton. You won't believe this, but in his eulogy, his brother told us a story about Ty that nobody knew."

She stopped herself realizing she was going on as if Clarence had all day. "Oh, my apologies. I hope I am not taking up too much of your time."

"Not at all. I'm intrigued. But I do have to go. Give me your number and I'll call later and we can continue this talk."

"I don't have a cell phone, so you'll have to call me on this one. My boss takes his naps in the afternoon between one and three o'clock. You could call then."

Okay, I have this number on my device, so I'll call right at one."

"Great! I'm looking forward to hearing from you."

And, she was anxious to hear from him and hoped he wouldn't forget. He called, but she'd had to wait until 1:15 before the phone rang. By that time, she was sure he had forgotten.

When she picked up the receiver, he said, "Okay, so what was the story?" He was starting right where they had left off.

"Well, Ty apparently hated Compton. His brother lived there, but he would never go to visit because he really thought of himself as a white person. He'd been around white folk all his life and didn't relate to neighborhoods in areas like I live in. When his brother was taking him back to his home in Compton where the burial people were, he said he could hear Ty, who of course was dead in the back of the car in a body bag, sayin' 'Don't you dare take me to Compton. I wouldn't set foot in that place while I was alive and now, you're taking me there for burial?"

Clarence laughed heartily. "That is funny." She loved his laugh. It was infectious.

"There must be customers waiting for you, so I'll let you go," she said, trying to be sensitive to his time.

"Yeah, but I want to know, you play the piano, too. Right?"

"Oh yes, I've played since I was a child. My aunt taught me."

"I love classical music. I hope you do."

"It's all my aunt would teach me. She hated modern music. She said it was nasty."

"Nasty? No kidding! This may sound a bit forward, but you sound like a nice woman and I have tickets to a concert this Saturday night. Would you be interested in going with me?"

Cleo was stunned. "You don't know anything about me. How do you know you would enjoy my company?"

"I can tell. I am a stranger to you, I know. But since we both like classical music and I have two season tickets without anyone else to take, I thought maybe you would like to go. I hope I'm not being too presumptuous and I promise I won't cause you any problems."

"Well, I suppose you are presumptuous, but I like it. Give me your phone number and let me check with my mom, make sure she can take care of my son Saturday night."

"You have a boy?"

"Yes, he's six years-old."

"There isn't a dad around?"

"No, no dad, except when he feels like coming around. He hasn't been to see Jamal, our son, for two years. We divorced some time ago."

"What's your name?"

They exchanged information and got off the phone just as Zack was waking from his nap and asking for a snack. Her mood had lightened considerably since the conversation with the stranger who had the honeyed voice, and she sang as she worked in the kitchen slicing some cheese and apple. "Clarence from Compton," she mused to herself.

Thirteen

IT WAS FRIDAY NIGHT and Cleo had already cleared Saturday night with Edith. Her mom would be happy to take care of Jamal since she 'didn't have anything else to do anyway.' But she cautioned Cleo about having a stranger come to the house.

"You know, you're right. It is kind'a dangerous not knowing him. It's just that I have a really good feeling about him and he knows he's coming to where I live with you and Jamal. Anyway, we can both check him out when he gets here. If he looks like a bad bet, I can beg off saying I have a bad cold or something."

"Oh… Well, honey, if you say so. It's just a little creepy not knowing exactly who you're bringing here."

"Mom, I think it'll be okay. He just sounds so nice and he is very considerate on the phone." A kind of joy gripped Cleo's heart when she realized she would get to meet Clarence from Compton in person and she was excited.

The bus was late. A bad accident had held them up for an extra hour. Fortunately, she was able to catch an evening train to her neighborhood. It was late summer so the sunset came a little earlier and the train let her off earlier, but not by much. The sun was beginning to sink and glinted off the iconic bronze statue of a hand reaching upward and letting go of a tiny bird which seemed to be flying away. She had seen the stunning sculpture many times located near the 103rd Street Station, but had never caught it in the light just this way.

It was pretty dark as she walked home, freaked out by the neighborhoods she strode through at that hour. Each was worse than the last, or so she imagined. All was a reminder of the night she was raped. The area seemed different to her, not like during the daytime. As it got darker and darker, the faces of the men standing around on sidewalks and porches, staring at anyone who walked by like they were possible prey, was unnerving. Gang kids roamed the streets, too, and liked to harass women walking alone. She was close to her house when a giant pale-skinned man walked by, lit by a street light. He looked her up and down as she scurried away. He hadn't been wearing a shirt, but the tattoos made him appear as though his entire upper body and all the way down his arms was clothed. She wondered if his whole body was inked. The tattoo patterns were as thick and as frightening as he was.

"Cleo, my god, where have you been?" Edith asked as she walked through the front door at last. The scent of brewing mint tea reached her nostrils signaling the safety of her home.

"There was an accident while I was on the bus and traffic came to a stop. I had a nice conversation with the bus driver though," Cleo explained while she removed her purse and sweater putting them away. "His name is Carlos."

"Are you getting to know him?"

"Yes, I guess I am. Somehow I always catch his bus coming home. He says I'm a regular, so, yes, I am. Nice dude."

"Hispanic?"

"Yes, I would say so. Whether first or second generation, I can't tell."

"He speaks Spanish then?"

"Seems to; has an accent."

"Jamal should learn some Spanish. He had a problem today with the kids on the way home from camp. I think they were all Hispanic."

"Did he get into a fight?" Cleo asked, alarmed.

"It didn't come to that—he was with Willie—but I was thinking. There's a woman down the street who has been passing out flyers. She wants to teach people how to speak Spanish. It might be a good idea to look into it, maybe have her teach Jamal. He might get along better if he understands what those boys are saying when they speak among themselves."

"That's a great idea, Mom. Do you have one of her flyers?"

"Yes, right here." Edith handed the paper to Cleo and she looked it over. "She knows how to use a computer. This flyer is well done; it's decorative as well as informative."

"Uh-huh. I thought so too."

"I'm going over there tomorrow and see what she's like. Maybe she can start on Monday. Sooner, better."

"Honey, I couldn't agree more."

The next day, Cleo got on the phone with the Hispanic woman whose name turned out to be Lupe Gonzalez. She sounded nice, intelligent too. They agreed on a time and Cleo went over to the house, which was only a block away, that afternoon.

The house was a lot like her own, a beige wood-frame two-story with a nice porch. It was probably built in the 1930s. The grass in the front was well-kept and the woman had some roses growing in a nicely trimmed flower bed. Cleo guessed the husband or a son might be a gardener judging by how well the yard was kept. Someone had to mow that lawn and trim the trees. She climbed the few porch stairs to the door and knocked.

"Buenos Dias," said the woman as she opened the door. "My guess is you are Cleo Henderson, and you're not from ICE."

Cleo chuckled. "No, I am definitely not from ICE. Buenos dias a usted, Senora Gonzalez."

"Habla Espanole?" Lupe was a fine-looking Hispanic woman of about forty years. She was mildly plump with lightly graying hair just off her face. She was dressed in a modern-looking, electric blue blouse and a pair of black slacks.

Cleo reverted to English. "No, not very much," then a splash of Spanish, "Poquito." Embarrassed, she said, "Sorry, I really shouldn't even try, my Spanish is so poor."

"Are you kidding? That's how you learn." The woman was very welcoming and cheerful. Cleo noticed she was Americanized, if that was the right word for it.

"Come on in!" She stepped back with a bit of a flourish and invited Cleo inside.

The home was fitted out in what appeared to be hand-me-down furniture covered with clear plastic to keep it clean, very common for the area. Her own home sported Edith's furniture, although they didn't have the plastic coverings. On the walls hung some Hispanic art prints, very colorful and some were historical. On one wall there was an upright piano with a guitar propped next to it. The house reminded her of her own place. She thought Jamal would feel at home here.

"My son has had some trouble with the Hispanic kids around the neighborhood," she said as she settled on the couch. "He's only six and pretty vulnerable."

"Oh. That happens, doesn't it? We try to keep the boys from picking fights, but it is hard to convince them to 'turn the other cheek,' no?"

"Yes, it is hard. There seems to be a lot of animosity between the Blacks and Hispanics. But I thought Jamal would do well to learn some Spanish so he could know what the boys are saying and maybe divert their abuse with some Spanish of his own."

"That might work. It is worth a try. My fee is very nominal and I would love to meet su hijo."

"I think he should meet you so he doesn't feel like he is being railroaded."

"Railroaded?" Lupe asked.

"Sorry. That means coerced. It's an American expression."

"Ah. That's a good one." She smiled. "Let me see," she took out a small calendar. "I have time on Monday to meet him. In the morning would be best?"

Cleo thought for a moment and said, "Yes, that would be fine. I'll bring him by around ten?"

"Sounds good to me."

They shook hands and Cleo left feeling like she had accomplished a very good opportunity for Jamal.

When she got home, she told Edith about the visit and the appointment on Monday morning. "Honestly, I'm not sure I should be taking the time off, but this is important for Jamal."

"Honey, you'd better call about a substitute now, so they can work on it over the weekend."

"Good idea, Mom. Thanks." Cleo grabbed the phone and looked up the number.

The scheduling clerk was on pretty fast. "Can I help you?"

"Hey Phyllis."

Phyllis was a middle-aged, brown-haired, green-eyed woman and Cleo liked her. She was very friendly.

"Cleo here. I have a personal problem and I have to get a replacement over at the Hughes' residence for Monday. It should be only half a day. I have a meeting with a woman who is going to teach my son Spanish."

"Are you sure you want to give your spot away like that?"

"What do you mean?"

"Well, Sweetie, we only have white and Hispanic women on hand. What if Hughes decides he likes the replacement better than he does you?"

"You know his issues with people of color?"

"Sure do. He called here a couple of weeks after you first started and complained about your skin color … And species, I might add." She said ruefully.

"Oh, man." Cleo felt defeated for the first time that day. She'd felt triumphant all afternoon because of the meeting with Lupe and a call to Clarence; she was able to tell him she could join him for the concert. He had seemed delighted with the news.

"And," Phyllis continued, "she'll have to work the whole day, not just half."

"Understood. It's a chance I'll have to take."

"If Hughes decides to keep the new aide, you know you would have to go to the back of the line over here. We have a few women and a couple of men who need the work and are quite capable of doing what you do."

"So far, I have developed a pretty good relationship with Mr. Hughes and I have to go to that meeting on Monday. It's about my son."

"Okay," Phyllis responded reluctantly. "I'll try to get the Mexican woman whose been bugging me about work. I don't imagine he's all that friendly with Hispanic people either."

"Thank you, Phyllis." Cleo was relieved and grateful. She hated the competition game. It made people suspicious of each other when camaraderie would heal so many wounds.

Cleo hoped she could get an hour in the middle of her Saturday errands to shop at the local dress store. Ebony's establishment had enough cool things and she hoped to find the "just right" outfit for the evening.

She found an all-black silk pant and top ensemble. The top had a scoop collar and the sleeves hung down just a little below her wrist, simple but elegant. The pants fit softly around her hips and hung loosely down her legs showing off her lithe figure as she moved. Edith had a necklace that would look perfect with it. The outfit was "vintage," second time owned; it wasn't expensive.

Edith was clever with hair and she fashioned Cleo's full mane into a respectable do with a pretty clip to go with the necklace. Feeling elegant in her new outfit and a nice hair style, she felt quite ready to meet the man with the honeyed voice like she had never heard before. What would he look like, she couldn't imagine? She laughed to herself—*He'll probably be short and ugly … not that there is anything wrong with it.*

She was ready, as ready as she would ever be to meet a complete stranger with the voice that made her melt. She hoped he would live up to her highest expectations. She headed down the stairs and her mom met her there with a look that indicated Clarence had arrived already and was out on the porch.

Edith reached up to pull a little curl down onto her forehead. "Okay, that's enough Mom!" She heard Jamal's voice as he screamed with joy. "So, he's out there with Jamal already."

"Yep. He's been here for fifteen minutes."

"Why didn't you tell me?" Cleo asked alarmed. She ran out to the porch to find Clarence from Compton with her son. They were laughing it up like they were old friends. As he rose from a white wicker chair, one of a pair her mom had bought when Cleo and Jamal moved in, she got a good look at him. He was thankfully tall and quite handsome in an Obama sort of way and, unlike Obama, he sported a short beard. His hair and beard were trim and he had an easy smile with sparkling eyes. He was dressed in a nice black suit, a white shirt with a red-striped tie.

"Cleo. You must be the beautiful woman I talked to on the phone. At least, I hope so."

Charming, too.

"Mom!" Jamal ran to her. "This is Clarence and he says he's going to take me skateboarding!"

"Oh really?"

"Only with your permission, of course," Clarence added.

He was polite and careful not to overstep. Good. She smiled. "Of course, Jamal can go if he has finished all his homework and house chores. He must do that before we go swimming or ice skating. Right, Buddy?"

"Wow Mom!" Jamal said with a stunned tone. "You look gorgeous."

"Thank you. Clarence and I are going out to a concert tonight."

She turned to Clarence. "Whose music will we be hearing?"

"Khachaturian, Aram Khachaturian's Symphony No. 2, written in 1943. If you aren't familiar with him, he was an Armenian composer. He conducted the Vienna Symphony orchestra during his career. Born in 1903."

"Wow, you know your stuff."

"I figured I'd have to since you said you play."

"I do know his music. I haven't played it, but, of course, I am familiar with it. My aunt taught me. She was very strict but I loved her just the same."

"You told me on the phone," he said covering his lack of knowledge about the composer.

"Sorry, I don't mean to repeat myself." She suddenly felt the heat of embarrassment.

"That's okay, I do a lot of that myself," he said as he took her elbow and they turned to go. "Peace, My Man," he said to Jamal as he extended his hand to do a 'high five', and the boy returned it with dap. Jamal gave it all he had, then ran to Edith to hang onto her.

As they got into the car, Jamal looked up at his grandma. "He said 'My Man!' Did you hear him?"

"Yes, I sure did, son. He seems like a very nice fella." She replied. And, *thank goodness* to herself. *I hope he isn't a fake.*

As Jamal climbed the stairway to his room, he repeated, "My Man," air-punching his fist, feeling very strong and grown up. When he got to his room and closed the door, he started to practice saying "Katituran, Katituran, Kati …" He wasn't sure he had it right but he kept practicing because he loved words, especially when they were unusual.

Clarence's car was a few years old, but a nice one. It was an Outback and was kept in good condition. Cleo thought this man was going to be one heck of a find if he continued to be as fine as he seemed. She did smell stale cigarette smoke in the car and hoped this didn't mean he smoked those horrible things. But she supposed he couldn't be perfect. That would be too much to expect.

"Hey, I really enjoyed meeting your son, Jamal. He's a cool kid," Clarence began.

"You won't get an argument from me about that. I think he's the coolest kid around."

He smiled. "I was impressed when he returned my 'high five' with dap. I didn't think he would know the whole routine."

"My son's pretty smart. I'm glad you got along so well."

The Khachaturian concert was as wonderful as Clarence advertised, and as they left the Concert Center, he asked her, "How about going to a bar to top off the evening?"

"A bar?" She asked surprised. "Somehow, I didn't take you as the drinkin' kind."

"I'm not. I was thinking of a dessert tasting bar. Have you ever been to one?"

"I've never heard of such a thing. Do they let you taste possible concoctions before you order?"

"Sure do."

They were downtown where all of the trendy things were, so she wasn't surprised at the new twist in bar venues. "Well, that's a new one on me."

"Come on, I know one nearby." He took her arm and led her to a small stylish café called Au Chocolate, Etc. that served tasty desserts and coffee. The venue was fascinating. It looked just like a liquor bar but instead of bottles of booze, there was a colorful array of sweet concoctions. Just as if they were in an actual bar, they sat on stools and tasted a few. Cleo chose a chocolate ice cream creation that dripped in the syrupy stuff. It was topped with a mound of nuts and whipped cream. She noted the artful presentation.

When she took a spoonful and tasted it, she nearly fainted from the richness of the chocolaty invention. "Oh my God, that's good."

"I know!" He laughed at her reaction. "This is the tastiest place I've ever found." Looking deep into her eyes, he took a spoonful of his dessert and tried to match her reaction. "My God! Where do people get ideas for these sweets? This is downright decadent."

They laughed and he reached to take her hand. "I hope you don't mind, but you are one of the nicest women I have ever met."

"Why would I mind?" Cleo smiled thinking she had found a real keeper. His sincerity was overwhelming. She did have one question on her mind. "Tell me, your car smells of stale cigarettes. Do you smoke?"

"I gave it up some time ago." He wrinkled up his nose and said, "The smell still clings to the upholstery, doesn't it?"

"It does, but I hope I'm not putting you on the spot. I was curious though."

"I gave it up cold turkey," he said proudly. "I was inspired by Obama."

"Good. I realize that must be difficult."

"Once I made up my mind, it wasn't that hard. A few days, is all. I had a few strategies like running for a mile or two and when I couldn't do that, I did jigsaw puzzles."

Cleo raised her eyebrows wondering why jigsaw puzzles?

"It was something I had done as a kid before I started smoking and it took my mind off the cravings. It worked."

"Well, that's great. I bet it was hard, though. I've heard smoking is a habit that's as hard to quit as some of the most harmful drugs."

"Yeah, I guess."

"You said you live in Compton."

"Yep, for as long as I can remember."

"Did you ever have any trouble with the cops there?"

"Yeah, only once. It was my fault. I got into a fight with a brother down the street from where I live and the 'Poh-Poh' came along to stop it. I got arrested. I deserved to get arrested but I didn't deserve the treatment I got. They roughed me up and then claimed I got the wounds in the fight."

"That's not really surprising, especially in Compton."

"Why do you say that?"

"My friend, Ty, told me about them. You know, his brother lives there and he said there is a supremacist cabal of police in Compton who do a lot of bad things to us. He said, they even have a symbol they 'ink' onto the back of their legs to declare themselves. It's real sinister."

"Yeah, I've heard about 'em."

After dessert, he took her straight home and kissed her on the cheek as he left her at the door. Walking away, he looked back and saluted his goodnight.

Cleo nearly danced her way into the house. Compared to Jesse, her ex, he was a real gentleman and it looked natural on him, not put on like some men she'd met who put on a nice act until they got to know her better.

"You look downright happy," her mom stated the obvious. "Looks like you had a great time."

"Oh gosh, Mom, I just hope he isn't a dream from which I will have to awaken."

"Dreams are meant to awaken you," she smiled. "Well, maybe I'm thinkin' of nightmares."

Fourteen

AS HE DROVE AWAY, Clarence thought about all that had happened since he'd met Cleo. He liked her a lot and it scared him. She was the first woman he'd met in a long time, or maybe ever, that made sense. He hoped he wasn't dreaming only to wake up to a reality like the one he'd just broken up with.

Etta Stone had been a horror show. He'd known her in high school and they got together just as they were about to graduate. She was nice at first, said she'd had a very sad life so far; it was drawn on her face and in her countenance. Being an optimistic guy, he thought he could cheer her up, but the opposite happened. It seemed the more involved they got, the sadder she became and the more demanding. She was controlling and argumentative. It must have come out of her childhood without a father and her mother, a white woman, who blamed her for everything that had gone bad in their lives.

He was glad he had been able to end it even though the breaking up had taken a long time. She'd get mad at him and he wouldn't call for months even though she called and left messages constantly. He wondered if the mother drank, though Etta never said.

Then the harassing began. Etta was determined to never let him go. She stalked him wherever he went. She had to work, but in her spare time, she dogged him until he thought he would have to call the cops. He didn't want to do that to her. So, he held off and took the harassment until one day about a year ago, he relented and took her out again.

She seemed so grateful that she behaved well for a good period of time. Then, suddenly they had a big fight. She was so unpredictable that he was taken by surprise. She threw things at him—shoes, bottles of booze, a silk robe that landed on his head and covered his face. Then, she threw him out of her apartment and told him to never come back as he was struggling to get the robe off his head. A neighbor who'd heard the fight peered out a door, then closed it quickly. Clarence felt embarrassed like he'd never been before. He decided that was it and he would never allow Etta back into his life again.

But, Cleo! What a delight. She was cheerful, positive, full of hope and determined to make her life work for her and her son, that delightful Jamal. He knew she couldn't be perfect, no one was, but he had high hopes for their relationship if there was to be one. He decided to call her in the morning and take her to breakfast at Charlie's, his favorite café. School was going well enough now that he could take a little time on Sunday morning to see her again. He hoped she would be willing.

His schooling was computers. He had a high ambition. He'd seen a movie recently that included CGI, Computer Generated Imaging, and loved it. He'd been clever at drawing as a kid, things like in the comic books he read. Since then, he had gotten so busy that he didn't have much time for drawing anymore, but he knew he had some talent and wanted to include that with his work learning computers. He'd signed up for advanced computer courses online.

He wondered about the dude Cleo was working for. She said he was severely racist. Zackary Hughes probably hailed from the south. His own mom came west from there and met his dad here who was on vacation from Baltimore, Maryland, where he lived. They each decided to move to California and got married. The match had not been a good one. Clarence's mom said that neither was suitable for the other which meant Clarence was reared by a divorced mom.

It had been hard since there was never any money. They ended up in Compton where she could afford to rent a small house. It was then and still was a small two-bedroom, one bath pueblo-style yellow stucco with a chain-link fence and a back yard with one tree growing in it. That had been a stroke of good luck because Clarence loved nature; it was where he'd spent most of his days as a kid except when it was too cold or it rained.

He loved being in the outdoors, climbing the tree, an old oak, and relating to the creatures he found there—squirrels, pigeons, blue jays, sparrows, crows and other birds, mostly the kind found in the city. He drew pictures of them and kept his drawings in a scrapbook.

There was only one thing missing in his life—his dad. The dude never showed up for anything, not even birthdays. Made him feel like a mama's boy even though he knew he was far too independent for that moniker.

He never understood his dad's reluctance to come around to see him. Wasn't he good enough? It was a loss that made him the kind of guy who feared bad relationships. Clarence never wanted to end up the absentee father.

Jamal had an absent dad, too. What a shame. The kid rocked. He even wanted to skateboard together. With only one meeting, Clarence felt like he could be a good dad for him. That was thinking way too far ahead, but the idea was tempting.

It had been a good life even without a dad. Clarence was athletic and loved skateboarding and he liked school well enough. He'd wanted to go to college, but it was out of the question without enough money, and his grades weren't the kind that generated scholarships. He'd considered a loan, but without employment to pay it back, he didn't qualify and his mom didn't qualify either. So, he'd gotten the job at Optimum-Care. It had been perfect for him and he excelled there making it possible to get a loan to manage the online computer classes. He knew he would be a good computer programmer. He really loved the class work and was excelling there too.

Yep, life was good, but he had to get out of his mom's house into a crib of his own. He hoped to find an apartment soon; was saving up for the first and last that was always required.

Life was okay and he liked Cleo a lot. Maybe too much for one date, but he had high hopes.

Fifteen

CLARENCE CALLED the next morning, Sunday, and asked Cleo to go for breakfast. She accepted, delighted he had called so soon.

Charlie's was a diner like so many she had seen. It smelled of hamburger grease with a counter for people who wanted to sit alone and stalls along the front by the windows with booth-style seating on either side of the tables. The tables were covered in linoleum and the vinyl seats were red. There was a clock on the wall that said 'Time to Dine' on the face.

"You remind me of a warm cup of coffee," Cleo said as her large, dark eyes peered at Clarence over a steaming mug across the coffee house table.

"How's that?"

"Well, you add warmth, strength and plenty of stimulation; you are the perfect shade— like a little cream in my coffee and your coloring is the perfect shade for my cup; and, you are providing me with the 'break' I need from the responsibilities of my life. So, why wouldn't you remind me of the perfect cup?"

"That is a very flattering thing to say."

"I'm not trying to flatter you; I am complimenting you for your effect on me."

"What's the difference?"

"Flattery to me is disingenuous, like trying to butter you up. That's not me. I am sincerely complimenting you. You are all those things." Suddenly embarrassed that she had made such a big deal out of it, she took a big sip from her cup. "My mom reminded me that I don't know your last name," she continued changing the subject. "I'm embarrassed that I don't know."

"No problem. It's Delacroix. Clarence Delano Delacroix," he said proudly.

"Wow! That's quite a moniker. Delano comes from Roosevelt I suppose?"

He nodded.

"And, Delacroix is a French name, isn't it?"

"Yep. You're right. We are descendants of my great, great, great, great grandmother who escaped the Delacroix Sugar Plantation in Louisiana, on the isle of Delacroix. The family owned the whole island. She had been impregnated by the family's only son and escaped running away in one of Harriet Tubman's breaking free campaigns. She's a family legend for the chances she took to be free. She gave her son the Delacroix family name even though she never married the man. She was very bold and very brave."

"I would say so. That's an amazing story. I love your name—it has a good sound and rhythm to it." Changing the subject, she said, "You know, no one ever drinks from a coffee cup or a mug anymore."

"That's true. They always drink from plastic or paper cups, don't they? I mean, we do, don't we when we aren't sitting here drinking from mugs?"

Just then, Cleo felt she had lost his attention. He was looking out the window as if he'd seen something.

"What is it?" She asked? "I lost you there for a minute."

"Nothing, nothing. I just saw a car I thought I recognized, a red Toyota, but it turned out to be nothing."

He continued their conversation. "Where did you get your name; Cleo Henderson, isn't it? Their order of eggs, bacon and coffee arrived. "Cleo Patra?" He asked as he moved his arms and chest back giving the waitress room to set his plate down. Cleo noticed his slim and muscular build through the white T-shirt.

"Goodness no. Patra didn't come with it. My mom liked the name, Cleo, but I always hated it. I heard once, from a school mate who was teasing me, that only cows were named Cleo. I think she was right."

"I don't think so. It sounds exotic to me. The name Cleo is like Barbara Streisand's nose. It isn't traditional, but it is classic."

She laughed with a cackle. "Now, you are flattering me."

"Am not."

"Are, too."

They giggled as they brought their warm mugs of coffee to their lips.

"Mmmm. Tastes just right." Cleo declared.

His eyes widened.

She realized a little late the implication of her comment. She couldn't help herself and started giggling again like a school girl. He chimed right in. The two of them seemed to melt together like two ice cream cones on a hot day.

Sixteen

WHEN CLEO ARRIVED at work on Tuesday after taking Jamal to his Spanish lesson on Monday, she hummed around the house while doing the chores. When she brought Zackary his lunch, he took a bite of his sandwich and between chews mumbled something about her cheerful mood.

"True. I am cheerful. I am happy in a way I haven't been in a long time."

"That's nice to hear. What makes you so happy? It must be a man," he said, answering his own question. "But I thought you had a meeting with some teacher yesterday."

"Yes, and it went quite well. Jamal, my son, is taking Spanish lessons from a neighbor woman to help him deal with the Hispanic children in summer camp. Her name is Lupe Gonzalez. She and her family are from Mexico. She's really nice and Jamal seemed to like her. I wasn't sure he would."

"Oh, well I hope he does well," he said a little unsure where the value was.

"I do too. We are very lucky to have her in our neighborhood. It doesn't always happen that way. There's a lot of animosity between the Blacks and Hispanics in South-Central. The kids toss their used sneakers over the telephone lines to mark their territory, like animals piss on trees and bushes to mark theirs."

"Sounds right."

She looked at him curiously wondering what exactly he'd meant by the remark.

"Is that why you are so happy today?"

"What, the Spanish lessons?" Then, "Oh, no. Not exactly. I'm very glad about the lessons, of course, but you're right. I've met a man and we had our first dates this last weekend."

"Oh. The whole weekend?" He asked with suspicion in his voice. "I hope you don't get all caught up in a man."

"We went to a concert Saturday night. Then, he called on Sunday morning and took me to breakfast at a place called Charlie's," she answered curtly; then pointedly, "So, no, we didn't spend the night together, if that's what you think.

"Well, it is what I thought, but never mind. You must have had a wonderful time if your mood is any indication."

"It was great."

"It sounds like you've found someone you really like."

"Oh, yes, I do."

"Right," he grumbled.

After she had done some more dusting in the house, she returned to take his lunch tray. "By the way," she said before going to the kitchen, "I'm grateful you didn't replace me. I'm sorry I had to take the time off."

"You thought I would replace you?"

"Well, yes. I was warned you might like someone else better."

"I like you just fine, Cleo."

"Thank you, Mr. Hughes."

That afternoon, she took him to a doctor's appointment. The struggle to get him and his wheelchair into the aging white Mercedes Benz, which had been stored in the garage for some time, turned out to be comical. Zack actually laughed. It was the first time she had heard him laugh at all. The old Mercedes coughed and choked a little before it would start, but she thankfully got it going.

The jocularity didn't last. The doctor was running late and they had to sit a long time in the waiting room. The place was dark and the setting old. It hadn't had an update in years. Paintings on the walls were prints by old masters and only dated the waiting room in a depressing way. By the time Zackary got to see the physician, he was in a very cranky humor and let the doctor know exactly how he felt. "On top of your lateness, you have spoiled this young woman's glorious mood of the morning."

The doctor could do nothing but apologize profusely for the problem. "I hope you can regain whatever happiness you had earlier," the man said.

"You know, if I hadn't been such a long-time customer of yours, I would be tempted to find another doctor," Zack cackled with glee.

"Well, Zack, if that's how you feel." The doctor had the sparkle of a knowing look in his eye as he pushed Zackary's shirt up and listened to his heart with a stethoscope. Both men laughed at the absurdity.

It had been a long and arduous day by the time Cleo arrived home. It was the first time she had a good chance to talk to Jamal since their meeting with Lupe the day before. She had gotten home from grocery shopping after he'd gone to bed and the morning was rushed which left no time for conversation. But tonight, she made sure there was enough time. After dinner while they lingered at the kitchen table, she asked him how he felt about the Spanish lessons.

"I hate Spanish!" Jamal objected. "And, I hate all those kids who speak it."

"I can understand how you feel," Cleo responded. "But, when you can speak and understand their language, they will like you better."

"I don't care if they like me. I hate them," he cried.

"Please Jamal. Try to learn Spanish. Even if you never use it with those students, it'll help you when you get older."

Edith had been listening while at the sink doing the dishes. "That's true, son. There're a lot of people in this city who speak it and this is an excellent opportunity for you."

"I still hate it," he cried as he ran away from them and climbed the stairs to his bedroom. They could still hear his tears after he slammed the door.

"I don't know, Mom. Do you think he'll be okay with the lessons?"

Jamal's stereo blasted out some Rap drowning out the tears.

"Honey, maybe not right away, but if he likes the teacher, with time he'll be fine."

"Gosh, I hope so... Mom," she continued, "I don't know what I would do without you. Please don't ever leave me."

Edith smiled ruefully knowing there would be a day, maybe not soon, but someday.

Seventeen

EDITH'S TIME TAKING CARE of Jamal and living with her daughter was a blessing for a lot of reasons. Cleo had insisted she go for a complete makeover at Lola's, the local beauty salon. She'd gone and was surprised when they took her into a private room with a massage table and gave her a complete rub down from head to toe. Then they did her face as well as changing her hair color and style, taking the color back to the beautiful shade of ebony she'd had as a younger woman, with a splash of white in the front. Not only did she look better, she felt a lot better, stylish even.

After Alfred Martin, her husband, passed away at the unbelievably young age of fifty-five, Edith thought her life was over. She had been with him since they were teenagers and how to live without him was unimaginable. He'd worked hard at his job as a train conductor on the Red Line, then as a bus driver for the Metro Line for all those years. Even when physical problems began to plague him, he refused to quit. But soon, he was promoted to supervisor and he was proud of himself for having achieved that position. He never missed a day in all his life.

That responsibility alone was enough to take the soul out of him, and then there had been problems with Walter, their son. Cleo had always been a good child, but Walter had been a handful. He had ADHD, Attention Deficit Hypertension Disorder, so keeping him calmed down enough so he could study and stay away from the kids doing drugs, was a challenge neither of them had bargained for. Those days had taken a toll on both of them, and had counted a lot against a long, healthy lifespan for her husband.

When Alfred passed, Edith thought she would go soon as well. Her sadness took its toll until Cleo suddenly came crying to her about her marriage to Jesse. Edith had never thought it would last, so she was hardly surprised even though she had hoped Jamal's entry into their lives would keep them together longer. Jesse just wasn't the kind of man to hang in with too much responsibility. She had to give him credit for lasting as long as he did.

Cleo needed help, which for Edith turned out to be a life-saver. They moved in with her in their family home. Taking care of Jamal as Cleo went to school and then off to work was what kept her going. The child was a handful to be sure, but he was nevertheless a delight. He had his uncle's energy but was able to concentrate in a way Walter had never been able to. She hoped as he grew, he would continue to be manageable. Her experience caring for small children at a private nursery school before her own kids were born was perfect for the job at hand. Edith was very glad for those four years with young children which had prepared her for rearing her two, and now Jamal.

Cleo was a good mom. Her dedication to Jamal was equal to the dedication Edith had toward her children, and she was proud of Cleo's determination to never let life get to her.

As a teen, she had joined a high-school civil rights group and had united with many factions in civil rights demonstrations which showed her abilities to organize and do the hard work that was necessary. So, it didn't surprise Edith that Cleo wanted to go to nursing school. She wasn't the least bit surprised with her dedication to achieving her goals even when huge obstacles got in the way. Cleo was a survivor and she took hope from her daughter's resolve that made life well worth living.

It all made Edith's life worth living, too. She went to her doctor's appointments, adhered to the vitamin regimen and doctor's prescriptions faithfully, and she ate good fresh food, even though she had to travel quite a distance by bus to find that kind of produce. She did these things because she knew she was needed. Cleo's hope in a life that made sense, gave her all the reason she needed to keep on. Her job taking care of Jamal added a kind of joy she never thought she would achieve. Everything he did, even when he was being difficult, was worth all the love and life Edith had to give.

Eighteen

OVER TIME, CLEO'S JOB was going well. Zack seemed to accept her even though at times he used language that was offensive to her race. She tried to keep her tongue though she often thought he shouldn't be able to get away with his audacity. But then, she thought, he was awfully old and wasn't likely to change just because she told him he should. Working with him was difficult, though, and sometimes it was hard to keep herself from saying how she felt. She thought about her mom often during these times, knowing Edith would be proud of her and her efforts.

She played the piano for him. He seemed to take such pleasure in hearing the music. She was good at it and had come to appreciate the trouble her aunt had gone to teach her. She managed over time to gain Zackary's trust in her intelligence, enough to begin filling out the checks to pay the bills and to research things that were disturbing to him, like why the doctors made him take so much medication. He hated taking pills. She took up the job of ordering the medications when he was running low. It was an opportunity to talk to Clarence when she was able to access him on the phone.

With time, Cleo and Zack managed to forge a relationship based on trust.

One day, when she arrived, Cleo found Zack in tears. "What's the matter? You have been so cheerful lately. What's gone wrong?"

"Oh nothing," he grumbled.

"Come on, it can't be nothing."

"I was just thinking about my wife and how much I miss her. She was the most wonderful person in my whole existence and now she's gone, forever."

"I am so sorry. You know, I've never asked her name."

"It was Miriam. Would you mind taking me into the living room and playing *Moonlight Sonata* again? You do it so well."

"I don't mind at all, but don't you want to eat your breakfast before it gets too cold?"

The breakfast sat on his lap, uneaten with the usual scrambled eggs and bacon with toast.

"I can't eat now. I'm too depressed."

"Okay. Come on." She wheeled him into the living room and set him up so he could eat while she played. But she worried he would cry too much to finish the food.

She played *Moonlight Sonata* and followed it up with a recent composition by a writer name Renee Michell called *Beside You*. When she was done with the number, she noticed she had been right. The tears streamed down his face. So, she tried a Joplin piece, *Maple Leaf Rag*, Joplin's most famous work; she thought it might pick up Zack's mood. It didn't work.

When she was finished, he said, "That Scott Joplin's a nigger, isn't he?"

"He's no longer living."

"Take me to my room," he barked.

Surprised, but not wanting to make things more difficult, she did as she was asked.

"You know, Mr. Hughes, there are people of color who are intelligent and talented as was Mr. Joplin. I think you are wrong judging him the way you do," she said as she struggled to get him into the bed.

"You don't know what I know!" he countered. "I knew niggers in Georgia who caused a lot of trouble. They were accused of all sorts of terrible acts. Even rape."

"I'm sure they were. That doesn't mean all of the accusations were true."

"You don't know what you're talking about. They were resentful and did appalling things to let us know how they felt."

"Maybe their feelings were legitimate. Maybe they were suppressed enough that they could justify their reactions to the oppression they must have felt with the Jim Crow era to deal with. Your education about black folk is very limited in my opinion."

"Who asked for your opinion?" He barked.

It was the first argument they'd had. Zack escalated his rhetoric. "They deserved to be punished even in the worst of ways."

"Oh, you mean by lynching?" She accused.

"Yes, that's exactly what I mean," he answered curtly. "God mandated they be hung. If they couldn't be prosecuted for their actions by the authorities, then ordinary people had to step in and take charge. You defend them, but you don't know what you're talking about. Whenever they broke the law, they always got a fair trial for their insolence. But some of the things they did …" His voice had grown slowly quiet and his eyes clouded over as if by ice.

Cleo wondered what was on his mind, but chilled by his demeanor she decided to leave him alone and left the room.

Angry now, she used the energy to dust and clean up the living area, especially the Steinway which needed to shine like it did when she first saw it. Tears filled her eyes as she thought about how insensitive he was. "Lynching!" she said to herself. "My God, how horrible." She was aware of some of the things that happened at lynchings—dismemberment, incineration, finger nails pulled out, and more tortures—all things that happened when the poor soul was still alive.

She was enormously grateful when Elsie showed up at six. She and Zack hadn't spoken the whole day after their quarrel.

Depressed, she made her way home after quietly doing the chores and, with Elsie, dealing with Zackary's needs. Cleo didn't know how she was going to be able to work in his employ from then on and spoke to Edith about it.

"He'll get over it, honey, and you will too."

"I don't know Mom. I was actually getting to like him, even care about him."

"All the better. He should feel that you care and that will make this all better."

"You are being far too positive this time. I can't imagine getting over his attitudes. He is so hateful when he talks about us. It's really bad. It's like he wants to punish people he doesn't even know."

"Maybe. I don't know because I'm not there, but you've said he is fine in other ways."

"Sure. But maybe he will learn to hate me just like he hates other blacks."

"Anything's possible, but I don't believe you will give him any reason to hate you. You are far too nice. By the way, your young man, Clarence, called and left a message not long ago, just before you got home."

That picked up Cleo's frame of mind. "Why didn't you tell me?"

"I just did."

Cleo ran to the phone and dialed. Clarence asked her out for dinner Saturday night. She accepted.

They had been dating for some time and she was grateful he had been such a gentleman. She thought maybe it was time to take things to the next level. She just didn't know how to broach the subject. Maybe she should tell him she wanted to have sex.

That Saturday night after a casual dinner, they went bowling nearby. The lanes had been crowded, but they got one as soon as it was available. She hadn't been bowling since high school and felt rusty. Nevertheless, she managed a couple of strikes and even a spare and felt really proud. Clarence was something of an expert at the sport, but he didn't minimize her abilities in the least. There were a lot of laughs between them as each worked at making the evening successful.

Clarence was watching as some other bowlers made strikes. "Wow, look at that group! They are good."

Cleo looked over a couple of lanes down. There were four women, all black. One, who moved toward them when she realized Clarence and Cleo were watching them, was very attractive but not beautiful. She was a light-skinned black woman. Her face was stern and her eyes sad like she had never smiled before. Her hair was done in long dreadlocks, in cornrows hiked up to the top of her head, and quite lovely. She wore a lot of makeup, especially long eyelashes that were obviously not her own and shiny red lipstick. She looked like she was going on a date instead of just bowling with the girls. She seemed more intensely interested in Clarence than the others; that's why Cleo noticed her. "Well, they sure do look good playing," she playfully chided, elbowing him in the ribs.

"Are you implying I'm interested in them?"

"No, not exactly. But you did take them in."

"Oh well, there's that one woman I know. But that's not important." He got off the subject of the others quickly which Cleo appreciated.

Nineteen

AS WAS HIS CUSTOM, Clarence asked her to go to breakfast the next morning. He picked her up at the usual time.

"About the women last night? Especially that light-skinned woman who seemed to know you," she asked. "What *was* that about?"

"Nothing. I told you, I just recognized her. She's bowled there before. She's good at it, that's all."

He smiled at her across the table trying to make light of it and, deciding to dismiss the woman of the previous night, Cleo finally told him her story about Zack and complained about their difficult time together all week.

"He'll get over it. I bet you are the best healthcare worker he could have, and he knows it."

"You and my mom are both so positive. I don't know, Clarence. Zack is intractable. He can't seem to get over how he feels about our race. If you had to deal with him every day like I do, you might change your mind."

"I might. But I do have a little perspective. So does your mom. You'll be fine. I'm sure of it. People can't carry grudges forever."

"He's really a hateful old man. And, look at where he lives. I mean Glendale? By the way, I almost forgot what happened on my way home one night about a week ago."

"It must have been very serious if you didn't remember," he chided.

"Oh, it was serious," she chuckled. "It's just that the situation with Zack has so-overridden just about everything."

"Okay, what happened?"

"Well, I was sitting at the bus stop in Glendale waiting for my usual bus to come along. There was an older woman sitting with her granddaughter at the same stop… at the other end of the bench, of course." Cleo stopped. "Maybe I shouldn't tell you. It'll sound like I'm whining."

"Come on. Out with it. I won't think anything. You have a right to feel how you feel no matter what it is."

"Well, I guess she didn't think I could hear her, or maybe she did and didn't care. The child was about six, around Jamal's age. The woman said to her 'Don't pick your lips that way. They'll get huge just like that woman's over there.' The girl's lips were dry and the skin was sticking out while she picked at them trying to get the dry skin off. I tried not to notice, but it was impossible to ignore them. Then the girl said, 'What's wrong with her lips? They're beautiful.'"

"Wow! She was right on," he said. "They are beautiful."

Cleo smiled ruefully. "Thank you, but that's not what the woman was trying to convey to her granddaughter. She was warning her and she smacked the child's hand as she reached for her lips. I wanted to run away from them. The woman was so insulting and I couldn't do or say anything."

"I'm sorry. That must have hurt you a lot."

"It did, especially with Zack acting the way he did. Maybe I'm being too sensitive."

"I don't think so." He took her hand and gently kissed it, with *his* full lips.

"Cleo, what if I proposed a time away, say renting a room near the beach, maybe up the coast a bit?"

"Oh, well, I'd be up for that. Where are you thinking?"

"How about Big Sur?"

"Wow! That's ambitious."

"Yeah, it is a little, but not out of the question. The beaches up there are outstanding. I remember places to rent that are kind of primitive, cabins with wood stoves. My mom and I went up there a long time ago, when I was little. I could research it and find out if those kinds of lodgings are still possible. Would you go if I found a way to do it?"

"Yes, I would like that. We would be leaving Jamal behind, right?"

"Oh yeah. I don't think he would enjoy it as much as we would," he chided sardonically.

"I have a feeling he wouldn't. So, we'll leave him with my mom," she said pointedly.

He smiled. She smiled.

The kiss from Clarence had been soft and strong, at the same time making it easy for Cleo to commit to the trip they were about to take. She managed to get a substitute for the week of their journey even though Zackary complained that she had to take the time off. Zackary was unhappy and thought 'the young man' was beginning to take too much of her time. She reminded him there were two 'young men' in her life, her son, Jamal, who had been the cause of the first interruption and the other was Clarence, her new boyfriend. Yes, it was true she did have a life outside of work, but it wouldn't interrupt the important things she did for Zackary. At least, she hoped it wouldn't. She still needed the job and hoped their relationship would improve with time. She didn't know whether there was a God, but she prayed nevertheless.

"I wouldn't let you, you know, but you seem to like the young man so much. Did you say his name is Clarence?" He asked as an afterthought.

"Yes, it is and I am very grateful for the time. Thank you, Mr. Hughes."

"Heavens, haven't we gotten beyond last names yet?"

This surprised her. She thought he would fire her after their last encounter. "Of course, Zackary."

"You know I prefer Zack, so call me that instead. Okay?" He said in his ancient gravelly voice.

She left that Friday evening with great hope that she had won Zack over.

Twenty

SCHOOL HAD BECOME a boring accumulation of numbing lectures and class work. Angus' graduation from high school would come soon, but not soon enough. He was anxious to get on with his life and high school seemed an impediment to the transformation he was looking for.

Until one day he saw her. There was a new girl who'd come to the school from some other state. Wow, he thought. What would it be like to go to a new school in the last year? What about all the friends who would be left behind? Of course, he wasn't thinking about all the friends he would be losing after graduation when they dispersed to unknown parts of the country, to colleges and universities across the great 3000-mile expanse called the United States of America. He would be left behind in California, and they would soon be gone. It was hard to wrap his head around the big changes that were coming, some welcome and some not-so-much.

The new girl was pretty with tawny hair and a tanned complexion, tall and lanky: a lot like he was. He was envious of her tan. She must have a pool at her house to get a tan like that, or maybe she spent a lot of time at the beach. He wondered if she was a surfer. Tanning wasn't something he could do easily. He mostly got red and if he was lucky his skin would turn a light shade of beige.

That first day he saw her, she was wearing tight Levis and a short-cropped top that exposed her midriff. He thought she was thoroughly sexy. She was taking World History in the same class, the one that started the day off with a lot of boring facts that had to be memorized. He hated it and thought a lot of what he was learning was just propaganda.

Right after class, he followed her to see where her locker was. He hoped it would be close to his and, miracle of miracles, it was, right across the hallway. This gave him a stellar opportunity to say 'hi' and maybe get her to talk to him.

He was shy, but determined. He thought a purposeful bump into her would be a good way to start things off. So, once he got his books out for the next class, he backed into the hall, trying not to look too obvious and successfully crashed his way into her backside at just the right moment. He knocked her books right out of her arms which gave him the perfect opportunity to pick them up for her as he gasped out apologies for the 'accident.'

She looked at him askance, not believing his 'accidental' crash into her. Then, she recognized him from history class. "Hey, didn't Ah just see ya'all in class?" She asked, with a slight southern accent.

"Uh, yeah. You're the new girl, right?" He hoped he wasn't making a fool of himself.

"Yeah. Mah dad just got a great job as head chef in a restaurant. It's in Burbank. Mah mom didn't like Burbank when she saw it, so we moved heah."

"Are you from someplace in California?" He asked trying to make conversation.

"No, we'ah from Texas. Dallas, to be specific. Why?"

"Oh, just curious, is all. I don't know anyone from Texas. I thought I detected a little accent there." Angus was thinking he'd struck gold. A girl from Texas was likely to think a lot like he did.

"What's yo name?" She asked.

He was sure he'd struck gold now. She was asking him his name! "I'm Angus Dunne."

"Angus Dung?!" She asked, alarmed not hearing him correctly.

"No, it's Dunne; D-U-N-N -E," he spelled it out.

"That's a relief," she laughed. Ah'm from cow country and Ah thought …"

"Yeah, I know. I get that a lot from guys I don't like." His humiliation was palpable.

"Sorry. Ah didn't mean to …"

"It's okay. Not your fault. My parents might have thought about that when they named me. I've lived with jokes all my life."

"Awe, that's terrible." She wasn't mocking him which was a huge plus. "Mah name is Sarah Griffith." She held out her hand to shake his.

"Oh, like the park?" He took her hand; it was warm and inviting.

"Well, Ah guess turn-around 's fair play."

"Oh, no. I didn't mean that in a bad way. It's just a way to remember your name. It's pretty, just like you are." He couldn't believe he was being so bold. "And, Griffith Park is a great site to visit. Maybe we could go there sometime, visit the observatory. It's a cool place."

"Ah'd like that."

He couldn't believe she had just accepted a date with him. Maybe the last semester-plus wouldn't be so bad after all.

Twenty-one

THE DRIVE UP the California Coast from Los Angeles to Big Sur was as stunning as advertised. The sun was shining and as Cleo and Clarence got farther out of LA, the sky became the most stunning shade of cerulean Cleo thought she had ever seen. Cumulous clouds rested over the hillsides and she mentioned it was the most gorgeous day she'd seen in a long time.

She had gotten Phyllis at the agency to find another fill-in for her at the Hughes' residence. A vacation was something she needed; it had been since early teen-hood that she'd had one, and that had been a short weekend with her girlfriends. It was the one time she had gotten high on pot and she didn't like the feeling at all. The only reason she had tried it was because she wanted to fit in with her friends. Then, she decided differently, not to be like them. At the time, she wasn't exactly sure what that would be, but she definitely didn't want to do things just because her 'Besties' did them.

This time, she hoped to get 'high' on Clarence. It was, at last, an opportunity to be together. She didn't think she would have to tell Clarence she wanted to have sex. That would be a given.

She had never seen so many big trees. They saw huge Redwoods here and there as they got closer to their destination. The area around Big Sur was lush with gorgeous pines. There was the beach, too. But Cleo loved the trees most of all.

Their rental cabin was tucked in amid the pines and other shrub she couldn't identify. The front was a dark brown wood-slat exterior with stone steps leading up to the small porch and doorway made from redwood; the porch roof was supported by tall pine logs and the pane windows were trimmed in redwood. It was warm and inviting. The chandelier in the middle of the living area was made of deer antlers and there was a wood stove parked in front of one wall. Someone had already started a fire. Logs filled a wooden container. The chairs and couch surrounded a round redwood slab on a short tree stump that stood in for the coffee table.

While Clarence was getting the luggage out of the car, she peeked into the bedroom and found a nice big bed and sliding glass door that led out to a wood deck with chairs and a table looking out over a garden surrounded by a tall wood fence providing privacy. The bathroom was clean and sported an old-fashioned soaking tub with clawed feet. The whole thing was charming and she felt lucky to be here. The kitchen was nice, too—functional. The farm-style sink back-splash was red tile, and underneath there were basket storage bins. Clarence came in with their baggage and took them into the bedroom. When he came out, he took her into his arms and asked, "To your liking, Madam?"

"It could be half as nice and I would have liked it because you're here."

"Good answer."

"I just hope you aren't spending too much money on this place."

"Honestly, it was the cheapest I could find within fifty miles."

"Let me help, then."

"Are you kidding? My manhood is at stake here. So, don't even think of going Dutch-treat!" With that, he kissed her and picked her up, carrying her into the bedroom where they made love for the first time.

They spent a few days wandering around Big Sur visiting the famous venues like Nepenthe before leaving to go back to L.A. The place was charming and interesting, but they had gotten unfriendly stares from some of the patrons. Not wanting to stay in a place where they felt unwelcome, they left and found a stunning beach nearby. Clarence parked the car. The beaches in this area of the coastline of California were very different from those in the southern coastal region of Long Beach or Santa Monica. It was rocky and the waves crashed upon huge boulders sending showers of ocean water into the air, into their hair and onto their faces. The sandy beach area was covered with seaweed brought up from the ocean with the tides. It was windy and the misty air smelled of seaweed and ocean.

There were no other people around. The chilly atmosphere didn't welcome sunbathing, so they sat on a giant rock and watched the waves silently, both thinking about the future and if it would be spent together.

Neither knew how the other felt. Cleo wondered if he, an unmarried man would welcome a ready-made family. He seemed to like Jamal, but her child was a handful, filled with a lot of energy and hard to control; stubborn too.

Clarence wondered if he could measure up to Cleo's expectations. Would he be good enough to take on a family with a child? However, both hoped there would be a future in marriage, maybe a long one, like 'til death do we part.'

And, Clarence worried about Etta Stone, his former girlfriend. She had been so demanding. She had asked him to marry her on their last date together. He tried to back out of the situation by making light of marriage in general, but finally he felt compelled to say 'no.' That was the blow Etta couldn't take. She had gone into a rage from which he couldn't talk her down. Finally, it had ended in the final breakup.

Ever since she had been stalking him. She would call him, sometimes as many as ten times a day. Etta left messages saying she was sure that God wanted them to be together, that the Holy Ghost was pushing her to marry him. That had been a while ago and he had managed to get a restraining order against her. But she had dogged him nevertheless and seemed determined to make him hers alone.

After a while he thought perhaps if he was a little nicer to her, on a platonic basis, she would calm down and realize he liked her but wasn't in love with her. He fantasized being able to talk her down from her obsession with a bit of time. In fact, that was why he'd gotten the tickets to the Khachaturian concert from a friend who had two season passes. Clarence asked Etta to go with him for the evening, then he would take her out for coffee and have a heart-to-heart.

But when he asked her to go to the concert, she thought, mistakenly, he was going to give her a chance. When he informed her he was looking for a platonic association, not a romantic one, she exploded again making a terrible scene and threatening harm.

The date to the concert was cancelled and he'd asked Cleo to go. But since then, Etta had become even more relentless in her pursuit, stalking him constantly and following whenever he took Cleo out. He was thoroughly done with Etta and didn't know what to do to get rid of her. She came around when he was out with Cleo, would meet him in front of the house when he got home, demanding to know what had happened, and he didn't know how to make her stop without engaging in another tirade. It was an impossible spot to be in.

Clarence had wanted to talk to Cleo about her, but it seemed a foolish subject to bring up in the midst of their new relationship which seemed so ideal. He knew it wouldn't always be perfect, but he didn't want to rush into the rough spots, not yet. And, Etta was a rough spot who couldn't be controlled. She had a temper that flared at the most unexpected times. He thought she was mentally unstable and in need of some serious therapy.

Twenty-two

CLEO WAS PLAYING with Jamal in the living room after they got back from Big Sur, trying to tell him about all the wonderful things she had seen. "You would love the giant waves that crashed onto the beach. It was really amazing and very different from our beaches here. You would have liked climbing around on the huge boulders and finding little crabs scurrying around."

His eyes grew big and he asked, "Mommy, when can I go?"

She promised to take him someday, maybe soon. It was an expensive adventure, so she wasn't sure how soon that could be. Even though she loved sharing her experience of Big Sur with Jamal, she wasn't sure she should have told him so much; it just whetted his appetite.

Soon she sent him upstairs to get ready for bed. Reluctantly, he managed to walk away and climb up the stairway to his room wondering if his mother would ever take him to see the giant waves.

"Cleo, I have some news, not the best news," Edith said as she joined her in the living room. Please, try not to freak out."

"What on earth?"

"Well honey, I got a phone call today, just before you got home, and I'm not sure what to make of it." Her mother's voice was hesitant. It was obvious she didn't want to broach the subject.

"Did it have to do with Jamal?" Cleo asked, alarmed.

"No, nothing to do with him." She paused hesitantly.

"Mom, please, out with it. I can't take it when you tease me like that."

"I'm not teasing. I'm just not sure how serious this is and I want you to be calm."

"I'll try my best, but what is it?" She said pointedly.

"Honey, the call was from a woman. Her name is Etta Stone and apparently she had a relationship with Clarence before you got involved."

"Are you kidding me?" She cried. "Clarence isn't the kind to play around."

"No, he isn't. But it seems those two concert tickets he had were intended for the two of them."

"The concert? Oh my God. I wondered why he had two tickets and no one to go with."

"Well, I guess they had a break-up a day or two before he asked you to go."

"If they broke up, then what's her beef?"

"Honey, I don't know, but the woman is wanting him back and you're in the way. She wanted me to talk to you about it."

"I sure as hell am not going to break up with him just to make her happy! Sorry, but I'm not that generous."

"I can guess how you feel, but this woman isn't going to be easy to get rid of. I mean, she called me while you were gone and she seemed to know you and Clarence had gone somewhere for the last few days."

"Oh man. What am I going to do? I need Clarence," Cleo whispered almost to herself. Then, "But why on earth would she think talking to me would do her any good?"

"Honestly, I'm not sure, but she sounded pretty determined. Said Clarence was the best thing to ever happen to her and she was willing to fight for him."

"Well, he's the best thing to ever happen to me and I'm very willing to fight for him, too. If she calls again, tell her buzz off and stay away."

"Okay." Edith wasn't sure she could be convincing and hoped this Etta would give it up on her own.

"I'll talk to Clarence. I'm pretty sure we're solid," Cleo added.

Twenty-three

ANGUS WAS BUSY EATING his lunch and trying to catch up on some homework for an afternoon class when Sarah showed up.

"Mind if Ah sit with y'all, have some lunch?"

"No!" He looked up startled that it was her. "No, not at all. I was just doing some science stuff for my class later."

"So, how's it goin'?"

"Okay." He'd never noticed her eyes before. Not that he'd had many opportunities; it was a busy time studying for mid-year exams. Her eyes were a glorious green color rimmed with dark lashes and they sparkled when she smiled. "Are your exams going pretty good?"

"Sho' ah. Ah don't have much trouble with it. Mah folks tell me Ah'm real smart and Ah guess they're right." She looked up at the sun, squinting. "The weather he'ah sho' is nice as advertised. He'ah it is, wintertime, almost Thanksgivin', and you'd never know it, 'cept for the colors on the leaves of the tree out there." She was referring to a maple tree on the lawn in front of the John Wayne Performing Arts Center. The tree was shedding its vibrant fall leaves.

"Don't they have good weather in Texas? I always thought they did."

"Sho'ah it is. It's okay most of the tahm. But there's somethin' special 'bout California. Ah always thought it was a lot'a hype, but it's really true. A' course, here in Glendale, there's a smog problem."

"You should 'a seen it before they got those catalytic converters for the cars. My eyes used to burn real bad. That was a long time ago, though."

"Well, mah eyes burn a lot he'ah."

"You're not used to it, is all. You'll adjust."

"Ah guess."

"You still want to go to Griffith Park to the observatory?"

"Sho' ah."

"We could go on the Saturday right after mid-terms."

"Sounds great. How'll we get ther'ah?"

"I can borrow my dad's car. He usually doesn't have a problem with me taking it if the occasion is important enough."

"Well, Ah hope he thinks it's important enough this tahm."

He smiled. He would make it important no matter what his dad thought.

Twenty-four

IT WAS SUNDAY and Cleo invited Clarence for dinner with her mom and Jamal. She spent the entire afternoon cooking the meal, baking a stuffed chicken in the oven, boiling red potatoes for mashing, which Jamal did with great gusto, and cooking fresh green beans with a garnish of fresh minced garlic drenched in butter on top. She also had time to bake a rich chocolate cake which she iced with butter-chocolate frosting.

Clarence brought a bottle of her favorite wine, a crisp Chenin Blanc, to go with their meal.

"My, my," Clarence marveled when they finished. "That was the finest meal I've eaten in a long time. My mom's a good cook, but I think you've topped her, Cleo."

"Thank you," she stumbled not expecting that much praise. "I'm flattered."

"Surely you must mean you're complimented," he countered with a smile.

"Of course, that's what I meant," she laughed. "Would you like to taste my talent as a piano player?"

Jamal laughed at their interchange. "You are sounding silly, Mom," he scolded.

"Okay, I'll try to stop then." She smiled at her son as she led them into the small living room where the upright piano stood. It was the instrument she'd stubbornly learned to play on all those years ago. She opened the lid and examined the keys. She hadn't played it for some time, testing it to be sure it was in tune. Deciding on something from Mozart and a Joplin Ragtime, she began.

When she finished, they all applauded with appreciation. "Well done," Clarence marveled. "No wonder Zackary likes you to play for him."

"I told you about his reaction to the Joplin piece, didn't I?"

"Sure, but your playing is excellent and I know he likes it when you play."

Edith had been sitting quietly watching their exchange, but she had a question of her own. "Clarence…"

"Yes, ma'am," he responded with promptness, almost jumping from his chair.

"Cleo told me you work the phones for that company that provides medications for folks who are unable to get to their pharmacies to pick them up."

"I sure do."

"Is it interesting enough for you?"

"Well, usually, but when it isn't, I do things to make it more interesting."

"Like what?"

"The other day I tried to help a woman who calls pretty regularly to order medications she's run out of. Most people do it by computer, but she is older and doesn't have one."

"What was her issue?"

"Well, she was having reoccurring dreams about falling into dark holes or finding herself descending an endless staircase."

"Oh my …"

"Yeah. I told her she would discover something new when she reached the bottom and not to be afraid."

"Did that work?"

"It did. She called back the next day and told me she discovered a rainbow at the bottom of the staircase and now she's looking forward to finding what's at the bottom of the hole."

"It's nice you took the time with her."

"I didn't mind and, well, she's a sweet lady."

"That's cool, Clarence," Cleo added.

"But what are your plans for the future?" Edith asked.

"Mom," Cleo reacted. "Clarence doesn't need to be grilled."

"It's okay, Cleo," he said. "I do have plans. In fact, I'm studying now to become a computer programmer. I don't mind that your mom wants to know."

Jamal jumped in saying, "I'm going to school, too! And, I am learning how to speak Spanish. Como esta usted?"

"Muy bien, gracias." He answered Jamal, fist-bumping him.

"You never said anything about going to school. Is it a secret you've been keeping from me?" Cleo smiled not wanting him to feel attacked.

"No, of course not. It just never came up. I would have told you otherwise."

"Well, I think that's exciting. What school are you going to?"

"It's an online course I'm taking. Makes it easier since I don't have to use my limited time traveling to and from a facility."

"That makes a lot of sense," Edith commented.

"It is easier and they're computer courses, so taking classes that way makes a lot of sense to me."

"That's smokin' hot!" Jamal sounded like such a grown up joining in their conversation.

"Yes, My Man. I think it is super-hot."

"Mom, when can I have a computer? I'm not an old person and you're not either. How come we don't have one?"

"Well, gosh. There's Christmas to consider and your birthday's coming pretty soon after that. I think you might be old enough now. I mean, you've grown your two front teeth so now's the time."

Jamal jumped up and down as he did so often when he was excited. "Wow! I'm getting a computer. Wow!" Then, he stopped. "And, what about a phone, Mom?"

"Oh, you want a cell too?"

"Well, yeah. All the kids have 'em."

"Let's concentrate on one thing at a time. Cells are expensive and we have a landline right here you can use to talk to your friends. I don't even have a cell and our phone works just fine."

"You had one before. What happened to it?" Jamal asked, sounding a little whinny.

"Didn't I tell you? I dropped it in the toilet and it got all wet. I couldn't get it dry fast enough and it never worked after that."

It was late by that time and Cleo walked Clarence to his car while Edith took Jamal up to get him ready for bed.

They stood together a moment before he got into the Outback. "You are an amazing woman, Cleo. You handled Jamal's requests skillfully, and thank you for the wonderful evening."

"Clarence, I have a question for you."

"Shoot."

"Well, my mom got a call a day before we got home from Big Sur. It was from a woman by the name of Etta Stone. Who is she and just why would she call my mother of all things?"

"Oh, Man, what the hell is she calling here for? I'm so sorry Cleo. She should never have done that. I wonder how she got the number?"

"I'm listed and people call me all the time. They tell me they got my number because it's listed, so that's probably how. But what is *she* all about?"

"What did your mom tell you?"

"That doesn't matter. Who is she and why would she call here?"

Clarence was clearly angered. "That little slut! Dammit, but she sure can horn in." He looked at her with contrite eyes. "I'm sorry, Cleo. Etta Stone is a desperate woman and she's made my life a living hell."

"You called her a slut. What's that about?"

"Like I said, she made my life extremely difficult. I couldn't take her anymore. She asked me to marry her and when I said no, she became enraged. We broke up, but she kept stalking me. I know that sounds extreme, but it's true. She wouldn't stay away. She's followed you and me a few times. I think she knows where you work with Zackary."

"My God. Are you sure you didn't lead her on in some way?"

"Well, we were intimate. That's why I didn't have sex with you for so long. I wanted to make sure I was clean. I got tested and I'm good." He smiled a sheepish grin wishing he didn't have to tell her all of it. "But to answer your question, no, I didn't *lead* her on. She's just a desperate woman. Neurotic."

"Well, sex can be a very important matter to some women."

"Ah, not to her. She was a player. There were always a lot of guys calling her on her cell, even when we were together."

"But I guess she took to you in an important way."

"I can't make any excuses. I was lonely and she seemed like she needed someone positive in her life. The kind of guys she was attracted to up to that point were … I don't want to label them, but they weren't nice. She needed a positive influence and I have to admit, I felt like I was up to providing that. I can sometimes have a big ego and it got out of hand with her; she was so needy."

"Yeah, I can understand that. You wanted to help her."

"Look, I am sorry she called here. Try not to make too much of it though. She'll probably get tired of stalking me and get on with her life. I hope so, anyway."

They stood together a moment longer before he got into the car. "You are a remarkable woman, Cleo. Thank you for the wonderful evening and for being so understanding." He took her head in his long-fingered hands and kissed her softly with his full lips and mouth. She fell into his body to let him know she was okay with everything. They held each other close for some time.

The red Toyota owned by Etta Stone passed by the couple unnoticed by both. The woman inside was razor-sharp focused on them.

Twenty-five

EDITH CLEANED UP the kitchen with a song on her lips. She was confident her daughter had found a good man at last. The girl had grown from being a gawky child who wore glasses and her hair in braids. That she got caught up with that loser, Jesse, was a misstep that any girl could take. That she had gotten herself pregnant at the age of eighteen because he made her feel special just as she was growing into the beautiful doe-eyed woman she ultimately became, was understandable. She wasn't the light-skinned Negro that anyone could accept, but the color that could make her proud; she was the color of hope. It was a shame, but Jamal was worth all of the worry Edith had spent on her grandchild. Mourning for her husband since his death two years before had been softened by her devotion to Cleo and her child.

Cleo had been such a bright girl. And, hopeful. She always seemed to be the one who held out the most hope in every situation. Edith tried now and again to offer doses of reality, but they were scoffed at as though reality would bend to Cleo's will. "It must be that Walter will be home on time to take me to the skating rink." Or, "Daddy's mood will be fine as soon as he realizes how good things really are." Or, "You will feel a whole lot better when you've had something to eat." How she got these ideas, Edith couldn't tell. Perhaps because she read so much. The books she read, aimed at young minds, were filled with stories that ended well. Edith herself had been more hopeful at the beginning of her life, so she supposed it was a trait that each shared. Innocence was so trusting.

But Cleo's hopefulness has spilled into her adult life like an unending river bubbling up with joy over the hard rocks that interrupted their flow. It was a wonderful attribute but, Edith thought, unrealistic in the world they occupied.

Maybe without realizing it, Edith had encouraged the habit. She had worked hard to make both Cleo and Walter grow into smart children, never letting them watch too much television, making them read books and write essays, practice the piano—Cleo did and Walter refused—or, study their math books. Cleo hadn't liked the math, but when she went to nursing school, she was very glad to have had that training. Edith never allowed them to speak ghetto-talk in their home. They had to speak the queen's speech. Edith didn't know if it was the right thing to do, but she did know it was necessary.

In her own youth, her mother had passed the tradition on to her after learning it from her mom who had been a very young woman toiling in the cotton fields on her father's farm which he worked as a share-cropper. Her mother made them learn a word from the dictionary every day after the day's labor was done and to always speak properly so that education would not be out of their grasp. Edith's family history was fraught with hardship, but that privation had created a strong bunch of people who passed that strength down one generation after the other.

Her daughter had learned well the hard lessons Edith was able to teach her children. Cleo's hope was relentless. Nevertheless, Edith was afraid it might meet a wall she couldn't climb, one that would thwart her best efforts.

Twenty-six

IT WAS THE SATURDAY after mid-term exams and Angus had talked his dad into borrowing the family car for the trip. "I have a date, Dad, and I promised to take her to the Griffith Park Observatory."

"A date? This is the first I've heard about in a long time."

"Yeah, well, Patsy didn't work out so well and I've shied away from *that* kind of thing." Patsy had been trashy, the kind of girl who liked sex and liked to put out for a lot of the guys.

"Not all girls are the same, Angus."

"This one sure isn't. She's real nice and she has the prettiest green eyes I've ever seen."

"Well, have a good time." His dad smiled and handed over the keys to the shiny new Buick sitting in the garage.

"Don't worry. I will. And, I'll be careful driving, so you don't have to say it." Angus' dad had always warned him to be careful.

His dad laughed a big guffaw and waved him off. "Go!"

When he arrived at the address Sarah had given him near the golf course, he was pleased to see it was the kind of house that would have a pool in the backyard. The house was a modern split level with sharp corners, painted a soft grey color, huge pane-less windows with tall, black double doors in the front. Two lofty palm trees, the kind LA County was famous for, stood on each side of the cement driveway. Stone slab steps led up to the house.

He knocked at the door and a nice-looking woman answered. She was a tall blond, dressed in a long terry robe and had the beautiful green eyes her daughter had. He assumed she was Mrs. Griffith, the mother. "Hello ma'am. My name is Angus Dunne and I've come to pick up your daughter to go to the observatory today." Feeling very bold, he held out his hand to shake hers.

"Hello, young man." She took his offer and clasped it in between her two hands in a very warm welcome. "Am Mrs. Griffith. My daughter'll be down in a minute. She's upstairs puttin' on all the final touches." She winked as if taking him into her confidence.

"Thanks, Mrs. Griffith." He noticed impressive gems on her hands. They sparkled.

"You can sit down in the livin' room right there while I go get 'er." She indicated the room she meant with a sweep of her other hand and headed up some stairs to the next landing to get Sarah.

It wasn't long before Sarah came skipping into the living room. "Hi Angus."

Her scent filled the space. It was apples and cinnamon. He took a deep breath, "Hi Sarah! You look great." And, she did. She wore a pair of black sweats that hugged her hips and figure, with a sage-green sweater that made her eyes look even greener than he remembered.

Unlike her mother, her jewelry was simple—a pretty, slender gold chain with a small pendant falling just above her breasts and simple gold-loop earrings, not the big ones that he hated but small loops, just the right size. There were two simple rings on her fingers, one that graced her index just above the knuckle. She would be comfortable walking around the observatory in her sneakers.

"So, how about we get going? My dad's car is right outside."

"Wait. Ah want ya to meet *my* dad." She pulled on his arm to bring him back into the foyer and yelled up the stairway, "Dad! Angus is he'ah. Come on down and meet 'im!"

"Honey," Angus heard a deep tenor-like voice yell down, "Ah just got out of tha shower. Why don't ya invite him for Thanksgivin' dinner and Ah'll meet him then?"

Angus hunched his shoulders. "We can wait until another time."

"Okay," she sounded disappointed.

"Come on, let's go."

It was still morning and the fall weather was breezy making the sky look a special kind of blue with clouds drifting by. "This is tha perfect day for a visit to the park, don't ya think?" Sarah marveled.

"You are the perfect person to be visiting it with," Angus smiled.

"Ah wish Ah'd made that picnic lunch I had planned. Mah little brother commandeered tha kitchen this mornin' makin' it impossible for anyone ta get in there."

"That's okay. We can pick up some fast food on the way. How old is your kid brother? I mean, a boy in the kitchen? That doesn't sound right."

"What do ya mean? He's old enough and he wants ta be a chef when he grows up like our dad."

"Oh yeah?"

"Yeah, he's makes the best home-cookin' Ah've ever known." She sounded a little piqued by his comment.

"Well, I just don't think of guys doing the cooking."

"Tha best chefs in the world are men, so you're way off the mark."

"My mom's the only one who cooks in our house and she says the kitchen's a woman's domain."

"So, she's wrong. Mah brother's a lot better at it than my mom, believe me. A'course, mah dad's the best."

"I guess it's possible."

"We eat nothin' but the best food at our house. It's all healthy, too. Mah brothah's very particular about that. Does his own shoppin' and everythin'!"

"Whoa. I wonder if he comes into the store where I work."

"He shops in our neighborhood store. Mah mom takes him, so …"

She lived off Cañada Boulevard, which was sort of close to where he worked. She didn't live that far away from Angus either. He just had to take Cañada up the road a bit from his street to Country Club Drive.

The visit to the observatory went smoothly. They got to attend the planetary lecture in the middle of the domed structure where there was a constructed view of the universe on the ceiling focusing mostly on the solar system. The seating was positioned so they could comfortably look up at the domed sky.

After that, they walked by the giant pendulum swinging back and forth in a deep well, depicting the movement of the earth on their way to view some science projects. It was fascinating and Angus really liked it. He was planning a science major in college and said so.

"What do ya wan'na to be?" She asked.

"Don't really know yet. I'm thinking about the military because I could fly jet airplanes."

"Do ya have ta know science ta do that?"

"Sure. You have to know and understand the science of aviation."

"Yeah, Ah guess so."

"You don't sound very enthusiastic."

"Oh no. You should do whatever makes ya happy. Ah guess Ah was just thinkin' about military life for the women left behind when their husbands go off to war and stuff like that."

"You planning to be my wife!" He was teasing her.

"Uh … no. Ah wasn't thinkin' that's all !" she objected. She squinted up at the giant white obelisk in front of the observatory on their way to the parking lot. "Mah mom told me about how mah dad was away a lot when he signed up ta go to Afghanistan. She didn't like it and as soon as his service was ovah, she insisted he get work close ta home. That was a long time ago before me or mah brother were born."

"It would appear that was a good choice. You live in a new place."

"Oh yeah, it was. He does really well as a chef. Learned how to cook in the military and he has a good position now, head chef for a hot restaurant chain."

"Does he have a military pension?"

"Yeah, Ah guess."

"Let's go on down to the park area and eat our picnic lunch," he said as they climbed into the car.

"Good idea. I'm starvin."

There was a blanket in the trunk of the car, so they spread it out and ate the take-out on the grass.

"Y'all have tattoos there, don't ya Angus?" She asked. They peeked out just above his Glendale High sweatshirt. The 'sweat' was red and the emblem on the front was black, the letter 'G' was located right over his heart. Red and black were the high school's colors.

"Yep."

"Ah have one, too," she bragged. "It's a tiny heart on mah ankle."

"Can I see it?"

"It's gettin' chilly and Ah don't wanna take mah sock off."

"Do you mind if I kiss you?"

Sarah blushed. She wasn't used to being asked. Most boys just dove right in. "Ah'm embarrassed ta make out right here in front'a people."

"There aren't that many folks around." In fact, there were only a few Armenian families and one Mexican family. They weren't close by.

"Well, maybe we should wait a little until we know each othah bettah."

"You're shy, aren't you?"

"Yeah, a little. Ah don't like boys who take me for granted. Just because we came here today, doesn't mean we really know each othah that well."

"Okay." He struggled to think of something that would change the subject. "The planetarium was killer, wasn't it?"

"Gosh, yes. Ah loved it. The thing about black holes is scary. Imagine everythin' close by, meanin' *millions of miles* close by," she had a wry smile on her face, "gets sucked up into those things."

"It's hard to wrap my head around. But I've been told in science class that nothing in the universe ever ceases to exist. Matter changes form but it is only changed; it never goes away completely. I wonder if those things that get sucked up that way cease to exist, or if they go somewhere else."

"Steven Hawkin' said once, they are completely destroyed and eventually everythin' in the universe'll get sucked up and will cease to exist and that'll be tha end of tha universe." She seemed to be awe-struck as she spoke.

"Well, maybe the end of *this* universe. Other scientists think there's more than one. Nobody knows for sure."

"Ah know, but didn't Hawkin' do the math ta prove he was righ'?"

"I don't have an answer to that one and he's dead now, so I guess we can't ask him."

They laughed together a lot and Angus felt like the day had gone very well as he drove her home winding up Country Club Drive.

"You take physics, don't you, Sarah?"

"Yeah, Ah do. It's real interestin'. Ah like the course a lot. Y'all like science too. That's what ya said."

"Yeah, I like it a lot. Aeronautics is my thing."

"Yeah, ya said. But the physics Ah've been learnin' about is fasci-natin'. Like Einstein.

Did you know he was wrong? He was wrong about time and space. Ah mean, who knew? Ah thought he was always righ' about everythin'."

"Well, what I've learned is about quantum physics. I've read a lot about it and I've watched things on TV that explain a lot," he replied.

"Yeah, Ah've watched that show. Ah mean, can you imagine? It's hard ta understand, but Ah guess, there's no time and space, everythin' is ... What was the word they used?"

"Entanglement."

"That's was it! Everythin' is entangled."

"Einstein thought there was time and space between objects, but in the quantum world there is no time or space. Isn't that awesome?"

Her green eyes sparkled with relish.

"Yeah, it sure is. I mean it sure does feel like there's a lot of time and space between us. I'd like to remedy that."

"Ah'm afraid that'll have ta wait. Ah'm not quite ready. Maybe when we get ta know each other."

He took her to the door and kissed her on the cheek. "Was that okay?"

"That was very sweet. See ya soon."

Angus loved it when she smiled like she was doing now.

As he walked away toward the car, she yelled, "Wait! Can ya come ta dinner on Thanksgivin' Day?"

"Oh yeah," Angus remembered. "My family does a big dinner for a lot of relatives who come by. So, I don't think so."

"How 'bout dessert?"

"Maybe. I'll see what my mom says."

Twenty-seven

WHEN CLEO ARRIVED at work on Monday morning, Zack was in a better mood. "Guess what?"

"I can't imagine. What?"

"It's my birthday this week. I'm turning ninety-five. Can you believe it? I never thought I would make it this long. I guess God makes us old codgers live a prolonged life as punishment for our sins."

She decided to ignore his comment about God. "Wow! We'll have a birthday party for you. When is it exactly?"

"It's Friday. But who the hell 're we going invite? There's no one left, as I have repeated endlessly before."

"Now, now. There are people in your life. There's Angus, the grocery boy and Elsie, the night nurse. There's Clarence who always helps with your orders for medication and there's the doctor you go to. He lives here in Glendale. There's my mom and me. I could allow her to bring my son, Jamal, for the evening."

"That's pretty ambitious. You only have a week to make plans."

"I've done it before; I can do it again," she said, elated that she had something she could do to make Zack feel better.

As soon as the dishes from breakfast were done and the kitchen was cleaned up, she got on the phone. Everyone she'd mentioned to Zack, plus the doctor's receptionist and Phyllis, the receptionist from the agency, said they could come. Clarence said he would pick up her mom and Jamal, and her mom said she would bake the birthday cake. Edith would do a great job; her cake decorating skills were awesome. And she said she would buy the numbers ninety-five as the candles to put on the cake, rather than risk garnishing it with the full count of ninety-five. Cleo thought that would be the best way to go as did Jamal who was jumping up and down with excitement in the background as they talked.

The week dragged on slowly because of the anticipation. Edith purchased balloons and other birthday decorations so Cleo could take them to work with her on Friday to decorate the house. With all the plans in order, Cleo felt she could do a good job creating the birthday event. Her eagerness was overwhelming.

When Friday finally came, she worked hard all day making the house look festive with balloons and birthday decorations everywhere. The housekeeper, who had turned down the invitation to join them, generously gave her plenty of room to do her thing.

The party would start when everyone was able to get there. That would be about 7:00 p.m., even though she had told everyone they could arrive as early as six. She decided to serve hot dogs on buns with all the condiments, chips, dips and watermelon. It was late in the season, but imported watermelon was available at the store when she went there as soon as Elsie was able to get to the house at her usual time.

No one had arrived before she got back except Angus the grocery boy. He had the usual smirk on his face. It seemed to be a permanent feature. She noticed the tattoos peeking from the top of his shirt, black ones that looked creepy even though she couldn't tell what they were. Most of all, his attitude turned her off. He was definitely anti-Black even though he had never said much of anything to her about that or anything else.

Elsie, ever the helpful one, was full of excitement that a party had been planned and reported that Zack had been sleepless all week in anticipation of the festivities. She brought potato salad to add to the hot dog offering. Everything was working perfectly.

Zack had been watching Fox News in the den. Cleo went to collect him and wheeled him in his chair out to the living room and got him situated just as the doorbell rang with the first of the invitees. They were the doctor and his nurse. Apparently, they were more friendly than had been indicated in their office setting. She was dressed festively with 'Happy Birthday' earrings hanging down her long neck. With pretty blond hair and glistening blue eyes, she was quite attractive even with the funny earrings. The doctor brought an offering of red wine for the table.

Then, her mom, Jamal and Clarence arrived. Jamal was dressed in his 'Sunday Best' which was a nice white shirt with his nicest pants and shoes. Edith had fashioned a tie to fit his small stature from one of her dad's. As Cleo noticed the familiar tie, she felt sad her dad wasn't able to be with them. But Jamal's excitement overrode everything. He was so pumped he was jumping up and down.

When she took him over to meet Zack, he suddenly became very quiet. Cleo noticed Angus standing off to the side of the room nursing a lemonade with that look of derision that was so frozen on his face.

"Zackary, this is my son, Jamal, and my mom, Edith."

Zack held out his hand to shake Jamal's, but Jamal was ready for a high five.

"Jamal," Edith interjected, "you're supposed to shake Mr. Hughes' hand. He isn't used to high fives."

Zack took Jamal's small hand and Jamal, encouraged, shook Zack's hand, hard up and down. "Well, son, how do you do?" Zack attempted to be polite in spite of the rough handshake and, Cleo thought, in spite of her son's black skin.

"Well, son, I see you've grown in your two front teeth," said Zack, looking at him closely.

"Yeah, the tooth fairy got the old ones."

"How much did you get for them?"

"Got fifty cents for each," Jamal answered proudly.

"I think that's only fair, don't you?"

"I wanted more, but I guess so."

Zack roared and his laughter got most of the room to join in. He also shook Edith's hand politely.

Cleo wondered just what he was thinking having to deal with so many black people in his home, something she was sure had never happened before. Clarence was next.

"I hear you are the young man who takes my orders for medication from this young lady who takes care of me in the daytime."

"Yes, sir. I am that."

"I am also guessing you are the young man who is making her so happy, since she has done nothing but radiate since you arrived."

"Well, sir, I am hoping I am that person. She makes me very happy, too."

Cleo burned with embarrassment. Saved by the doorbell, she ran to get the next arrivals who were Phyllis and her date. "I'm sorry I didn't warn you, but I have a date for this evening," Phyllis reported. They were both older, but obviously falling in love the way Phyllis was acting. Her date, a man named Marcus—or Marc for short, also brought a bottle of wine and a six pack.

When Phyllis shook Zack's hand, she wished him a very happy 95th birthday. This was the first time she had met him in person even though they had often talked on the phone.

The party went well. The food was very popular and the cake looked great with Edith's best decorations and the two candles on top. Zack wasn't able to blow them out and Jamal helped him with a big blow that came with a little flying spit.

"Jamal," Edith interrupted. "No one will want to eat the cake now with your spit all over it."

"I'm sorry," he apologized, not really understanding why this time was different from all the other times he had done the same thing on his cakes.

"Well, that isn't going to stop me from having birthday cake," Zack said bravely.

This was the first moment when Cleo thought there might be a chance that he was beginning to change his mind about their race.

Twenty-eight

ANGUS WAS FALLING IN LOVE. He and Sarah had been meeting regularly at the school quad to eat lunch together. They had awesome conversations about everything they could think of.

One of their favorite subjects was music. He loved Country and she loved Jazz. Neither one could agree about Hip Hop. Sarah didn't get Angus' fascination with Country; he didn't get her thing about Jazz. In sports, he was best at basketball and she was best at swimming. They both loved to watch baseball and the school football games were the most exciting times they had together. The whole school would show up and cheer louder and louder until they were purple with excitement.

He had asked Sarah to go with him to the birthday party, but she wasn't able to make it that night. Thanksgiving and Christmas were coming up and they were stoked about the time off from school. The kids were teasing them because they held hands as they walked to their classrooms and met every morning just before school started because they attended the same history class. It was a sweet romance getting started.

When Angus arrived at Sarah's house for Thanksgiving dessert in his new car, she seemed glad to see him and was happy for him to have wheels.

Meeting her dad was the reason Angus had been invited to Thanksgiving desert. But his job as head chef kept him too busy at the restaurant. It was Thanksgiving, Angus was reminded. Her dad had sent his regrets via Sarah who said he was looking forward to meeting 'her new friend.' He'd tried to get away from his job, but it just didn't work out.

The dessert was delicious, traditional pumpkin pie with whipped cream on top. The flavors were spicier than the pies he was used to. His mom wasn't the cook Sarah's dad was which made Angus embarrassed that he had questioned men as cooks.

Her dad had cooked the whole dinner and dessert with some help from her brother. Angus really wanted to meet the dad. He wanted to ask him if he could work in his restaurant part-time after school until next summer when he could work full-time. He conveyed his desire to Sarah and she thought that would be a killer idea.

They escaped the house after dessert and he showed her his new-used car parked on the street. He bragged it had been owned only once before. "I got it for $10,000."

"That's a lot'a change. Where'd ya get it all?" She asked.

"Well, I worked hard for a lot of it and my dad provided the rest. He's putting me on their insurance policy until I can afford to take over that responsibility. I have to pay for the gas and any repairs, so I have to be careful and I do work hard at the grocery store."

"Wow, that's really dope. My dad's thinkin' about gettin' me a car, too. But Ah don't have a job, at least not yet. Ah have ta go to college and then Ah guess Ah'll get a job."

"What do you want to be when you get out of college?" He asked.

"Ah was thinkin' of designin' clothes. Ah know, that sounds like a big dream, but Ah think Ah can do it. Ah'm good at designin' stuff and Ah'm good at drawin', which is part of the job. Ah'll show ya some of mah designs some time; they're awesome."

"Cool. I'd like that." He hesitated only a moment before he changed the subject and asked Sarah if she'd like to go for a drive in his new car.

"Shu'ah. Where'd ya wannna go?" She asked.

"Well, we could drive up to this place I know about that looks out over Glendale and part of the San Fernando Valley. I think you can see Burbank from there, too."

He drove the car up to a place where some of the kids parked. "I've been scratching to get up here since some of the dudes I know have been coming up for a while."

"It's a good view. Wow, look over therah! Tha freeway's movin' pretty good now, but there're a lot of cars. Makes me wondah where everybody's goin.'"

"Yeah, I suppose they're going to some Thanksgiving get-together. Families and stuff. Or they're coming home after."

"It's gettin' late. Some of tha cars down there're usin' their headlights. Maybe we out'ta go."

"Aw, come on. We got time. We just got here."

"Well, Ah guess."

"It'd be a lot more comfortable in the back seat, don't ya think?"

"You wann'a make out don't ya?"

"I want to know you better, Sarah. I really like you. Come on." He hopped out and opened the backseat door for her. "Come on; don't be shy. I promise I won't do anything you don't want to do."

"Oh, okay." She sighed. "But we can't stay too long."

He kissed her and nuzzled her neck. "You're hot, Sarah." They began to neck and it wasn't long before Sarah got worked up. Mouths opened and tongues began to probe. He reached for her breast and she didn't stop him.

It wasn't long before she was aching to be next to him and she lifted his sweat shirt. Sarah was kissing his chest when suddenly she stopped short.

"Oh, mah god! You've got tha president tattooed all oveah your chest. What tha fuck?!" She lifted the shirt higher and got a glimpse of the Swastika tattooed to his shoulder nestled in the dark hair of a maiden. "Mah God, Angus. What are ya, anyway?"

"Hey, I ..." He didn't know what to say. Pulling down his sweat shirt, he backed off, jumping out of the car. "I believe what I believe! That's all! I mean, you're too sensitive. No one would say that unless they were too sensitive! Why're you so upset?"

"Ya didn't tell me ya was a damned Nazi!"

He began to pace. "Hey, I just dig the president. What's wrong with that?"

"And, you got that Hitler thing goin' there too! What's that all 'bout?"

"It's what I believe in. That's all. You're just being hypersensitive, that's all."

"Ah'm not too sensitive, dammit!" She was screaming and crying all at once. "Ya got 'ta take me home, Angus. Now!"

He just stood there, stunned.

Jumping back into the front of the car, she took out her cell and punched in her home number. "Ah'm callin' my mom, Angus! She'll come and get me if ya don't take me home! NOW! Dammit!"

"Okay, okay. I'll take you."

"Mom," Sarah had gotten her mom on the phone as she sat hugging the door trying to get as far from him as she could. "Ah'm coming home!" She yelled into the phone. She could barely hold back the tears as she spoke.

They drove in silence … Most of the way.

Then he said, "Sarah, I'm in love with you. Please."

She didn't answer.

"Please. Can't we talk this over?"

"Ah was fallin' for you, too, Angus, but Ah can't go with your point of view. Hitler was willin' to kill people who were not considered Aryan an' so-called 'pure.' We ah in the same World History class, aren't we? Tha teacher covered World War II. You were there, weren't ya? Ah mean if ya really believe in that Nazi stuff, then we couldn't … Ah wouldn't be able to spend another minute with ya."

"Well, all I can see of the left is the overt paternalization. They are infantilizing the population, making them dependent and unable to take care of themselves. They don't work; they don't even try anymore. What you apparently believe in is taking care of people when I think people should take care of themselves! What's wrong with that?"

"Ya mean pull themselves up by the'ah *bootstraps*?" She mocked. Angus grunted.

"Well, Ah hate ta be trite, but what if there are no bootstraps, or even socks to pull yourself up with? An, what if ya don't have the so-called '*righ*" skin colah? What about people who come from other poo-rah countries, asylum seekahs, lookin' for the freedom ta succeed, only ta be kept out or incarcerated?"

"In America it's different. Everybody has a pair of shoes, at least."

"Really? Ya think everyone's endowed with tha *means* to get ahead? Ah mean, we are talkin' about today, aren't we?"

"And, people coming from all over the world to take away our jobs, especially the Mexicans!"

"Yeah, shu'ah! Tha jobs no American wants!"

"We are all endowed with inalienable rights!"

"Oh, foah God's sake, stop it with tha platitudes!"

"You did it!"

"Angus, Ah'm going to say just one thing more and that's all. People who believe in '*individualism*' are *alone* in tha world. Those of us who believe in community and that ALL are created equal, that no one person can do it alone, that we'ah all in this together, we who believe in this will nevah be alone. That may sound silly or banal to you, but it makes all tha sense in tha universe to me." With that she crossed her arms and sat facing the door, wishing she could be home ... now. "Anyway," she gestured with her hand, "that Swastika says it all."

When they got to her house, her dad was out on the porch waiting. Angus couldn't believe his eyes. Flanked by the giant palms that stood like sentries on each side of the driveway, her dad stood tall, an imposing black man with hands on his hips waiting for her to show up. He looked ready to take Angus on if needed.

When Angus got home, he ran upstairs to his room, stripped and took an icy cold shower. Finally, cooled off enough, he turned the water to hot and soaped down. He took the handheld showerhead and sprayed himself clean. Then, imagining himself with a sub-machine gun, he strafed the shower walls with hot water—rat-a-tat-tat—imagining his assault on the house that Sarah lived in with that black bastard who had smashed all of his illusions away. Sarah was half black!

Twenty-nine

SINCE JAMAL HADN'T COME with them to Big Sur, Clarence suggested they take the boy with them to the beach in Santa Monica. It was great fun having him along and he said he was 'stoked.' It was a beautiful day and just warm enough. They all went swimming together, diving into in the big waves, helping Jamal so he could experience what it was like. They romped together in the ocean lunging into the water like they had seen the porpoises do on TV, making noises like the playful creatures who smiled.

It was hard to get Jamal to come out once he was in, but their stomachs roiled with hunger and he finally came out with the promise of sandwiches and potato salad with Frito chips and lemonade.

Jamal was shivering when they finally gathered up their things to head home. Their suits felt uncomfortable with the sand caught in the creases and they tried to wiggle it out before getting into the car. They laughed at their gyrations trying to shake out the extra sand.

Cleo stood at her door putting some of her things in the front seat, still giggling.

They didn't see it coming; the red Toyota ran up on them in the parking lot going way too fast. Cleo and Clarence were still laughing over the uncomfortable sand and Jamal was at the back of the car putting his toys away. "Come on, Jamal," Cleo laughed, urging him to get into his car seat in the rear of the Subaru. He was dawdling as usual, and she was getting impatient wanting to get him strapped in.

The Toyota came roaring up so fast Cleo didn't see it with no chance to grab her son as he was hit and thrown several feet into the middle of the lot. The rear door of the car went flying too as the flash of red smashed the boy. Cars driving by screeched their brakes trying to avoid hitting him as he rolled helplessly. Most did avoid him. One car, its driver busy looking for a parking spot didn't see him and grazed him as he moved into its path.

"Jamal!" Cleo's scream was so shrill it could be heard all the way to the stratosphere. As she ran to him, cars halted in stunned disbelief.

Clarence caught sight of the red Toyota as it slipped away screeching out of the parking lot into oncoming traffic. It was astounding the car didn't get hit.

"Damn, fucking damnit!" He yelled as he ran after the fleeing Toyota.

People stopped and came running to the boy.

There had been the ambulance, police cars surrounding the incident, and people trying to see as they passed by. Jamal's neck was stabilized with a neck brace and his arm and leg which had been injured had supports too. The paramedics scooped Jamal's limp body onto a gurney once he was stabilized. The sirens screeched as they left the scene heading for the hospital.

A police car offered to lead Clarence and Cleo and they followed close by.

The emergency room at St. John's was crowded with people waiting to be helped, Jamal's tiny frame taking precedent with doctors and nurses surrounding the gurney. Cleo and Clarence watched helplessly, Cleo's face drenched in tears, her frame leaned against Clarence for strength. All of hers was gone.

"It's my fault," she sobbed.

"My God, Cleo," Clarence adamantly declared, "this had nothing to do with you. It was Etta. I saw her car as she careened out of the parking lot. She caused this. She did it."

"My God! Etta?" Cleo was astonished. "How did she find us? She would do something like this?"

"You bet. She probably followed us the whole day and spied as we were enjoying our time together. She's crazier than I thought. Don't worry. She will pay! She will pay!" His voice was grave with determination. He held Cleo tight. "Don't you worry, we will make her pay."

Thirty

JAMAL HAD A CONCUSSION with a broken arm and leg. Being so young, his body was supple and it managed to take the shock pretty well when the car hit him. "Knocked the breath out him," said the doctor. He'd set the boy's arm and leg and Jamal was in a medically induced coma to allow him time to heal from the blow he took to the head and his small frame.

Cleo and Clarence sat vigil with him until, exhausted, they slept on cots in his room. When he finally awakened, they were beside themselves with joy to have him back with them and out of danger.

"Hey Jamal." Cleo carefully gave him a big hug when he awakened, intensely grateful that he would survive, even thrive in spite of what happened.

Soon he was getting counseling from a social worker for PTSD, Post Traumatic Stress Disorder, which Cleo and Edith were especially glad about. He was reporting bad nightmares in the hospital, symptoms of the disorder.

They talked for a while about school. He had started first grade. Jamal didn't feel like talking about lessons and how he would manage them. The doctor reported that it would take time for him to heal and he would have to do his schooling on-line.

Clarence found an old lap-top computer and restored it himself, part of his curriculum. He gave it to Jamal; it came in handy for the school lessons. And, he loved the video games.

When Cleo got home finally after the long waiting at the hospital, she had some time to think about this Etta Stone. She wondered at the audacity the woman had to call her mother at home, when she knew Cleo and Clarence were away, and demand that Edith make her stay away from her man so that Etta could have him back. What kind of a person does that? Then, she runs Jamal over in the parking lot, maybe thinking Cleo would become frightened enough to give Clarence up. That was utterly crazy. It was preposterous and foolhardy for her to think anything would stop Cleo from her new Ba'e. She loved him too much. He was far too perfect for her and Jamal and she simply had to have him in her life. There was nothing, nothing that would keep Cleo from loving Clarence, no matter how utterly insane this woman became. Cleo would have to die first.

Thirty-one

THE L A NEWSPAPER his dad read and the local news channel had carried the story. Angus Dunne read the news article recognizing the names, 'Cleo Henderson and Clarence Delacroix and her son, Jamal Henderson, the woman's son from a previous marriage.' He'd recognized them from the birthday party. The boy's school picture was featured.

"Parking Lot Rage Explodes," read the lead-line. The story was on the front page, a small article beginning down at the bottom. It described how a red Toyota was spotted as it rammed the boy and the Subaru Outback, catapulting the six-year-old boy. The Toyota was an older car driven by and 'African American woman.' The boy was hit by an unsuspecting car behind them. Angus felt bad for the boy. He was only six years old.

Angus was only six one holiday; he couldn't remember which one, when he recalled his extended family sitting around the dining room table enjoying the holiday feast. A cousin had recently married a colored woman and the family couldn't help themselves making jokes about the marriage and the potential children that would come from that union. His dad was laughing while he made a comment about the kids coming out 'polka-dotted'. Angus had never seen a polka-dotted person. He wondered if they got rid of the polka-dots by scrubbing them right after birth. Maybe that was why he had never seen a person with polka-dots. He'd never forgotten the incident and asking some teachers and school friends, he had to wonder about it because they all said no, there was no such thing. That had been a long time ago, when he was still little.

But he had taken his dad seriously and believed what he'd said; to him it made a lot of sense, even now. He'd seen a commercial recently with a young woman scantily dressed. Her skin was white but she had big brown dots all over. It really surprised him and he thought maybe his dad had been right. She looked polka-dotted.

Maybe, if he went to the hospital, he could gain entrance to the neo-natal unit and see what his dad was talking about. If he could see the babies before they did whatever they did to them to take away the dots, he could confirm with his own eyes what his dad had said.

Since his breakup with Sarah, he'd been depressed. He didn't know what to do with himself. He tried studying for class work and playing video games, then he would just mope around the house.

His mom was anxious about his moods. "You need to get out, Angus. Do something with yourself. Get outside and enjoy the sunshine. You know, we don't have sunshine in California for nothing."

He couldn't shake his feelings for Sarah. Even though she was half black, he'd fallen for her and it didn't feel like a little sunshine would help him forget. But he took his mother's advice seriously. He knew he had to get on with his life.

Angus concluded Jamal must be at St. John's Hospital because of its proximity to the Santa Monica beach where the accident happened. Angus' used car was in for repairs the day he got his inspiration and decided then and there he would catch a bus and get down to St. John's. He wanted to see the tragedy being played out in the hospital like those medical dramas on TV. He was sure it would be exciting. And, he was certain he would see polka-dotted newborns if he could gain access to the neo-natal unit where the babies were kept. He wondered about Sarah and if she'd had polka-dots when she was a baby. She was light-skinned just like the lady in the commercial. Angus could imagine she had the same polka-dots that woman had.

He left the house on his bike early one morning, not without being spotted by one of the boys from school, his neighbor, James. He didn't know the boy's last name, but that boy knew his and he hated him—He'd called Angus 'cow dung.' Knowing his fascination with white supremacy and the Ku Klux Klan, he'd even referred to him as 'Black Angus' wanting to get him riled up in the short hairs where it really hurt. Angus had never heard of a Black Angus, so he researched it on the Internet. There were Red Angus and Black Angus, but there were no White Angus. It said their rudders could be white.

Not wanting to stop and get into a fight, he passed James by trying to skim him close and maybe knock him down.

"Hey, you fucking Cow Dung. Watch where the fuck you're going," the boy screamed at him. Angus felt gratified he'd elicited that reaction and he smiled big as he whooshed past him and down the street.

He got the bus, hanging his bike on the designated bracket, and made all of the transfers to get to his destination. It took a long time. Nothing in LA County was easy to get to by bus or train. It would have taken a long time on the freeway even if he'd had his car.

Once there, he found the enormous hospital and, locking his bicycle to the rack, made his way into the main lobby. "I'm looking for Jamal Henderson," he told the gray-haired lady behind the desk.

Noting the tattoos on his arms she said, "Well, you can't be a relative, so who are you and what is your business?"

Angus didn't have a good answer so he told her to mind her *own business* and walked off, the woman looking after him with suspicion. After he made sure she wasn't watching him anymore, he looked for the pediatric section on the hospital information board, took the elevator to the designated floor and began his search.

First, though, he wanted to check out the neo-natal unit. So, finding it near the pediatric section, he went in to check out the new-born babies. There they were in their little plastic beds. There were quite a few dark kids and some white ones, too. But his interest was in polka-dotted babies. He could see black babies and he could see tan ones, but there were none who had the polka-dots his dad said would be there. Angus was disappointed in a way he had never been before. He'd always taken for granted that his dad was honest and would never lead him on. But it was what it was and there was no denying his own eyes.

He stopped a nurse and asked if there had ever been any polka-dotted babies and what would they do if there were.

"Of course not, young man," she declared. "Where'd you ever get an idea like that?"

"My dad told me."

"Ah, your dad was just messin' with you."

"My dad wouldn't lie."

"No, I suppose he wouldn't, but this time he was just teasin' you, you know. Where are your parents anyway? You didn't come here alone, did you?"

He nearly ran away from the woman. His embarrassment made him turn a bright shade of red and he couldn't get away fast enough.

It didn't take long to find Jamal next door in the pediatric area. He was one of the few colored kids and he was younger than the rest. Most were teenagers, white kids just a little younger than he was, and a couple of Mexicans who were older than Jamal, about ten.

It was close to noon when he arrived at Jamal's door and someone was serving him lunch. It looked pretty gross, a dry looking wheat sandwich with cheese inside and a cup of juice with a straw. The kid just stared at it like it was shit—kind of what it was. After the guy who brought the food left, he wandered into the room like he belonged.

"Hey Jamal." He said it like he really knew what he was doing, trying to be a part of the normal stuff going on at the hospital. Angus didn't know what exactly that would be, but he didn't want to alarm Jamal. It worked. He was surprised the kid was so alert.

"Hey, do I know you?" The boy asked. "Are you a vol-un-teer?" He pronounced the word haltingly like he was afraid to say it wrong.

"Yeah, kind'a," Angus answered, noting the kid's careful speech. But I met you before, a while ago at a birthday party for a very old man. Do you remember?"

"Oh yeah, my mom put it on for Zack. He's old, isn't he? I don't think I've ever seen anyone *that* old."

"Yeah, I remember; you blew out the candles on the cake. They said that he turned ninety-five. Isn't that awesome?"

"Yeah, it sure is," Jamal answered. "My mom really likes Zack. She thinks he has a lot of good qualties."

"I think you mean qualities."

"Yeah, I do."

"Well, that surprises me. I didn't think she liked him at all."

"Hey, you look a little shaken up, man. What's the matter?"

"Ah, nothin'. I was just in the neo-natal unit and a nurse didn't want me there, is all. So, does it hurt?" Angus changed the subject.

"Well, yeah it does."

"Sorry. I thought they'd drug you up so you wouldn't feel anything."

"They do a little, but it still hurts. Lots of things in life hurt. No big deal." Then Jamal smiled, "'We would never learn to be brave or patient if there were only joy in the world.' That was Helen Keller," he announced proudly.

"Huh? Who the fuck is Helen Keller?"

"You dropped the 'F-bomb'!" Jamal seemed excited he'd caught him saying something bad.

"Yeah, well, who is … Helen Keller?"

"Oh. Clarence told me she was a lady who couldn't hear, see or talk," he said proudly.

"Wow. Then, how the he…." Angus stopped himself before he said 'hell'. "How the heck did she *say* anything?"

"Glad you asked. She learned how to sign, that's how."

"Sign?"

"Yeah, you know, like sign language." Jamal was feeling pretty smart next to this guy. He moved his good hand and fingers like he was signing.

Angus, feeling unsure of himself, wanted to change the subject. "So, your mom likes Zack?

"Yeah. She put on that birthday party for him, you know."

"Hey, what's going on in here?" A nurse came into the room to collect the lunch tray. "Who are you, young man?"

"He says he's a vol'nteer." Jamal's voice still sounded uncertain.

"Okay, time's up. This young man needs to eat his lunch and get back to school."

"School?" Angus asked, wondering what the nurse meant.

"I just started First Grade this Fall," Jamal grumbled. "I don't want the lunch."

"Yeah, he has class work from his school he has to do." The nurse didn't like the looks of this guy. "You're not wearing a volunteer's badge. So, scram."

Angus smirked at the reference to scram, an old person's word. "Get lost."

"Oh, yeah. Sure. I'm goin'." He sauntered from the room.

Angus decided to hang around for a little while longer hoping to see Cleo or Clarence. He didn't want to talk to them, but spying was one of his favorite things to do. He found the chapel and since there wasn't anywhere else to be, except the waiting room which he wanted to avoid, he decided to sneak in and pretend he belonged in case anyone else came in.

It was a quiet space and Angus kind of liked it. It looked like they didn't want to be too specific about religion. He didn't have a religion, didn't want anything to do with the God thing, unless you counted the Klan as religion. A member did have to believe in it and they touted the Jesus guy and God a lot, mostly as a weapon against Jews and niggers. They believed, and he did too, the Bible was for the white race and against mixing races. He'd been to a couple of meetings and thought they were dope.

One thing that surprised him about the hospital was the lack of excitement. He thought the whole place would be like the emergency room episodes so popular on TV. The place turned out to be kinda' peaceful except for the occasional nurse running into a room.

As he sat there, he got to thinking about Sarah again and how it turned out her dad was black. That sure was a douse of cold water. He thought the guy was going to come after him when he brought Sarah home that night. He hoped she didn't tell her dad he'd tried to rape her or anything.

Wow, a black man and a white woman. He thought Sarah and her brother must have turned out polka dotted like his dad said. What if they got that treatment to take off the spots? Or maybe, like that nurse said, his dad had been teasing him. Angus was sure the nurse in the unit with the babies must have been lying to him about his dad. After all, he had seen that commercial with the lady and her brown spots all over. His dad was a strict man and Angus couldn't believe he'd lie to him even if he was just kidding. Of course, that had been a long time ago and he hadn't heard a thing about his cousin and his Negro wife's children in all that time. But he wanted to believe his dad would never lie like that.

He started to cry, wounded and feeling lonely without Sarah. He'd really fallen for her. She was the bomb, always a bright light in his day and with that smile and her tall lithe body; he couldn't help but think about her constantly. He had to realize she was half black, Mulatto. That meant she was like a crossbreed like between a horse and a donkey. Didn't it?

An older man walked in. He was black, had a graying beard and was dressed casually with a dark grey jacket that matched his steel gray hair. He saw Angus and sat down next to him.

"Hey there, pal, what're you cryin' for?

"I'm not cryin'! Just got something in my eye 's all."

You a friend 'a Jamal's?"

"Why're you askin'? It's none of your business."

"Oh, yeah, I guess it isn't, but I 's curious. Saw you talkin' to 'im in the room."

"You spyin' on me?"

"No, not exactly. Curious 'bout the young boy 's all. Read he had a bad accident in Santa Monica at the beach."

"Yeah, car hit him bad, took the rear door off the Subaru. He ended up splattered in the middle of the parking lot with cars comin' at 'im. I guess you could say it was real bad."

"Yeah, I guess ya could. What's your relationship with 'im?"

"He ain't a friend if that's what you're implying. I just know his mother. I work for her employer, Zackary Hughes."

"Righ."

"What business is it of yours?"

"Oh nothin', just curious's all."

"Hey, do you know if half black, half white babies have polka-dots?"

The man looked at him like he was crazy. "Where'd you get a' idea like that, boy?"

"My dad told me."

The man broke out into a hearty laugh. He seemed overcome with amusement and Angus was embarrassed.

Still chuckling, trying to get his breath, the man got up. "Hope you git that what eve' it tis out of you eye." He left without saying another word.

Angus sat there wondering who the man was and why he wanted to know so much. A kind of feeling of—what?—guilt came over him. It was unfamiliar and he didn't know what to make of it. Pictures of flying doves and sunlight coming down into the place made him think maybe that was why he felt odd; or, maybe the man laughing at him.

It was getting late and he wanted to get on with it. He emerged from the chapel and went back to Jamal's room hoping to see Cleo and Clarence. His hopes were gratified. They were there standing by the bed, Cleo holding Jamal's good hand, the one without a cast.

"So, the doctor says you can go home soon, but going to the school will have to wait until you can get around a little better."

"That's okay, Mom. I like school with my computer. It's dope. The teacher can talk to me."

"That's really good, sweetheart. But, don't you want to see your friends?"

"I like a couple of the brothers, but I don't like those Mexican kids."

"They're Hispanic," she corrected him.

"They're Mexicans," he insisted. "Why do you think they're Hispanics?"

"Because not all of them are Mexican," she replied patiently.

Clarence chimed in, "Some are from other countries, man, like Guatemala, Honduras, Peru. Places like that."

"Yeah, well I don't like 'em. They just want to beat me up all the time."

"I know. Life is hard sometimes, but we have to try to be friendly even when the other people aren't," his mom added.

"Why?" Jamal asked, not understanding.

"What you see isn't all there is. They aren't *only* Hispanic; they're people just like you are. Would you like it if everyone saw you as a black kid—not as a person?" She asked.

"Remember what I told you about learning to be brave and patient, bud?" Clarence asked.

"Yeah, but…"

"Well, you know, I've had trouble with Mr. Hughes sometimes," his Mom said. "He can make me really angry and I've wanted to cream him."

"You have a right to how you feel, honey." Clarence said.

"Well, sure. I know how I feel, but I choose not to act on those feelings."

"I might not be so nice to him the way you are."

"Come on, Clarence. You know it isn't right to fight when there's another way."

"Well, I may know that, but doin' it can be another mat-"

"Let's just say," Cleo interrupted, "I try to let it go until later when I have better control of myself."

"I have to admit you're right, sweetheart." Clarence nuzzled Cleo in the neck.

Jamal was embarrassed.

Angus stood outside listening to their conversation, then slipped away not understanding Cleo's assertions and not understanding how he felt either. Helen Keller?

The black man with the grey jacket and graying hair stood aside until Angus left. Then, he knocked on the jam of the door to let Cleo and Clarence know he was there.

Clarence looked around and stopped cold. He wasn't sure he was seeing right. "Dad?" He asked.

"Hello son."

"What the f..." He stopped himself, knowing Jamal could hear him. "What 're you doing here?"

"I'd like fer us ta talk, if ya don't mind."

Not wanting to expose Jamal and Cleo to the coming conversation, he suggested to his dad that they go to the cafeteria.

Clarence turned to Jamal and gave him dap, as much dap the boy could handle with only one hand. They hugged. "I'll catch you later bud." Clarence left to go with his dad.

Thirty-two

CLEO STAYED WITH JAMAL while Clarence went down to the cafeteria with his dad—The man he hadn't seen in twenty-odd years.

"I have to admit," he said as they sat at a table, "I'm shocked to see you here. What made you come?"

"I read about tha accident in tha paper and wan'ed to be sure Jamal was okay."

"Well, now that you see he'll survive, don't you want to be on your way?" Clarence asked bitterly.

"Understood, son. Sorry."

"Sorry for what? You've been absent from my life a long time. Are you just now sorry that Jamal's been hurt?"

"No, I been sorry for a *long* time, for the *whole* time I been away."

"Well, nice of you to say." Clarence was not convinced by his father's words. "I've wanted you to come a lot of times, like my birthdays or Christmases, and you never showed up." Clarence felt cheated and hostile. He wasn't sure he could accept a simple 'sorry'.

"I'know, Son."

"Hey look! Don't keep calling me 'son' like that. You haven't been a father to me since I was just a little kid, barely four years old. You have no right!"

"Yeah. I's true. I have no righ."

"You never got in touch for any occasions … Nothin'! What the fuck! I don't even know why I am sittin' here with you now."

"I know, there're no words I could say ta make this okay."

"You bet, there aren't. So, why the fuck did you leave?"

"Look, I can see you ain't ready for this yet."

"Ya think? I don't even know what could make me ready."

"Maybe the truth. But I don't know if ya're ready ta hear it yet. It ain't pretty."

"I'd like to know the truth."

"You'd just think I was tryin' to make excuses, to make it all okay, and it ain't. Da whole thing's rotten to the core. I'm rotten to da core."

"I can't disagree with that." Clarence wanted this meeting over. "Look, why don't you get your 'truth' together, whatever the fuck it is, and maybe … some other time."

His dad stiffened. "I guess you neve' had to be a no nigger, huh boy?"

Clarence looked at his dad, disgusted, got up and walked out.

Thirty-three

ETTA STONE WAS ARRESTED on charges of hit and run, assault and battery and went to jail. The red Toyota was confiscated and her driver's license suspended. Etta apparently posted bail and was released with some restrictions. She wasn't allowed to go anywhere near Jamal or his family. She borrowed her mother's car to get around and drove illegally.

Jamal came home soon after their visit in the hospital. He had to spend a lot of time in bed while he healed, then he had to learn how to use crutches. His youth made it easy for him to adapt even though he was bummed that he couldn't go to school yet and show off his leg and arm casts. He wanted to get his friends to sign the leg cast.

Cleo offered to invite those kids over so he could get the job done.

"Hey, Mom, that would be so dope! When?"

"I'll find a time, don't worry." She kissed his forehead.

Thirty-four

WHEN CLEO ARRIVED at Zackary's home the following Monday after being absent for a couple of weeks, it was raining pretty hard. She loved rain, but not when she had to travel in it. She was soaking wet and after the usual run-in with Angus at the door, she made her way into the family room to find Zack finishing up his breakfast.

"It's raining," he noted. "You look like you drowned in a swamp."

"Good morning to you, too, Mr. Hughes."

"You've been away a long time. I was beginning to think I'd never see you again."

"It has been a stressful time. I'm sorry I had to take so much time off."

"We had a good game of Monopoly going there and I wanted to beat you. You didn't give me a chance."

"No, but not entirely my fault. I'll try to make my absences briefer in the future." She shed her outer rain gear and stuffed it in the closet along with her bag. "How have you been?"

"I've been okay. The lady they sent was moderately acceptable. She didn't cause any trouble, at least. I heard from Angus your son was hurt pretty bad in that accident. I read about it in the newspaper too. The woman who hit him, did she do that on purpose?"

"We think she did. She was arrested for hit and run, but she's out on bail now. Jamal will be okay with a little time. His arm cast has been removed and he wears a support device; it frees him up a little so he can do his schoolwork on the computer."

"Computer, huh? He knows how to use it?"

"Oh yes. Kids today seem to dive into it like breaching whales. It was harder for me when I first learned."

"How're the Spanish lessons going?"

'He's learning but it is slow. He isn't that enthusiastic. The teacher is real nice, though. She came to visit Jamal in the hospital."

"Sorry I couldn't make it."

"I didn't expect you to be able to, Mr. Hughes … uh, Zack." She corrected herself. "No mind. I'm glad you're doing okay. Why don't I take your tray and we'll take up the Monopoly game again?"

"We'll have to start a new one. Angus knocked the other one over. It scattered all over the place. He's such a clumsy bastard."

"I noticed he had a car in the driveway today; I guess because it's raining."

"Yeah. He was able to get a used car with some help from his dad. I guess he figures he's getting too old to be bicycling everywhere."

"Yes, I would say so too."

She took his tray to the kitchen, washed the dishes up and when she came back, he was sound asleep.

"So much for the Monopoly game," she whispered to herself.

Thirty-five

WHEN SHE GOT HOME from work that night, Jamal was excited to tell her all about the day.

"My friends came over just like you said they would. It was raining but they came over after school anyway. Look at my cast! Isn't it dope?"

The writing on the leg cast was in all different colors. The words were pretty colorful, too.

"You've said that word 'dope' before. What does it mean exactly?" She asked.

"Mom, you can't be *that* old."

"Just tell me what it means."

"It means cool, I guess. Like it's really 'bad.'"

"Honestly, I don't know if I understand why good is 'bad.' I know it's been that way for a while, but I don't get it."

"It's just rad. You understand 'rad' don't you?"

"I suppose I do. Maybe I've been too square all my life, too involved in my studies to take on all that kind of talk."

He laughed because she said 'square.' "It's okay, Mom. You're okay. I love you anyway because you're so dope."

They giggled together. "I really like your cast, Jamal. It looks very dope."

Clarence came by after Jamal had gone to bed. "I missed you," he said. "We've spent so much time together lately that I find it difficult to be without you."

He picked her up and asked where her bedroom was, then carried her up the stairs, silently creeping by Jamal's door. "Is your mom in bed yet?"

Her mood was so light, she couldn't help but answer him with a big, wet kiss on the mouth.

Cleo had dreams that night—nightmares. The one she could remember was crystal clear. She was dreaming of being in a strange place and trying to fix it. There were a lot of things that needed fixing and a lot of people getting in the way, and she struggled to get it all done in time. In time for what, she didn't know, but she was certain it must be extremely important.

"For what?" For what?" She cried and awoke with a start. Gasping for air, she discovered Clarence there trying to hold her as she thrashed—trying to get it all done.

"Oh my God," She cried. "What a terrible nightmare. I thought I wouldn't... My God, it's you. You're here."

"And, I don't plan to go away, if you'll have me." He propped her up on the edge of the bed as she slowly regained consciousness from the deep, terrifying sleep. They were in her bed and she remembered he had taken her up the stairs to her room; they had made love and had fallen asleep together.

"It's okay, Cleo. You're safe now. Jamal is safe too. You don't need to worry. I love you. I love you so much and I want to take care of you and Jamal." He held her tight. "I want us to be together forever."

She was barely awake and the words sounded like they were coming from a long-lost dream she'd had when she was far too young to understand what those words really meant, only that they were special.

"What are you saying, Clarence?"

"I'm asking you to marry me, Cleo. It's been on my mind for a while and I want to make it real."

"My God!" she cried. "Are you sure marriage is what you want?"

"Yes, I am sure. I don't think I have ever been more certain about anything in my whole life.

"My God, my God." She couldn't stop the tears.

"Can't you say anything other than 'My God'?"

"My God. You are asking me to marry you?" She asked incredulously.

"Will you? Will you be with me for the rest of our days, Cleo? I love you more than my own life and I need you to be with me forever."

"My God."

"Is that all you can say?" He was smiling with tears in his eyes.

"No, of course, I can say… Yes! I do want to marry you and I do want to be with you for the rest of our days. Yes, I want to grow old with you. Yes, I want to have more children with you. I can't think of anything I would want more." She was crying now, releasing all of the pent- up emotions from all that had happened.

He took a small box from the bedside table and opened it. It contained a ring of white gold that was mounted with a small diamond. "Cleo, will you be mine? Will you be my wife?"

As he placed the ring on her finger, Jamal came hopping into the room with his leg still in the cast. Edith stood at the door monitoring Jamal's entrance.

"Yes!" he screamed. "I want us to marry you, too." Jamal was elated and jumping up and down on the bed creating quite a commotion. The bed covers flew and the pillows landed on top of his head. "Yes! Yes! Yes!" he cried. "We love you. Yes!"

The three of them frolicked on the bed yelling with joy and abandon as Edith watched, a wide grin on her face and tears in her eyes.

Thirty-six

CLEO'S WEDDING PLANS were very simple. She wanted to marry Clarence at her home and she hoped she could put on a nice party in the backyard afterwards. Edith helped her, of course, and after Cleo met Clarence's mother, Eunice, she offered to help, too.

Eunice was a lovely older woman a lot like Cleo's mom. She had been a hard worker all her life having a child to rear and a house to keep. She worked as an executive assistant and sometimes bookkeeper which afforded her the ability to cope as a single mom in their rented Compton house. Eunice told Cleo all about how she and Clarence had managed all those years up to the present. They had been very close and Clarence was a good son. She told her how she had insisted he go to school no matter how tempting the "social life of Compton" was. She had kept a close eye on him, never allowing him to get off course, insisting he take school seriously, speak well and avoid associations with gangs and street trouble. Cleo thought she had done a great job keeping Clarence in line and away from danger. There had been "one time when he got into a fight with a brother from the hood. That caused him the trouble of being arrested and roughed up by police. He had to spend a night in jail, but was released and never charged . . "Thank God," she'd said. Eunice, as a divorced mom, had to work all her life. She let Cleo know she was marrying a 'good man.'

Cleo asked Jamal if he would be willing to escort her down the small aisle they had planned in the living room.

"What's escort mean, Mom?" Jamal was too young to know the word yet and she explained that the man of the house, usually the father of the bride, would take the bride down the aisle to meet her new husband at the altar. "What's an altar?" He asked, perplexed.

"Well, in some churches the altar is at the head of a long, tall room where the people sit in pews. You've seen that on TV sometimes. At our church there are two aisles heading down to the head of the church and the altar is that big table at the front." They had been to the local Baptist church only a few times and never developed the habit of church attendance.

Jamal still looked perplexed so she continued. "We're going to have a little aisle here between the people who will stand on each side, so that you can walk me down it to meet Clarence at the fireplace which will sort of stand in for an altar. I know it's a little confusing since you haven't spent much time in church, but we want to make this seem like that. I'll come down the stairs in my dress, with my flowers. I'll meet you at the bottom of the stairs and we will walk together down the aisle from there. How does that sound?"

Jamal just shrugged because he didn't know what to say. Then, a thought, "Will I have to wear my 'Sunday Best' like before at the birthday party?"

"Yes, you will. Is that okay with you?"

"No. But, I'll do it if that's importmant," he said, mispronouncing the big word.

She smiled, "It is. And, we'll have some flowers and candles. It'll be very simple, but I hope elegant."

Jamal just shook his head, unbelieving. He still didn't understand what was going on. He was willing to do whatever his mom wanted, but he thought it was kind of stupid making believe they were in a church like that.

Edith, of course, insisted on baking the cake which wouldn't be huge (maybe three layers) or elaborate, but she intended it to look very elegant with pretty flowers draped down the sides. "Should I put a bride and groom on the top?" She asked.

"Sure, Mom. You do whatever you want. It's your job and I know you'll do it good."

"You know I'll do it *well*," she said to remind Cleo.

"Yes, Mom, you'll do it *well*. That's what I meant to say." She smiled at Edith knowing how strict her mother was about English.

Eunice insisted on contributing the flowers which Cleo knew would be expensive. She was grateful. Cleo liked her new mother-in-law. The last one, Mrs. Henderson, had been a 'piece of work' as she had often conveyed to her mom.

She made out the guest list to include the friends she had neglected. Many of them, her 'Besties,' had called when they heard about Cleo's engagement to Clarence and they all insisted on coming to the wedding, forgiving her abundantly for her inattention. They understood how busy she had been; they had been busy, too, but declared it would never happen again. She also invited Phyllis and Elsie. Neighborhood invitees were Lupe Gonzalez and her husband, the Hayes' family down the street, Kisha and her family next door.

Cleo sent an invitation to Walter, her brother, but he declined saying he couldn't make it on that date. She wondered about his excuse, if it had to do with current drug use. She hoped it wasn't that, of course. Maybe he had a job to go to. Whatever the reason, she was disturbed he couldn't come. He had not been an active part of their family for some time and it hurt her a lot. She thought it must hurt Edith too. But she would say, "He's only working on making a life for himself, which is what he should be doing."

There was one invitee Cleo knew would not be able to afford the trip. Her Aunt Dorothy would have loved to come, but it just wasn't practical. She sent a small gift of a sugar and cream set which Cleo loved. It was decorated very prettily with little blue bells dripping down the sides. Cleo was astonished she hadn't sent something more to do with piano music.

Eunice invited a few of their friends, hers and some of Clarence's childhood gang which included a mix of ethnic and white boys. Clarence had always been devoted to widening his choices of friends into an inclusive mix. He invited a couple of friends from his job at Optimum Care, too.

When Cleo saw Zackary again, she invited him to the wedding.

"No, no. I'd be too much trouble in the wheelchair. I don't want to disrupt anything."

"You would be fine. How would you disrupt my wedding?"

"You'd be surprised. Maybe with a big fart."

She laughed. "Okay, if you don't want to come, I understand. But please know I want you to be there."

"Thank you for being so generous. Elsie will tell me all about it. I won't miss anything, except you, of course, while you're on a honeymoon."

"We haven't planned that just yet."

"Do you have to go on one?" He asked sheepishly. "They cost a lot of money, you know."

"Clarence hasn't said anything about that yet, so try not to worry."

Cleo took Jamal to the doctor and he was able to have his cast off, at last. He walked unsteadily at first, but got his bearings in no time.

The next time Cleo saw Clarence, he told her his plans for their honeymoon.

"I hope this will be to your liking. An uncle of mine died—not close or anything. You know my dad and I haven't been close for many years—but his brother, my uncle—his name was Thomas Delacroix—left me just enough money to take this trip. I want to go to the Island of Delacroix to see where my ancestors lived. It's in Louisiana. Does that sound like a good honeymoon destination?"

She loved the idea. "Of course. That would be a perfect place to go. I'll ask Zackary for enough time off. He won't like it, but I'm sure he will be okay."

Thirty-seven

THE WEDDING WASN'T a big gathering, but it was enthusiastic. Clarence's dad declined, probably for obvious reasons. He didn't want to face his ex-wife and the fact that he and Clarence didn't get along easily. Their last encounter had not ended well. Clarence, once again, felt abandoned by his dad.

The good news was Walter. He had decided to come at the last minute. Cleo was delighted to see him. He had dressed nicely with a white shirt, coat and tie over his Levis. He wasn't as tall as Cleo, but thin in build and she was surprised he was clean-shaven and wearing a short dread style.

Cleo wore a long off-white dress with no sleeves and a short train in the back. It was silk with a few clear sparkling sequins around the neckline, and she didn't care to wear a veil, just some pearl earrings and a necklace. Edith planted some yellow roses in her hair when she did it up. There were candles and flowers adorning the mantle of the fireplace and everyone stood for the short service lead by the local Baptist minister.

Clarence was very handsome, looking very tall, in a simple black suit with a silk tie to match the yellow flowers. Eunice and Edith were beautiful in their lovely outfits. Her mother's lacy dress was an ivory shade and Eunice wore gold satin. Everything was perfect, just as Cleo had hoped. The weather wasn't too warm and there was a nice breeze outside so their lunch after the ceremony would be fine.

Since Walter had come, he took his place beside Cleo to walk her down the aisle.

Jamal walked her too, as they had planned, on the other side. He was visibly relieved to be freed of the entire responsibility. As Cleo reached the bottom of the stairs, she couldn't believe how blessed she was. "Hey, Whitey Wally, thanks for coming," she whispered.

"I couldn't miss your wedding. That would have been the biggest mistake I could have made." He smiled.

Everything came off without a hitch and after the big kiss, which embarrassed Jamal—he hid his face in Edith's dress—they all wandered into the back yard where chicken thighs, potato salad, chips and watermelon were served along with wine and wedding cake. The young people had lemonade to drink. Some adults drank champagne. The skies were a clear blue with fluffy clouds, the kind Cleo always dreamed of.

What no one at the wedding knew about were two people. Neither knew about the other as well. Etta Stone, still out of jail on bail, managed to watch the wedding in the living room through a window from an alley between the houses, and Angus Dunne hid behind the fence to spy on the party. Etta imagined she would run into the house calling Clarence to her side and they would run from the altar. Etta would somehow inspire Clarence to flee from Cleo to do no less than marry her. She failed to execute her plan, struck by their blatant love and joy and somehow feeling chastised by her intensions. Her mother would be proud that Etta felt corrected. She felt stupid when she realized how impossible it would have been to pull off. But her mind was still intent on messing things up for Cleo.

Angus didn't have such overarching fantasies, only a minor fantasy compared to Etta's. But he wanted to make their lives miserable somehow, maybe a fire-bomb or tear-gas thrown into the middle of the party while everyone was toasting the couple with champagne. When he witnessed the gathering of mixed races, something began to grow inside him that he'd never expected. He left the property feeling vaguely ashamed of himself, but only vaguely which he overcame almost instantly, recalling how enthusiastically Zack had encouraged him. He wondered how the old man would have viewed the occasion—probably with scorn.

Thirty-eight

THE TRIP ALL THE WAY to Louisiana had gone off without a hitch which neither Cleo nor Clarence expected. They had flown economy and it was crowded, but bearable. When they got to New Orleans, they rented a car to drive the rest of the way to Delacroix Island. It was just thirty miles southeast of the city and across a bridge.

The island was bare of old trees and foliage and was sparsely populated, sporting a whitewater tower that looked more like a UFO propped on top of metal postings.

Quickly, they found an acceptable motel and rented a room with a bathroom. It was a tiny bit seedy, but as it turned out, was the only motel in town or on the whole island. Clarence was told that by another customer down the hall at the ice machine. Cleo was impressed that Clarence was so careful about how he spent his money. He found the best deals for the car and, of course, the motel was pretty cheap.

"Ya know, you ain't gonna find much around here." The man at the ice machine was full of information. "It's nothin' but a small fishin' village. Hurricane Katrina pretty much wiped out tha whole place and tha oil spill surely didn't help. What used'ta be Delacroix Island has diminished from erosion and bad economic conditions. It sure ain't what it used'ta be when the Spanish arrived back in the day, I kin tell ya that."

"Wow. I read some things about the place before we came and I knew about the hurricane and the oil spill, but isn't there something of a tourist thing going on around here?"

"Well, yeah. There's some good crab and shrimp eatin', and a village to look at. There're fishin' boats in tha marina, but not much else."

"I was hoping to find something about the plantations here back in the eighteen, nineteen-hundreds. My ancestors were from here. They owned a sugar plantation."

The man laughed. "All that's gone with all tha hurricanes that've come through here year after year. Yer way too late fer that."

"Bummer. Well, thanks anyway for the info. It's good to know what to expect." Clarence was clearly disappointed. He'd imagined there would be something left.

"By the way," he asked the man, "What brings you here?"

"Me? Oh, I'm a buyah. I buy up as much crab and shrimp 's I can, and sell it ta restaurants north 'a here."

"Is that a good business?"

"Shore is. I wouldn't be doin' it if it weren't." He smiled.

Clarence smiled back and headed for the room. When he got there, he found Cleo dressed for the evening. "You look damned good, but I'm afraid too good for what we're in for."

"Why? What do you mean?" She asked.

"I just found out there's nothing much here. There's a small fishing village and we can go there for dinner, but I'm afraid we've come a long way for pretty much nothing."

After he told her what he'd heard, she changed to more casual attire, pants and a light top.

Calling from the bathroom she said, "Well, as far as I'm concerned, we came for a very good reason. It is our honeymoon for one and this is where your ancestors came from. That's worth a lot."

"You know, you're right as usual. Thank you, Cleo. I was afraid you would be as disappointed as I was feeling."

"No way, husband. You're worth everything to me and anything you need is what I want."

When she came out of the bathroom, he hugged her warmly and they left the room to explore the village.

"Hmmm, you sure smell good," he said as they walked out the door.

"Thanks. It's a perfume my girlfriends gave me as a wedding gift."

"I'll have to thank them when we get back." He smiled.

The village was quaint, no doubt, but nothing like either of them expected. They found a small eatery where they could get a dinner of fried crab or shrimp served in red plastic baskets with coleslaw. There were candles on the tables which added a nice glow.

Clarence told her what he'd heard about the island and what was left.

"That's terrible. I expected much more," she said after he finished.

"I know. So did I."

"You must be really disappointed."

When they returned to the motel the night clerk told them about a house where they could learn a little about the history of Delacroix. It was the town museum, such as it was, they were told.

"Oh well, we have a room and it's got be good for something," she said, trying to be cheerful.

Clarence was in a low mood. He had expected so much more. Cleo removed his shirt and massaged his neck and shoulders to relax him. His neck was as taught as a tightly twisted rope.

"Don't you worry about me, Ba̖e," Cleo whispered in his ear. "I'm fine with what's here. All I really care about is you, anyway."

He turned to her and kissed her, bringing her down to him on the bed. "You are all I care about, too. So, what's the matter with me?" He chuckled. "All I want is you. Are you okay with that, Mrs. Delacroix?"

"You bet I am." She kissed him full on the mouth to let him know how she felt and they made love as a married couple for the first time.

The little house on Isleño Street had the address for the museum. It was early when they arrived the next morning. The lady who lived there answered the door. "What ya wan'?" She asked warily.

"This is the town museum, isn't it?" Clarence responded.

"Shore is." Her tone lightened. "But it'll cost ya a bit to come in an' look aroun.'"

"Sure," he said as he reached for his wallet. "Our name's Delacroix and we've come looking for some history about the Delacroix family." He took some bills to indicate he was willing to pay her fee.

She looked at the wad with widening eyes. "That'll be ten dollahs," she returned. "Oh, an' another' ten for th' lady. Ya understand this is a donation."

"Sure," he replied skeptically.

She let them in after accepting the money, which was obviously the maximum she charged. "Yer name's Delacroix? That don' sound righ'. The Delacroix's were whites, Spanish peopah."

"You're right. They were. My great, great, great, great grandfather was a white man, the youngest son of the family. His grandfather was actually French, but he'd met his wife somewhere in Spain before they came here and established the plantation. My many times-great-grandmother never married the grandson, but when she went north, she took his name for her new-born child. She felt it only right since she, being a slave, didn't have a proper name," he explained.

"That righ'?" She answered cagily. "Well, then that's a fake name fer ya."

"Well ma'am, I beg to differ. It is my name and I claim it legally. It became our legal name even though she never took the name for herself. She was raped by the man and she felt shame. The story goes that she kept her own first name, Lilah, and went only by that for the rest of her life."

"Ah see."

Cleo thought Clarence had handled the situation well, even though the woman clearly took the information with disdain. They were African-American and she was white, after all. They couldn't expect a white woman in the South to be accepting of black folk.

She showed them around the tiny house and they found a couple of worn tin-types of the Delacroix sugar plantation, but not much more. As the story went, the Delacroix family was sent by Spain during the American Revolution. It was the Canary Islanders who came first and populated the southern Louisiana coastline and the island.

There was a Frenchman named Delacroix and he apparently married his young wife in the Canary Islands. When they arrived in the U.S., they purchased land on the Spanish-American Island and developed a farm, cultivating the rich soil of the area. Initially, they produced vegetable and fruit crops, which eventually became a sugar plantation. By that time, they had purchased the island. Delacroix learned Spanish since that was the language that predominated the land. He and his wife produced a large family and the name continued from generation to generation until finally hurricanes had their way with the plantation and the island. But that was long after Clarence's many times-great-grandmother escaped and took herself and her unborn child north.

Cleo and Clarence decided to tour New Orleans for the rest of the trip after seeing the tiny museum of history the island provided.

As they explored the New Orleans area, they came across an abandoned old apartment project that looked as if it had become the canvas for an artist. A good one, they thought, as they slowly passed by it examining the images that covered the entire horseshoe-shaped building facade. Cleo wondered out loud who the artist was. "This work should be in a museum," she marveled.

"This is the museum," Clarence remarked as the car passed by it.

"I suppose you're right," she agreed. Then, she changed the subject. "You know, we're on our way to Honky-Tonk Town. Are you sure we want to do that?"

"Hey, we're okay."

"Are you sure?"

"I will make sure you're okay. I love you and I will protect you."

"Clarence, that is never what I worry about."

"Then, there's nothing to worry about." He smiled that cock-sure way he had of making everything feel perfect.

That night, they ate dinner in New Orleans at a very nice restaurant they found that offered 'Good ol' Southern Cookin.' They ordered giant prawn dinners with grits, collard greens, hush puppies and a tasty white wine to go with them. When they were served, Cleo looked at her dish with dismay. "The prawn is looking at me. I know it's dead, but its beady eyes are a little too much."

Clarence laughed and took her plate, cutting the creature up so it wouldn't look at her. "There. That better?" He asked.

"Much better. I really don't like to eat things that can look at me."

The meal was exceptional and they were as happy as the newlyweds they were. They made their way back to the car.

"Hold it!" A white police officer had driven up to check them out. As he got out of the squad car, he held his hand on his weapon. "B'fore ya go 'nother step, I wanna know who yew are and if that cah really belong to ya."

"Yes sir," Clarence said, planning fully to honor the request. He reached for his wallet to take out his ID and the rental agreement with the car leasing agency.

"Hold it righ' thar," said the cop. The man took out his gun and aimed it at Clarence.

Cleo knew how to be when an officer stopped folks. She'd learned it from her brother, Walter. She'd learned to never reach for something unless told to do so by the officer, and Clarence had not followed that rule. She tensed knowing things could easily escalate.

Taking a chance and noting the man's name on his shirt, she said, "Officer Hamilton, please don't worry. Clarence is an honest man and he would never do anything but follow your orders."

The officer stiffened.

Clarence froze. He knew from what she'd said and the gun aimed at them that he shouldn't have reached for the wallet. "Yes, sir." He put up his hands. "We're from California and here on our honeymoon. We're staying at the Delacroix Motel on the island and we've rented this car from the Mississippi Auto Agency located at the airport. We mean no harm, I assure you."

"Well, yew sure sound funny, all formal and all." The officer softened a little. "But I wanna see yer proof fast. Take yer wallet out slow, young man." He emphasized the word 'slow'.

Clarence complied, being as easy about it as he could trying not to indicate anything improper. The cop took his ID and the paperwork and looked them over while still keeping a steady eye on Clarence and Cleo. "Delacroix huh? Yew got the same name 's the island?"

"Yes sir. Got it from my four-time-great grandmother when she escaped north. It is our true name. Came down from the Delacroix family there."

"Okay, I guess this 's proper ID." Still holding the gun on them, slowly taking his flashlight, he peered inside the car to check if there was anyone else in the backseat and looking at the Vin numbers to see if it was the rental indicated on the papers he held in his hand. Then he checked the license plate. They matched of course. Warily, he returned his gun to its holster and gave Clarence his ID and the paperwork. "It all looks in ordah," he said cautiously. "I guess thar's no reason ta detain ya any longah. Yew folks have a good evnin', ya hear? An', congratulations."

Relieved, they felt like they had escaped one hell of a problem when he let them go. They knew how easily things could escalate when dealing with the police. Clarence, slowly at first, opened the passenger side to let Cleo into the car. He suddenly felt an urgency to get his bride out of harm's way. He rushed around the back and jumped into the car fast, pumped with adrenalin.

"I guess I got to be that 'nigger' my dad was looking for," Clarence laughed lightly and jammed his key into the ignition to start the car as fast as he could. The wheels screeched as he took off. Startled, the cop pulled his gun again and began shooting. The car rolled off into traffic and hit another car as it was moving by. Shocked by all the gun fire, Cleo looked over at Clarence to see why he had lost control only to find him with blood pouring from the back of his head.

She screamed uncontrollably. Everything came to a screeching stop as other cars hit them and the world as she knew it was inexorably changed.

Clarence was slumped over the wheel, dead.

Lights from the patrol cars and the ambulance that gathered were blinding as she held Clarence who was laid out on the cold pavement. Blood from his wound drenched her clothing. A medic pulled her away and they gathered him up onto a gurney, covering his body completely. His hand dangled out from under the shroud and she could see the gold ring, the ring she had placed on his finger only the day before. Cleo reached out for his hand as she sobbed uncontrollably. An officer took her by the shoulders and ushered her away from the scene into a waiting police car.

She resisted. She didn't want to leave. Her mind kept racing back to the moment when she could have altered the outcome, something that would have made a difference. She should have warned Clarence not to hurry. Why did he feel he had to rush? The officer had let them go. Why did he hurry?

There had been no cameras on the police officer and none that were operational during the incident. Authorities checked with the restaurant and other businesses close by, but none produced a scintilla of evidence that the cop had panicked and shot Clarence for nothing other than the desire to get his bride away from a harrowing situation. It was Cleo's word against the policeman's, who was adamant that Clarence must have been guilty of something to have acted the way he did. "He was runnin', 'n I knew I had to fire mah gun."

"You murdered my husband, you son-of-a bitch!" she screamed, spitting the words into the face of the cop.

"My husband was only guilty of being 'A NIGGER,'" she roared at the reporter who was trying to get a statement.

The officer's statement to the reporter—"He took off like a shot and I knew he must have somethin' he was hidin'"—was believed, even though there was no evidence to support his assertion. As the officer walked away from them, Cleo could barely hear his last words: "Oh well, he was just another niggah from the left coast."

The murderer, Officer Hamilton—she would never forget that name—was never laid off, fired or prosecuted for killing her husband. *I hate him! I hate him!* she screamed in her sleep.

Cleo returned home in an interminable stupor. Dazed and in shock with only a searing pain plaguing her heart, the whole trip was a blur and everything that happened seemed surreal. She couldn't believe Clarence was gone forever. The days that followed Clarence's 'murder,' as she had formed it in her mind, were endless. She hadn't slept much or eaten and when Edith picked her up at the airport with the help of her brother, Walter, she couldn't conceive of the reality she now faced. It was unimaginable.

The question lingered—why did he hurry?

The only clear memory she had of the funeral was Jamal's hysterical wailing. He was as inconsolable as was she. The faces of the other mourners, Clarence's mother who stood stoically almost like a statue with no expression on her weary face; his dad, who cried inconsolably; an elderly grandmother and grandfather and some friends were mostly a blur seen only through her tears. There was some conversation with Clarence's dad, Jamal being the focus of the discussion. She had met him only that once before at the hospital. Cleo was too bereft to focus on their conversation and what it was about.

The old Negro hymn, "Ooh Lord, Remember Me," which had been played during the service, echoed endlessly through her head, its haunting sadness taking her deeper into despair.

Oh Lord, remember my Ba'e.

Why did he hurry? He must have had a reason. Why?

Then, she began to blame herself. It was her fault for not stopping him, keeping him calm so the cop wouldn't get the wrong idea. *Why, why hadn't she stopped him?* became the mantra that reverberated endlessly through her head.

Thirty-nine

THE *LOS ANGELES TIMES* didn't use up much room reporting her husband's murder. Cleo found a small fourth page story that said, "LOS ANGELES MAN KILLED BY POLICE IN LOUISIANA." The article mentioned Clarence's name and briefly covered the incident claiming he was a black man who had fled from police after a brief encounter causing the officer to believe he was afraid of getting caught. Since there had been no cameras, there was little detail and no mention of Cleo or her presence in the situation. The truth was predictably glossed over.

There were so many incidents of a similar nature that reporting had become commonplace.

Her life became tedium. The heavy, searing pain in her heart was constant.

That cop didn't have to shoot. Clarence didn't have a weapon. But he had rushed and the cop reacted. There was no reason to shoot. He could have just said "Halt!" Why did he have to shoot? The endless questions kept coming and they wouldn't stop. They wouldn't let her sleep. They wouldn't let her eat. She couldn't think of a reason to shower or get dressed. Most of all, Cleo felt like she had lost hope.

Then, at last, she slept and ate when she could, and sat staring at the walls. Exhausted, she slept again. Her mother took over all of the care of Jamal who crept around sensing his mother's desolation and how intense it was.

Edith told him to be quiet and to leave her alone.

Cleo's sleep was filled with horrible nightmares of death and blood, guns and police badges with name plates attached. There was a recurring reel of Clarence slumped over the wheel of the car, unmoving and blood-soaked. In one dream she was looking all over the city of New Orleans for the cop who murdered her new husband. She lurked down alleys, darkened streets, and finally down a central, well-lit street where she saw Officer Hamilton, his nameplate, an enormous plaque worn as a badge of honor on his chest, strutting confidently down the center of the roadway with a smirk curling his lips. She found she had a gun and with an unspeakable rage, she fired it straight into his chest. The bullet deflected off him like a swatted fly. He never stopped smiling smugly, and he never stopped strutting down the street. Her screams were silent, unheard by anyone. She awakened, startled, her heart beating wildly in her chest, unable to breathe, unable to speak or scream. She couldn't function.

Edith called Phyllis at the agency asking about the job with Zackary Hughes. Phyllis reported the job was still Cleo's when she was ready, but that Hughes was getting upset and unable to cope with the people she sent over. She'd sent over numerous candidates, but none sufficed. He was never satisfied and complained bitterly that no one was as competent as Cleo was. Phyllis was running out of healthcare workers to send. She was glad he hadn't gone to some other agency.

Finally, Cleo got up one morning saying she was ready. She was far from cheerful, but thought she had to get on with her life and put this "murderous episode" behind her. She had to place it in a context, a context that was foreign to her because it lacked any hope at all. But she was determined to get back to normal, whatever that was.

It took all the guts she had to shore up her strength to move forward. She had to because Jamal and her mom depended on her. Whatever she had to do she would do. The difficulty lay in her heart. It was heavy, cumbersome with memories of that horrible night in New Orleans. She wanted to weep; somehow the tears wouldn't come. They were jammed down in the pit of her stomach like a bale of cotton, dry, unmoving and absorbing any relief there was to be had.

Forty

WHEN CLEO RETURNED to Zack's house that Monday, she found a disgruntled man who was unable to put things right. Neither Elsie nor Angus had been able to deal with him in a reasonable way. He was furious with the last replacement the agency had sent over to handle his needs while she was away.

"She was a slob," he bawled. "You should never have left—you should never leave me again!" Zack was inconsolable. The nurse had apparently been old and ugly, "like an ape," he'd lamented. "You should never leave me again, you hear?" He repeated. He was in top form, angry without reason.

"Okay, what can I do to make this better?" She asked.

"For one thing, you can get me a warm breakfast. I haven't had a hot meal since you left, damn-it."

"No problem. Coming right up," she said as she removed her jacket and put her purse and jacket in the closet. She nearly ran to the kitchen, so anxious to make things right for him. As soon as breakfast was done and put on a tray, she took it to him, placing it on his lap. "Would you like me to rub your neck, help you relax a little?" She asked.

He reluctantly allowed her to massage him, his neck and shoulders. Then he asked her to play the piano for him—"Just not anything from that Joplin guy," he insisted. "By the way, I heard about the trouble with your new husband. I'm sorry. It must've been a terrible thing."

"Yes, Zack, it was. I am trying to get myself back to normal, if that's at all possible."

"I understand."

She wheeled him into the living room and set him up next to the piano with his breakfast on his lap as she had done before.

Deciding to keep the music soft, Cleo played mostly Brahms. The need to concentrate made playing the music doable. It was hard though to hold the tears back as she played with thoughts of Clarence crowding her mind. But the Brahms was successful and Zack seemed to be calming down and needing a nap as soon as he finished his breakfast and she finished playing the Steinway.

"Are you sure you don't want to read the paper first?" She asked, sincerely wondering why he was deviating from his usual habits.

"No. I'm tired. I've been tired all weekend waiting for your return. Neither of them, not Elsie or Angus, could do anything right," he lamented. "Everything was wrong. Everything! I can't deal with it when it's all wrong."

"Of course, you can't. I understand." She was sympathetic. She knew exactly how he felt. "I know I have trouble when things go wrong like that. Life can be difficult for me and I can imagine it must be even worse for you sometimes."

She rolled him into the bedroom, changed his diapers and got him into bed. He grumbled the whole time. Fortunately, he fell off to sleep almost immediately and she quietly left the darkened room to do the dishes and straighten the house, which was in a chaotic state. She wondered why Elsie hadn't been able to do what needed to be done over the weekend, but surmised the woman's mind must have been distracted by something else, either something at home or Zack's irascible attitude… or both.

When she finally finished all of the chores, she sat in the den on the couch waiting. For what she didn't know. The feelings she had been harboring ever since her new husband, she was afraid to think of his name, had died, kept coming up like a bad stomach wishing to cleanse itself. She wanted to throw up and she couldn't. She wanted to cry and she couldn't. She wanted to die and she couldn't.

It was late when Zack finally arose from his nap. He hadn't been able to sleep the whole time she was gone, or so he said. Cleo fixed him a late lunch and he read his newspaper after he finished. The soothing crackle of the paper as he thumbed through it, turning the pages and folding it back, reminded her of her dad as he sat at the end of a long day reading the *LA Times*. It was a comforting memory accompanied by sadness that her father was gone now. He'd died too young. Clarence died too young.

She was exhausted by the time Zack concluded the crossword puzzle.

"How are you feeling now?" She asked. "Have you had enough time to rest and recover?"

"I guess I'm okay, but I can't find my medicines. That stupid woman hid them. Neither Elsie nor Angus could find them."

"Oh. How long have you been without them?"

"Just this weekend."

"That's a long time to be without your blood pressure medication."

"My pain medication, too," he complained.

"I'll look around and see if I can find them. If I can't, I'll call Cl…" She started to say 'Clarence,' but stopped herself in time … "Uh, I'll call Optimum-Care and ask for replacements. They can have them here by tomorrow." She paused. "Actually, that would be far too long to wait. I'm sure I can find them. Let me look."

She looked all over the house, even went upstairs to the darkened unused portion of the residence. It was gloomy and foreboding, but she turned on a couple of lights and investigated the rooms thoroughly. They were neatly done and hadn't been touched since the last yearly cleaning. It took her a long time and she found nothing. It was getting late and she needed to catch the bus.

"I'll check your bedroom once more and see what I can find in there." She left him in the den watching Fox News as was his habit.

Thoroughly checking the closet and drawers, she found nothing. There were two more drawers to check. She had never wanted to invade the bedside tables because she imagined there would be private things there that he might not want her to see. She checked one bedside drawer and then the other, reaching her hand deep inside to make sure she missed nothing.

Her hand struck an item in back of one of the drawers, the last one she would check, and she drew out a small box. It was made of tin and clasped shut like an Altoid's container. She knew it wasn't big enough to hide his medications, but curious she opened it anyway. In shock, she examined the contents. There were the skeletal remains of a severed finger and beneath it was a folded piece of yellowed newsprint.

Trying not to touch the ghastly finger, Cleo took the paper out and unfurled it to reveal an old newspaper article. It was dated July 24, 1946. The one paragraph article described four bodies of Negro origin, two men and two women, found near Moore's Ford Bridge, crossing the Apalachhee River. They had been shot many times. It was characterized as a lynching.

Apparently, the finger was a souvenir of the event. Cleo had read about many lynchings when, as a teen, she visited the National Memorial for Peace and Justice (some call it the national lynching museum) in Birmingham, Alabama. Her parents had taken her on a vacation to visit some of her father's relatives. While there, they saw many disturbing depictions of Negro lynchings during the Jim Crow era. They were often described as being entertainment for a town's residents with pictures of hundreds of smiling people, children even, and severed parts of Negro bodies kept as souvenirs. She had been deeply affected by the things she saw. The memorial's displays were gut-wrenching in their depictions of the injustices her people had been subjected to for centuries. It was still happening.

It had been a dark day in Birmingham as rain dampened their visit. She had thought that God was weeping with her as she viewed the thousands of names etched upon steel columns.

And now, appalled by her find -- nearly dropping the box in disgust—she regained some semblance of calm, cold as it was, and walked to the family room where she had left Zack.

Trying to maintain her composure, she asked, "Just exactly what is this, Zackary Hughes?"

He looked up and saw what she was holding. Smiling, he declared, "That, my dear, is the finger of a black nigger-bastard. His name was Roger Malcomb and he was lynched as the man who assaulted the son of one of my father's closest friends and neighbors, a man by the name of Barnette Hester who owed a cotton farm in Georgia where we lived. Malcomb would have murdered the young man given the opportunity, but only sent him to the hospital with his insides torn apart—over a dirt-poor nigger woman of all things."

"He was lynched?" She screamed the question, unbelieving.

"You bet. They let him out 'a jail and he would 'a escaped if it 'd not been fer the brave intervention of a team of white men who took the law into their own hands. Rightly, too, I might add." His speech had regained a bit of its southern origin.

"There's nothing right about it." Cleo was horrified with what she was hearing. "Lynching is murder, nothing more."

"You're so stupid, Cleo. You don't know what you're talkin' about. The man was guilty and he was out 'a jail. There was nothin' more to be done about it but what was done. Execution was the only solution. It always was." He had raised his voice to match hers. "It's God's will, I tell ya."

"I can't believe what I'm hearing. I suppose you were there. Did you participate in the murder?"

"It was a justified lynching. No, I did not, but I watched an' I was glad of the thing. Those niggers deserved what they got."

"Those *Negros*?" She asked surprised, emphasizing the corrected word.

"You bet. They rightly killed the whole lot of them, the nigger whore over whom this whole brouhaha was fought and her friends. There were four of 'em. Four more coloreds we didn't have to worry about any more. It was a real coup." Zack's gravelly voice took on a sinister tone.

He said it with such pride, she couldn't help herself and threw the box with the finger in his face.

"Damnit, you whore! You're no better—You're a black stain upon this nation, a parasite, a louse, a jackal, a screaming monkey!" he roared. "You're no better than all those nigger bastards. They deserved what they got, damnit. You're a god dammed 'Coon', I tell ya!"

Cleo's anger hit a peak she had never known before. She could feel it, hear it rising up from the pit of her groin to her stomach, to reach her throat in a low-pitched bestial growl. It spewed forth in a rage forcing her body to flare as her hand flew across his face. She barely managed to nick him as he drew back to avoid her. The weight of his move made him topple over from his wheelchair, his head hitting the corner of the coffee table.

Behind her, she heard something, "My God! No!" Cleo never saw whose voice she'd heard—she ran straight from the house.

Angus Dunne had watched as Cleo attempted to hit the old man. Zackary was out cold when he examined him. Callously, he went to the kitchen just off the family room. Finding what he sought, a small, sturdy paring knife with a serrated edge, he returned to the room where Zackary lay. Wiping the knife clean of his own finger prints, he placed it near his body. Then, he picked up the landline phone and dialed nine-one-one. "There's has been an assault on an old man here. Please send an ambulance and call the police." He hung up the receiver before any questions could be asked and sat down on the couch to wait.

Forty-one

IT WAS UNIMAGINABLE, the drone of the room, mumbling voices of the other inmates and the clang of cell doors. It all faded in and out of her consciousness as Cleo tried to remember what had happened. The others, they were all women, dressed in the same yellow tops and blue pants with the words 'LA County Jail' emblazoned on their backs, except the female guards in their uniforms looking like soldiers unable to think for themselves. They stood frozen in place largely in the same position, arms behind their backs, guns in holsters watching God knows what; the women there?

The gathering was mostly black with three white women and one Native-American who was older with graying hair. They were surrounded by metal bunk beds and sat on folding chairs in an over-crowded jail in downtown LA. There were big round tables for them to sit at and the floors of the room were covered with sage-green linoleum tiles cracked and bare along where people had walked back and forth through the place. The room had no windows. They were surrounded by jail cells, all full. The place was cold and dank with the smell of some disinfectant.

Everything became a haze. It came from her eyes—they were watering. Tears formed, blurring her vision. Her heart was heavy with memories of Jamal, Wally and her mother, Edith, standing on the tiny lawn behind their house's barbed-wire fence, watching as the police took her away in handcuffs. The pain clouded their eyes not knowing what was happening. And, the neighbors including Lupe Gonzalez, the Hayes family and little Kisha from next door were there watching. How could she tell them she had been arrested for elder abuse, assault and battery, charges that couldn't be true? The only relief she felt was that Clarence wasn't there to see this. He would have been terribly disappointed in her allowing Zack to get to her enough to send her into the custody of police. Then again, if he had survived, none of this was likely to have happened. The pain was more than she could bear.

She hadn't purposely hit Zackary. Her arm had flung out in a dark rage and somehow it landed on his chin, just barely. She remembered he'd dodged her flying hand, backing away and fell over from the wheelchair, hitting his head on the edge of the table. She'd heard a voice behind her. Was it Angus? She wasn't certain as she ran from the house, down streets reaching the corner where the bus would pick her up.

She'd forgotten her jacket and had been cold standing there crying. The old woman with her granddaughter sat on the bench watching her as if she must be mad. The bus, Carlos, the Hispanic driver, taking her without her handbag or bus pass, the blur of passing headlights, then running the length of Flower, passing the woman who'd had the white bag and little dog—the white bag missing, the little dog still straggling behind on its leash grimier than before. And endless homeless people, always there, lining the walls of the buildings and occupying the gutters.

Suddenly seeing her brother Wally, God bless him, his car waiting for her as she approached the train station. He'd never been there before. Why was he there this time? She didn't know, she was simply grateful to see him. When she got into the car and hysterically told him about the fight with Zackary, he held her. "There, there. It'll be alright. He'll be okay and so will you."

How could he know that nothing would be okay again?

There had been the judge behind his raised desk, not a simple desk but a huge façade blocking her or anyone from accessing him directly because of the great expanse between him and the prisoners and their representatives, an expanse as vast and dry as a desert mesa. The court where she was being arraigned was the Superior Court in Glendale. She didn't have a lawyer to defend her. Feeling small and inconsequential standing there before the judge, she pleaded that she was innocent. "It was an accident," she cried.

"You'll have a public defender assigned to your case." She was to remain in jail until bail could be raised to get her out. It was a huge sum and she was certain her family would not be able to raise that much money.

Then, the unimaginably long ride to, of all places, the Century Regional Detention Facility in Lynwood. The jail, which was cold and dark and smelled of a strange cleaning solution, was memorable for the hollow sounds of clanking cell doors and the forlorn look of the prisoners.

She worried about things such as her safety in this environment. Checking with the black woman next to her while they ate, she inquired about how the woman stayed safe.

"Me?" The woman asked, surprised that anyone would talk to her.

"Yes. I've heard rumors about police brutality in places like this. I've heard names like the 'Vikings.' Do they bother the women?"

"You're asking the wrong person. I've only been here a couple of days. I haven't seen or heard anything bad … or good about the place."

"Why're you here?" Cleo was genuinely curious.

"One thing I do know, people don't talk about themselves and questions like that are not welcome. So, I'd keep my mouth shut if I was you." The woman turned away from Cleo not wanting to encourage anything that could get her into trouble.

"I see."

But Cleo wondered if she would ever see her son again. And, how would Edith be able to come see her on a bus? So many unanswered questions plagued her weary brain.

Everything seemed so surreal. These circumstances were never anything she thought would happen to her. She felt a stranger in her own skin—this new person, a felon, a criminal, a widow and a black woman who didn't know her own strength, her own cruelty, or the kind of sinister rage, the fury that had brought her to this jail. Her head throbbed with the indignation of it all. Why would she be accused of elder abuse?

Zack had said earlier that she should never leave him again and yet she had been accused. They argued, yes. But this was an extreme reaction. Or, maybe not, given his past. Perhaps he was right. She was unstable, unable to control herself, a black animal to her core.

He was there at the lynching of those four people, not all of them guilty—he'd said that only one had been accused of assault. And, he said it was God's will. What kind of a belief was that? The two women were certainly innocent, and the other man was simply present, yet they had been killed too. There had been no judge, no jury, no conviction, yet there had been an execution, an execution of the innocent. It was astonishing when she thought about it, a modern-day lynching, crude, barbarian, uncivilized.

Zack had been there, apparently as a young man, so the lynching had happened sometime in the middle of the twentieth century. She knew there had been lynchings all along since Reconstruction into the eighteen, nineteen and twentieth centuries, even to this day, but it all seemed so primitive a reaction when most people had become sick of those killings for so long. The whole idea of lynching was primitive. She figured she must be naïve having such high expectations in the goodness of folks.

Edith would have an opinion. There were current police killings happening all the time that seemed terribly unjust and inappropriate. People all her life had told her about the brutality from gangs within the police departments, white supremacist cliques that took pride in punishing blacks often for nothing more than a missing tail light, or an out-of-date license plate. Clarence, her own husband had been unfairly and unreasonably shot in the back of the head, killed, and her mom would say it is a practice that wouldn't cease until whites had to pay for it with their jobs, long prison sentences or maybe their lives. Cleo had to admit her mom was probably right. She'd had such high hopes that civil rights activities would have a much bigger impact than seemed to be the case. Michelle Obama had been such an inspiration to Cleo's best instincts, a yardstick by which to gauge right action. She had encouraged the highest standards, to maintain a sense of worth— ethics that stood for the finest values. "When they go low, we go high!"

Was it all for naught? Did none of it matter? It didn't seem to matter to many white folks. It hadn't mattered to the white policeman who had murdered Clarence.

Hamilton, his name had been Officer Hamilton. It was a name she would never forget.

It was hard for Cleo to understand why whites were so prejudiced against the people she knew. Of course, there were bad blacks as well, but there were bad whites, Hispanics and Asians. Native Americans had both good and bad in their ranks, too. There was always a combination of both in all races and societies. Why was it so hard for white people to see and understand that? Then again, white people seemed to lump all ethnicities into one hardcore, unmanageable group, angry and violent.

Cleo's hopes for equality between the races were so out of proportion to the reality she had to face. Perhaps it was true, one rotten fish would putrefy the whole catch. Were her actions going to spoil everything she ever knew, stood for, fought for? Would they spoil her family, her son? Would Jamal grow up to be a rotten thug, a drug dealer, a murderer, her example more than her little boy could overcome?

What were the charges? Assault and battery—Elder Abuse? The whole thing had been unimaginable from the time of her wedding until now … all of it incomprehensible. She wondered if she was in the middle of a nightmare from which she might awaken. No, there was no hope, no chance this would all be a terrible illusion.

Zack seemed to have such an outsized sense of his privilege, as if he and his father were entitled to kill black folk even though they were innocent. And the cop had been so suspicious. Was it because

Clarence and she were black? It had to be. There was no other reason to stop them. They were doing nothing but being a happy couple celebrating their marriage, their love. They had been walking toward the rental car, innocently holding each other with no other thought than the lovemaking they would finally get to after a long day. How could Officer Hamilton misconstrue such innocence?

White privilege, the mantra of a disadvantaged people—a score to be settled, a debt to be paid, a reparation to be met. And, she, the proof that all blacks, 'niggers' as Zack had called her and her people, were unredeemable, a black mark on society that could never be expunged. She had become a stranger to herself, to herself as human, as worthy of justice in a white society.

Yet, it couldn't be true. There was still a tiny part of her that knew she was worthy, knew she had value, worth in any society. She had to hang on to that, to her sense of worth as a human being. Clarence had found her to be precious and they had married. She was human, dammit, fully a person of value, of significance, merit, meaning. She had to come to terms and stand up for herself. She could not allow Zackary Hughes, that Officer Hamilton, not any white person to define her and her worth.

Forty-two

THE ASSIGNED PUBLIC DEFENDER sat across from Cleo with his briefcase and documents. Shuffling through the papers that pertained to her case, he asked her to tell him the truth, only the truth. He was duty-bound to defend her and would have to know exactly what had happened to do a decent job.

He told her his name was Adam Barnes. He was a black man, serious, with a receding hairline and facial hair that gave him a look of dignity. His eyes were sad. He had seen a lot of pain in his life, mostly the pain that belonged to others, but she was certain, pain of his own as a Negro, a man who elicited fear among whites, people who would cross the street rather than face a person of color walking down the same path.

The room was small and stuffy and she wished they could meet outside somewhere. She needed to see the sun, feel fresh air caress her face, her skin, and hear the life of a planet filled with people, birds, creatures of all kinds. She wanted to smell something other than some disinfectant.

"I've been told," she started, "that you public defenders are so overloaded with cases that you can't do a good job. Is that true?"

"I've practiced law for *many* years, Mrs. Delacroix, as a public defender." His race was a blessing but she wondered if he'd have the time to do justice to this case. "I am committed to doing the best possible job defending you or anyone else I am assigned to. I will give your case all I have to give." He paused for only a moment. "It is my pride that keeps me doing my best."

She liked what she was hearing. Coming to the conclusion she had no choice, she told Mr. Barnes her story starting with the nasty racist attitude of Zackary Hughes and how he had thrown it in her face at most every opportunity.

Then, Cleo launched into the time when she had found the tiny tin box with the severed finger and the news article, how she had thrown the box and the finger in Zackary's face, though that recollection had been vague in her mind.

Barnes tried his best not to show any alarm, but was unable to when faced with the chopped off finger. "I must admit that is shocking. I can't imagine finding such a thing. It must have been horrifying for you. I might have done the same thing."

He seemed to be sensitive, which was a plus to Cleo. "Even so, I didn't mean to harm Zack. I'd actually grown to like the man, to care for him even with his intractable attitude. But this was too much and my rage overwhelmed me—I guess with all those months of taking my boss's abuse, I just lost my ability to cope. And, my husband who was recently murdered by the police in New Orleans ... All of it came crashing down on me."

"Oh, I am sorry. That's very understandable. Although proving that to a judge or a jury might be difficult."

"Will I have a choice?"

"A choice?"

"To have a jury trial or...

"Or, a bench trial?" He added. "A bench trial is adjudicated by the judge only, but I must warn you Mrs. Delacroix, judges are typically very conservative."

"So, what do I have to look forward to? I have a small child at home. My mother is looking after him, but how long she can go on without my help? I'm not sure."

"I hope she will be able to manage. I won't lie to you. Unless you can come up with the bail money, you are going to be here for a long time."

"Oh God," she cried. "What will I do?"

"Do you have a friend who could help? If not with money, maybe they could raise something through a 'Go Fund Me' program."

"That's an idea. I just don't know how many people will be sympathetic."

"You might be surprised. Not a lot of people know that lynching lasted well into the Twentieth Century the way it did, how it happens even today. There's a lot of confusion about what lynching really is. A lot of people believe it's a lynching only if a rope is used to string a black person from a tree. We, of course, know it is killing a person perceived as guilty and getting away with it. And, it probably occurs a lot more than any of us on the west coast can imagine. There was an unconvicted man and three innocent people killed in this, so folks may be sympathetic. You could emphasize the men who did the lynching acted as judge, jury and executioner, clearly against the US Constitution."

"You're right. I'll talk to my brother about it. He's computer savvy and he'll be willing to try."

The Go Fund Me drive didn't go as well as they thought and Cleo had to remain in jail until the trial. The money they did collect was well-used in her defense. Barnes had to hire a detective with connections in Georgia which was costly.

Forty-three

CLEO DIDN'T HAVE many opportunities to talk to Edith and the single phone available to use at the jail finally became accessible at a time she could call.

"I'm pregnant, Mom. It's Clarence's baby. It must have happened that one night we had together on our honeymoon."

"Oh, my God!" Edith cried out. "That's wonderful, Cleo."

"Yes, it is. I have something really important left of Clarence and I am going to make my life work in spite of all that has happened." She stopped for a moment in thought. "I'm going to name my baby Clarence, or Clarissa if it's a girl. They are both wonderful names, don't you think?"

"Oh honey, this couldn't make me happier. It is so righteous. I just pray this baby won't be born in prison."

"Me, too. I would hate to have to give it up right away."

"Oh no, honey," Edith replied. "You are going to be acquitted of this terrible charge; I know it in my bones. I know it like I know my own name. In any case, your brother and I will raise the child if you can't for some reason."

"Thank you for being so positive. I can't say I feel quite the same way. I did strike out at Zackary. I may have missed, but he did fall out of his chair and hit his head because I lashed out at him that way."

"I know. But he caused his own troubles. They were all his own. I know you believe in yourself, Cleo, so I'm not worried. You will come out of this okay."

Forty-four

IT WAS FINALLY TIME for the trial. It was past the Christmas holidays by the time the ordeal finally started. It felt like they had waited forever. Cleo had missed the holidays and missed the opportunity to give Jamal a present. There wasn't enough money left for that.

She was glad Clarence had gotten an older computer that needed help. He restored it as part of his class work and managed to make it into a PC that was like new. When Jamal got it in the hospital, he was excited and was able to get the schoolwork done while he was unable to go to class. As it turned out, the computer was the last gift Clarence gave Jamal. It helped him a lot, even now that he was in the classroom.

Cleo's mom told her he was still having trouble with the Hispanic kids even though he was trying to learn Spanish and had tried using it a couple of times with them. But they had laughed and he felt humiliated. Thankfully, that experience motivated him to study harder so they would never laugh at him again.

Cleo asked to be adjudicated by the judge and against a jury trial which she figured would be populated with a majority of white folk. She wished she could count on the fairness of white people, but the truth was she couldn't. She wanted more than anything to be able to, and she'd had high hopes that the Black Lives Matter and other civil rights movements would be able to turn the country around.

But her hopes, especially lately, had been dashed. She felt alone and, as if in a war for her survival. It *was* a war for her survival. If she was convicted, she would be sent away for a four-year prison term. Her son and her mom needed her. Her baby would, too.

The white women who had come and gone while she was incarcerated had proved their fear and hatred for her and the other black women in the jail. Oddly, the black women could be just as callous toward each other. The hatred was endemic and her hopes, as strong as they had been in the past, had been dashed against the rocks of intractable fear and animosity in the whole population. The situation made her incredibly sad, but there was little she could do. Negro people were angry at the system and they took it out on each other, even themselves.

Her lawyer, who looked intelligent with glasses and a well-trimmed mustache, who always wore well-pressed suits and been well-groomed, was an asset. He was bright and thorough. She felt confident her mother was right, that she would come out of this horrible situation with some dignity and would be found innocent of any intention to harm Zackary Hughes. She also hoped Zack would find her innocent of any intent to harm him.

Barnes had proposed she plead guilty and take the plea-deal that had been offered to cut her time in prison down to a minimum. She said 'no' adamantly. There was no way she would plead guilty because she didn't feel guilty. She felt bad she had lost her temper, but she had not been abusive and had not really caused Zack's injuries. He'd pretty much done that himself. And, she needed to be able to work in her job as a health-care aide. How would she be able to do that if she pleaded guilty to elder abuse?

She sat at the defense table with Adam Barnes. He had worked hard to make sure she got the trial she wanted. She felt confident in him.

As she looked around the courtroom, Cleo felt perplexed that it was so bare of the kinds of accoutrements she thought were common to all courtrooms. There were no tall dark oak panels, no tall windows, no pillars, no pictures of ancient politicians like the first president or

Thomas Jefferson, the author of the idea of equality in the Constitution; nothing authoritarian at all. Actually, the place was plain, the wood paneling was a wainscoting in dark oak and the gallery was dark wood. It was almost empty except for a few scattered people who were likely waiting for their own cases to be called, or perhaps they were curiosity seekers there to see the dealings of evil intent. The floor was carpeted in dark brown matching the wood paneling. The whole room was two-toned with the dark brown against creamy white walls. The jury box stood empty and the only things of authority beside the judge were a medallion with the symbol for justice etched into it hanging directly behind the judge's bench, the American flag and the flag of California with its ubiquitous bear, both of which hung regally next to his desk. Of course, there was the bailiff, whom she supposed had some authority, and the guard who had brought her in. She thought the paraphernalia of authority were well represented even in this drab, two-toned environment.

Edith and Walter sat in the gallery right behind her, separated by a low wooden barricade with a low-slung door. She wondered if any of her old classmates would show up. She had been so busy getting married, having her baby, divorcing, then going to school, working and getting married again; she had neglected her 'Besties'. Now she wished she had paid more attention to them. They would have been supportive. Some had come to the wedding and while they may have wanted to be here for her, she knew they all worked and likely couldn't take the time off anyway. At least, that's what she told herself.

As far as Cleo knew, there was only one direct witness. Apparently, Angus Dunne was there that night and his was the voice she'd heard behind her.

Wally and her mom were here to be supportive; that was all on her side. On the side of the prosecution, there sat Zackary with a new caretaker—a white woman, older and quite stern and efficient looking. Behind him was Phyllis, the clerk at the agency, and Elsie, the night nurse. They had not been at the scene, so they would not be witnesses. Cleo supposed they were there to be supportive of Zack-ary, although she thought Phyllis should be more neutral, maybe even Elsie. She had to remember that Zackary was the one with the money, so he would be the one with the most support. He was also the white victim.

The judge entered while all stood; he sat and gaveled the court-room to order. He was an older white man with white hair, red cheeks and a well-trimmed beard. He almost looked like Santa except for the black robe, and there was no twinkle in his eyes. They looked stern and authoritative.

The two attorneys, the prosecutor and her lawyer made their opening statements. They were basically boring and unremarkable which bothered Cleo, especially when it came to her lawyer. She had expected more from him. Her head swam with disappointment.

Then, without warning, the first witness was called. The prose-cutor called the name of the complainant, Zackary Barnette Hughes. Cleo had never known his middle name. He was rolled in his wheel-chair to the front of the courtroom near the witness stand and asked to swear to tell the truth. Of course, he did swear, but she wondered just how much truth would be told.

The prosecutor asked, "Mr. Hughes, how long was Cleo Delacroix in your employ and what were her duties?"

Zackary answered as best he could in his ancient, gravelly voice. "She was my daytime health-caretaker for I'd say a few months, maybe a half a year. She was there during the week, cooked my meals, helped me do some of the things necessary to living, she even played the pia-no to entertain me. She seemed very nice."

"On the evening of the attack…" The prosecutor searched his notes. "On the evening in question, Mr. Hughes, can you tell us what happened?"

"Certainly." Zackary's voice took on a note of authority. "I was watching television when Mrs. Delacroix came into the family room and started ranting about God-knows-what. I had sent her into my room to look for my medications and she came back with a box in her hand screaming at me as if I were some sort of criminal. I'm an old man and had no idea what she was letting on about."

"Did you argue?"

"Yes, her tirade turned into an argument of sorts. I just wanted her to lay off and leave me alone. But she wouldn't let up. At some point, she threw that box at me."

"Did she say what was in the box?"

"She did. She said it was some finger. I didn't know what the hell she was talking about."

"Then what happened?"

"Well, she lost it. She raised her hand and struck at me. I tried to avoid her lashing out like that, but couldn't and was knocked off my chair—that is, the chair and I went flying."

"And, you were injured, were you not?"

"Oh. Yes. I was. My head hit the corner of the coffee table hard. I heard it crack and I wondered if I had a brain concussion or something terrible."

"What happened after that? Do you remember anything?"

"I heard the voice of a man. And Cleo, Mrs. Delacroix, fled out the door. I haven't seen her since until today. Then, I passed out."

"Was your relationship with the defendant cordial up until that time?"

"Yes, I would say it was. I never had any complaints."

Cleo listened in shock. The way Zack put it one would think she had suddenly lost her mind for no reason.

"Your witness, Mr. Barnes."

Barnes got up and approached the witness stand. "Mr. Hughes, based on your testimony so far, would you say Mrs. Delacroix was an abusive caretaker?"

"No, up until that moment, no, she had not been abusive."

Cleo felt relieved. At least he hadn't accused her of mistreatment or neglect.

"Mr. Hughes, it is my understanding you are from Georgia. Is that correct?"

"Yes, it is. I lived there in Monroe County until I was twenty-four. Of course, I spent some of that time in the Army training, but for the most part that was my home."

"Do you remember what happened on the day of July 23, 1946, in Monroe near Moore's Ford Bridge?"

The prosecutor suddenly rose. "I object Your Honor. This has nothing to do with the incident in question."

Barnes answered. "It does your Honor. It will clear up some details in Mr. Hughes' testimony. I assure you."

The judge said for the defense to continue with the line of questioning.

"Mr. Hughes? Do you have a recollection?" Barnes asked again.

"No sir, I do not. What happened?"

Barnes smiled incredulously. "Mr. Hughes, you know very well what happened because you saw what happened."

"Sorry, but I am an old man and there are a lot of things I don't remember. You'll have to help me because I have no idea what you're talking about."

"It was the murder of four innocent black people, Negros. It was a lynching as it is called."

"Oh yes, I heard there was something like that, but I didn't see anything."

"Mr. Hughes, you were there and you witnessed the whole affair. After the event, onlookers hovered around and you were one of them. There was a tooth of one of the victims removed and the *severed finger* of Roger Malcomb, the man who was accused of attacking a friend and neighbor of yours and your father's. Does that help you to remember?"

"Malcomb was a poor laborer and he did attack his boss's son, Barnette Hester. I do remember that now."

The name Barnette surprised Cleo. Wasn't that Zackary's middle name?

"You were the person who severed the finger of Roger Malcomb, were you not?"

"I don't understand. What are you talking about?" Zack was understandably defensive.

"The severed finger of Roger Malcomb was in the box Mrs. Delacroix found in your bedside drawer, was it not?"

"I don't know what Mrs. Delacroix found, or thinks she found."

"Mr. Hughes, you are lying to this court. Do you know the penalty for lying?"

"I am not. I know what I am talking about and you must have the wrong person when you talk about that damnable finger!" Zackary's voice roared.

"That will be all, Mr. Hughes." Barnes said pointedly, then turned to the judge, "I reserve the right to recall this witness, Your Honor."

"So noted," the judge replied.

After Zack was returned to his place behind the prosecutor's table, the next witness was called. His name was Angus Dunne, the only witness Cleo knew about, though she didn't know how it was that Angus was there at that hour.

Angus was allowed through the back door and walked a little unsteadily through the swinging barricade up to the front of the courtroom where the judge sat. He ordered him to sit to his left in the witness box.

After the formalities, the prosecutor asked his name and why he had come forward with his testimony.

"I couldn't forget what I knew. I care about Mr. Hughes. He has been a good friend as well as an employer."

"Tell me, Mr. Dunne, what is your involvement in this situation?"

"I was there. I saw what happened," he said with pride in his voice.

"You said you were employed by Zackary Hughes. What did you do for him?"

"I worked primarily for the local grocery store where he liked to shop before his stroke. The store assigned me the job of delivering his groceries since he was unable to shop any longer. He asked me to fill in the time after the night nurse left and the daytime healthcare worker arrived in the morning. It was usually only fifteen minutes or so."

"How is it that you were at the home of the plaintiff at that late hour, Mr. Dunne?"

"I had some extra items he needed from the store and I was digging the bag out of my car when I heard screams coming from inside his home. They were loud and disturbing, so I thought I should investigate in case something was very wrong and I could help."

"Please tell us what you found when you entered the house."

"Well, they were yelling at each other, Mr. Hughes and Mrs. Delacroix, in a terrible argument. I couldn't tell exactly what it was about, but they were clearly out of control, especially Mrs. Henderson, the defendant."

"You said Mrs. Henderson?"

"Yes, sorry. That was her name before she recently married Mr. Delacroix. I sometimes forget."

"So, tell me in your own words what you saw then?"

"She had a knife in her hand and she was threatening Mr. Hughes with it."

Behind her, Cleo could hear Walter and Edith mumbling.

"What happened then?" The prosecutor asked coolly.

"Well, she, Mrs. Delacroix, came to an angry crescendo. She raised the knife and lashed at him with it."

Cleo was astonished with the obvious lie. Behind her both Edith and Walter said: "No, no, that can't be true."

The judge interrupted with the resounding clank of his gavel. "I'll have quiet in the courtroom."

"Mr. Dunne, there was no blood found at the scene. What can you tell us about what happened?"

"No, I suppose there wasn't. Mrs. Henderson, I'm sorry, Mrs. Delacroix," he corrected himself, "obviously missed with the knife but she knocked Mr. Hughes off his wheelchair. That's when he hit his head on the edge of the coffee table. It was horrible. I could hear the crack of his head against the table. I was certain he'd gotten a concussion. Mrs. Delacroix didn't hesitate and fled from the scene. She was his caretaker and she didn't stop for a minute to attend to his welfare, as she should have."

Cleo felt her head begin to throb. Where on earth did he get the idea she had a knife?

The day had been long and she was pleased when Edith and Wally came by to visit the jail before heading home. Wally had been kind enough to make sure their mom was able to attend the court sessions. They were told they had to come into the room to see her separately.

She heard the door click behind her to lock her and Edith inside. It was a creepy feeling being locked in like that. It was something she would never get used to. There was a giant mirror on the wall, but Cleo was aware enough to know it was a two-way mirror so the guards could monitor their conversation.

"Guess what?" Edith smiled big with promise as she sat down in the chair opposite Cleo.

"What?" She responded trying to meet her mother's brightness. They hadn't been able to visit since she was in jail. The phone calls had been brief and condensed, Edith supplying the most pertinent information she could think of.

"Walter got us tickets to see a special showing of *It's a Wonderful Life* at the Pantages Theater in Hollywood the week of Christmas. It was a wonderful experience. Jamal was excited to see it on the big screen." Edith added, "You know he had never been in a movie theater before."

"It isn't a centennial year. I wonder what the big occasion was."

"I believe it is the work of one of the actors, the little kid who was hanging off Stewart's leg in the final scene. Of course, he's a grown man now, and he does something special every year. Wants to keep the tradition alive. Isn't that a hoot?"

"That's exciting. I'm sure Jamal really enjoyed the experience of going to a big theater like that. And, I don't believe he has ever seen a movie in black and white before. It must have been an enlightening experience at the very least."

"It was a welcome distraction from all that has happened lately. Walter has been so good to Jamal. I think he realizes the boy needs a strong male influence." Tears formed in her eyes. "It has been horrible for Jamal to realize Clarence will never come home again."

Cleo couldn't help herself. The mention of Clarence's name was like a knife reopening the wounds so recently stitched closed. She fell into Edith's arms weeping as if it had just happened.

The guard came to the table and separated them. "No touching," she said.

After they cried their goodbyes, Wally came into the room and Edith left.

"Thank you for making those special arrangements for Jamal and Edith at Christmastime," Cleo said as she wiped the tears from her eyes.

He looked at her curiously.

"You sent them to see *It's a Wonderful Life.*"

"Oh yeah! It was a good experience for them. And, me. I went along too. Great movie. I've always like it, ya know what I mean?"

She wanted to hug him, but of course it was impossible. So much was impossible these days and again Cleo wanted to cry, but held back the tears.

"I can't believe Angus' testimony. It was a boldfaced lie. The only thing I had in my hand was that little box with the severed finger in it. I guess I threw it at Zack."

"Evidently, he was at Zack's house that evening. Curious. But I guess he had a reason."

As Walter was preparing to leave, Barnes entered the room where they sat.

"I'll wait outside," he said.

"That's okay, Walter. I have to talk to Mr. Barnes and you needn't wait. Take Mom home. Jamal can't stay at the Hayes' residence too much longer." They had asked Mrs. Hayes to take care of Jamal after school so Edith could attend the trial. The woman was glad to be of service.

"Okay, Sis. Take care."

Barnes sat down. "So, what can you tell me about this Angus Dunne?"

"Not much. He's been there at the Hughes residence every morning when I got there. Never missed a day as far as I know. He was riding a bike for a long time, but now he has a car."

"Can't you think of anything else?"

"Not really. He never says much to me. He's obviously prejudiced against black people. He always looks at me in a kind of menacing way. He dresses nicely in button-down shirts and Levis. I suppose the store requires that. I've noticed some tattoos creeping above his shirts and some on his arms. I think they're snakes."

"Do you know anything about his relationship with Mr. Hughes?"

"I'm not sure. They talked sometimes during that period before I got there. Maybe they discussed things that pertain to white supremacy. They had a connection of some kind, though at the time, I didn't know what it was. And Jamal said Angus came to visit him when he was in the hospital. I thought that was odd."

"That is. Do you know what they talked about?"

She smiled. "Jamal said he'd caught him dropping the F-bomb."

Barnes smiled. "Is that all?"

"That's all I know about. Angus has always seemed a little odd to me. I've never been quite sure what to make of him. He's so quiet and never says much to me. But when he does speak to me, he can be very derisive. I can't say I like him much."

"Well, I'll have to cross-examine him tomorrow and I need all the info I can get." Barnes stopped for a moment in thought. "Is there anything else you can tell me about him that might be useful?"

"I'm sorry, Mr. Barnes. That's all I know. But it was odd that Angus showed up that night. He says he had more groceries to deliver, but as far as I could tell he'd delivered the usual order that morning. What else could there be?" She stopped a moment and then said, "You might want to ask Elsie Larson about Mr. Dunne. She might know more than I do."

"By the way," Barnes said, "my detective received this and passed it on to me." He took a newspaper from his briefcase. It was the *Glendale News Press*. On the second page was an article with the lead saying, 'Glendale resident, Zackary Hughes, found attacked in his home.' Naturally, the article repeated Angus' claim that his assailant, 'his African-American caregiver,' attacked him with a knife. In a town like Glendale, that was all that needed to be said. Fortunately, Cleo's name was not mentioned.

Forty-five

THE NEXT DAY, Barnes cross-examined Angus Dunne. "Mr. Dunne, what were you doing at the Hughes' residence on the evening in question?"

"Like I said yesterday, I had some items from the store to deliver."

"Didn't it have more to do with your relationship with Mr. Hughes?"

"Sorry, but I don't know what you mean."

"I have information from the night nurse, Elsie Larson, that you have been at the Hughes' residence in the evenings on many occasions."

"Occasionally, I do go there, yes."

"For what purpose?"

"For deliveries."

"Can you tell me why you stay for long periods of time?"

"Because Mr. Hughes and I talk."

"What do you talk about?"

"I don't know if that's any of your business."

"It is the business of this court, Mr. Dunne. And, you have sworn to tell the truth."

"I know that," he said defensively. "Well, we talk about ourselves and what we believe."

"So, you would say you have philosophical discussions?"

"Yeah, you could call it that."

"Tell the court, please, just what *philosophy* you and Mr. Hughes hold together."

Angus was clearly uncomfortable with the questions. He looked like he wanted to run or hide. "Well, uh, I guess you would say we believe in the white race."

"Do you believe the white race should be the only race?"

"Kind'a. We believe that God provided this country to us white people and others are here illegally, or were brought here to be workers; you know, slaves."

The courtroom erupted into a quiet din. The judge used his gavel to quiet them.

"Mr. Dunne, do you hate Mrs. Delacroix because of her race?"

"Well, I … I guess … yes, I do."

"Mr. Dunne, what did you see when you arrived at the house of Mr. Hughes the night in question?"

"Uh, first I heard yelling and a woman shrieking. So, I ran into the house to discover Mrs. Delacroix with a knife in her hand. She raised it up, like this," he demonstrated what he meant, "and she lashed at Zackary with it."

"Are you sure you saw a knife?"

"Yes, sir, I am very sure." He said it so definitively Cleo almost believed it herself. She wondered what the judge thought. She looked at the man to see his expression which was stoic. There was no way she could discern what he was thinking.

"Mr. Dunne, do you believe, in your philosophy of life, that Mrs. Delacroix should not be allowed to exist in this country?"

"Yes, sir. I do."

Zackary harrumphed his approval.

"Why do you think Mrs. Delacroix had a knife and lashed out at Mr. Hughes with it?"

The prosecutor yelled, "I object, your Honor! Calls for speculation."

"I am only trying to establish this witness's philosophical position, Your Honor," replied Barnes.

"I'll allow it, Mr. Fredericks. Please continue Mr. Barnes."

"Mr. Dunne, tell the court what you think."

"I think she wanted him dead."

Edith and Walter behind her choked out, "No, no. That can't be true."

Cleo's eyes stung with tears. *No, dammit, I don't want to cry! Not here, not now!* She whispered to herself.

"Quiet in the court," the judge called out. "I'll have you removed if you can't contain yourselves."

After quiet was restored, Barnes asked one more question. "Mr. Dunne, Mr. Hughes did not mention in his testimony anything about a knife. Why do you suppose that is?"

"I dunno. Maybe he didn't see it," he mumbled. "Or maybe he forgot. He is old, ya know."

"I can't imagine anyone forgetting a knife aimed at them," Barnes added.

"Your Honor!" Fredricks yelled.

Barnes overrode him. "That will be all, Mr. Dunne. Thank you."

"Do you have any further questions of Mr. Dunne, Mr. Fredricks?" The judge inquired.

"No, Your Honor, I do not." He sat down heavily.

The next witness to be called was the police officer who arrived at the scene. His name was Officer Brownley.

The prosecutor began, "Officer Brownley, what did you find when you arrived at the home of Zackary Hughes on the night in question?"

"Well, sir, Mr. Hughes had hit his head on the corner of the coffee table and the paramedics were there taking him to the hospital. He was tied to the gurney when I arrived."

"Was there any blood?"

"No, I didn't see any blood anywhere at the scene."

"And, how did you know he hit his head?"

"Mr. Hughes was able to tell me what happened and there was a young man there. His name was, uh," he peered at his notes, "His name was Angus Dunne. He said he had witnessed the whole event."

He continued to tell the court what he saw and what he was told, including the testimony by Dunne about the knife. There was nothing remarkable about his statement until in cross, Barnes asked him if he found anything at the scene.

"Yes, I did. I found a tin box; it was small, about the size of an Altoid's container. And, nearby I discovered the skeletal remains of a severed human finger."

"Did you find a knife, sir?"

"Yes, I did."

"Was the finger a fresh severing?"

"No, no. It was quite old, as I said; it was the skeletal remains like it had happened a long time ago."

"So, the knife didn't have anything to do with that finger?"

"No, it did not."

"Did you ask Mr. Hughes what the finger was doing there?"

"By that time, he was gone, had been taken to the emergency room."

"Could you tell the race of the person whose finger it was?"

"I think it was the finger of a Negro person. There was a little flesh still remaining, but as I said, it was mostly skeleton. There was an old newspaper clipping and it said something about a lynching in 1946. It was the lynching of black people." He reached into a folder he was carrying and drew out some photographs. "I have pictures of the evidence and the scene at the house right here."

The judge took the photos and examined them. "It appears the house is well-kept, in good order. Interesting."

"Yes, Your Honor, I thought the same myself. Most homes are not so neat and tidy."

"The finger is disconcerting, to say the least."

Barnes continued his questioning. "About the knife. Was there any blood on it?"

"No. No blood and we had it tested in the lab. There were no prints and no DNA either."

"Thank you, Officer Brownley." The officer left the courtroom as had Dunne after he testified.

"Do you have any other witnesses?" The judge was asking Fredericks.

"Yes, Your Honor, I would like to call the emergency room doctor who attended to Mr. Hughes."

"So ordered."

The doctor told all he knew which was about the injury incurred by Hughes. It was not as remarkable as the prosecution tried to imply. Zackary had been released that evening into the care of Elsie, his night nurse. The medical report said that he recovered quickly and no permanent damage had been done.

Then, it was Barnes' turn to call witnesses. "Your Honor, I want to call the defendant, Mrs. Cleo Delacroix to the stand."

Cleo had agreed to testify; had insisted in fact, against Barnes' strongest advice. She nervously made her way to the front of the courtroom. It felt like a long walk, maybe the longest walk she had ever taken, and took her seat next to the judge.

After she was sworn in, Barnes began. "Mrs. Delacroix, can you tell me exactly what kind of a relationship you had with your employer, Mr. Zackary Hughes?"

Adjusting the microphone in front of her, she cleared her throat and began by describing how she came to work for Zackary, how he began the relationship by letting her know exactly how he felt about 'niggers,' as he put it, and how she had been offended but was desperate for the job. She told how she tried to keep the association with him on a higher level by not opposing him, by playing the piano for him, and by trying to be a pleasant and responsive person in his life. She also told how he continued on occasion to be abusive with his words about her race and species, how he seemed to think that Negros were of some substandard genus.

Elsie fidgeted in her seat. She was clearly uncomfortable with the testimony.

"But there were other things he said that indicated he was quite human with a heart and with love for his deceased wife. He told me about his relatives and how they had all died leaving him alone in the world. He also told me about a Negro nanny for whom he had feelings of love when he was only a babe in arms. And, he told me his father had fired her because of those feelings, hiring an older white woman to replace her." Before she finished, she smiled and said, "He told me the older white woman was 'very mean.'"

That testimony brought on a quiet "Harrumph" from the current old white woman who tended to Zackary. She squirmed in her seat.

"How did you come to feel about Mr. Hughes?" Barnes asked.

"Actually, in spite of his obvious racism, he had a good side that I came to appreciate, even care about. He is very old, as you can see, and I felt he had been misled by his culture and his father, who didn't appreciate him, to believe that black people are bad. When he turned ninety-five earlier last year, I put on a birthday party for him and he seemed to enjoy it. Since he didn't have many people left in his life, I invited my mother, my son, Jamal, and Clarence," her voice caught with emotion for a moment when she mentioned Clarence's name, "the man I had been dating and then married." She continued haltingly; her voice raw with emotion. "Mr. Hughes didn't seem to mind even though he never had black folk in his home before. We had a good time and I felt that he had changed his mind about my race."

"So, what happened that night, the evening in question?"

"Well sir, it was getting late when he asked me about his medications. He said the woman who cared for him the month before—I had been out of town on my honeymoon—she had been careless and lost them. Even though I had a bus to catch, the last bus available, I went searching for them because he hadn't had his medications all weekend and it was Monday already. It was important for him to take them."

Cleo heard some mumbling at the table where Zack sat with his attorney.

"Please continue, Mrs. Delacroix," Barnes said.

"He told me to look in his bedroom and of course I did. I looked all over and although I was concerned about invading his privacy, I searched in his bedside drawers for the first time. In the second drawer, I found a small box and inside there was the finger of a man. It was mostly the skeletal remains, all shriveled up and old. It was shocking and creepy. It startled me and I almost dropped it. Also, in the box, there was an old newspaper article with information about a lynching that had taken place the day before the article appeared, July 23rd, 1946. The article was dated July 24, 1946. I had to assume the severed finger had come from the incident. Taking souvenirs of lynchings was very common."

"What did you do then, Mrs. Delacroix?"

"I was astonished and repulsed. But, when I gathered my thoughts, I went back to the family room to confront him. I had to know what that finger was about and why it was there."

"Did you argue at that time?"

"Oh yes, Mr. Hughes was very defiant and told me exactly what it was, where it came from and how proud he was to have it, to have saved it all those years. He told me about the incident in 1946, the lynching, and how necessary it was to murder black people."

Cleo could hear Elsie and Phyllis squirm with cries of disgust. She could hear Zack grunt although he had been very quiet throughout the proceedings.

"Quiet in the courtroom!" The judge insisted. "Go ahead Mrs. Delacroix."

"I was incensed, horrified and told him so. That's when he called me terrible names—'a black stain on the nation, a parasite, a louse, a jackal, a screaming monkey. He called me 'a god dammed Coon!' I'll never forget those horrible words coming from his mouth."

"Did you threaten him with a knife, Mrs. Delacroix?"

"Oh no. I didn't have a knife. I had that box with the finger in it and I guess I threw that at him during our argument which I vaguely remember. But after he called me those names, I just lost it. All of the abuse for all of those months came roaring back, and … well, my new husband had been killed by police on our honeymoon. I was so distraught, I lashed out at him. But I didn't have a knife and I only nicked him on the chin with my hand because he dodged to avoid me. I can't really say, but it seems he knocked himself and his chair over and hit his head."

"Then, what happened?"

"I heard a voice behind me. I thought it must be Elsie, the night nurse, because she was due to come at six to relieve me. Or, it occurred to me it was Angus, the grocery boy. That's why I left. I thought Elsie or Angus would be able to handle the outcome. It was wrong for me to flee like that, but I was late for my bus and I didn't even stop to take my purse or jacket from the closet. I was horrified by what had happened and I didn't know what to do. I am ashamed that I lashed out at him and then ran like that, but I simply didn't have anything left."

"Thank you, Mrs. Delacroix."

"Excuse me," she interjected. "I have one more thing to say."

"Go ahead, Mrs. Delacroix."

"All of my young life, I have been involved in Civil Rights causes. John Lewis told us to get into what he called 'Good Trouble.'" I failed that day, because what I did, lashing out at Mr. Hughes that way, wasn't Good Trouble. It was the kind of trouble I have always rejected. I didn't reject it that evening. I thought only of myself and how *I* felt. I failed to think about anyone else and how they might feel and for that I am deeply ashamed. And, because of my intransigence, my family has suffered. For that I am especially sorry. They didn't deserve to be put through this."

The judge cleared his throat. "Mr. Fredericks, do you have any questions?"

"No, Your Honor." Fredericks seemed pleased. He obviously felt she had impugned herself and he didn't have anything to add. She thought he was right as she made her way back to her seat feeling very wobbly.

Barnes arose next to her to speak. "Your Honor, I would like to recall Mr. Hughes back to the witness stand."

Hughes was wheeled back to the stand and told he had already sworn to tell the truth.

"Yes, Your Honor," he answered.

Barnes resumed his questioning of Hughes seamlessly. "Mr. Hughes, isn't your middle name the same as Barnette Hester, the man who was attacked in 1946 by Mr. Roger Malcomb, one of the victims of the lynching?"

"Uh, yes, the name was given to me by my father."

"Why did your father give you that middle name?"

"He and the senior Mr. Barnette Hester were best friends in school and after. They were life-long friends."

"So, you had a special relationship with Mr. Malcomb's employer?"

He hesitated for a moment before continuing. "Uh, yes, I did, because of my father. Mr. Hester was also my Godfather. His son of the same name was a dear friend. He was the Barnette Hester who was viciously attacked."

"The senior Hester was your Godfather?" Barnes replied, seeming to be surprised by the revelation. "And, you were present when the lynching took place?"

"Your Honor," Fredericks rose to object.

"Sit down, Mr. Fredericks. I want to hear the rest of this."

Zack looked shaken. "I don't remember."

"Oh, come on Mr. Hughes. You remember very well because it was your father who led the gang of twenty-five white men in the murder of Roger Malcomb, his innocent wife and his wife's innocent friends, the Dorseys, was it not?"

Zackary blanched. "I—I…" He looked confused.

"And, it was you who severed the finger of Roger Malcomb at the time of his death and kept it as an ignoble souvenir of the lynching your father led."

"My father was a good man… He loved me," his voice grew weak. "He tried to love me." Zackary grabbed his chest and his breath became labored. "I wanted him …" he wheezed and struggled for breath… "to be proud … of, of me," he said choking out the words. "He was proud when I brought the finger to show him…" Looking pale, he cried in pain. "It was never enough …" He was gasping for air and clearly in grave trouble. "His love for me … was more important than … But it was never enough." He was gasping for air. "Oh God, please help me." His breathless plea had no strength behind it; clearly, he was having a heart attack.

Cleo rose from her seat screaming, "No, no! You can't die Zackery!" She ran to him as he fell forward from his chair to the floor, grasping his chest, moaning and unable to breathe. She turned him over and began CPR, vigorously pumping his chest in an effort to save him.

"No, No. You can't leave us now, Zackary. You have to live! Do you hear me?" Someone behind her tried to pull her off him—the bailiff, the guard? She put the full force of her small frame throwing them off and into driving the life back into Zackary. There was pandemonium around her as she kept up the struggle for five, then ten minutes while waiting for the paramedics to arrive. She kept it up with tears flowing and her heart breaking as he clearly succumbed.

She cradled him in her arms. "No, no, Zackary, come back to us," she wept. "You can't do this. Please, please!"

Walter picked her up and led her away, the paramedics replacing her with a stethoscope to hear his heart which never resumed beating again.

Cleo Delacroix was in shock, tears flowing down her face as she realized the enormity of what just happened. "He's gone. He's gone. Oh, God no. Zack is gone. My husband and now this … Oh no!" She moaned.

When the court quieted after Zackary had been removed, the judge rang down his gavel. "Case dismissed," he said with finality and he released everyone left in the court.

"What?" Cleo was stunned. "What did he just say?"

"The case has been dismissed, Cleo. You are free to go. You can go home to your family now," Barnes said, stunned but relieved.

"You're kidding. How can that be?"

"It is the judge's decision to dismiss the case. You're are free, Cleo."

Forty-six

FREE. The words resounded in her dreams. *"You are free."* She could see Clarence's face in her dream, and he was saying, *"You are free to go home with your family, Cleo."*

As she began to awaken, she could feel her mother's arms around her. "You are, Cleo. You are free." She repeated. "You're safe now. It's all over and you are home where you belong."

The barrier that had held the pain in for so long erupted. She wept for Zackary who had died in her arms. She wept for Clarence; he wasn't here. She finally wept for herself that she would never again see the only man she would ever love.

"But Cleo, you still have his baby inside you. Remember?"

She couldn't forget, of course. She held her stomach as she wept, spilling all of the enormous tension that had held her together for so long. The torture of knowing she was alone now that Clarence was gone had enveloped her every moment like a deep steel wall built around all of her hopes and dreams. Now, she was free from the jail and the judgment of the courtroom, but she would never be free of the memories of that terrible night in New Orleans. Clarence, her new husband, only trying to save his new wife from the humiliation of that policeman's harassment, shot in the back of the head, the blood spilling down his neck; an innocent man without any malevolence in his soul, only kindness, love, caring and the same kind of hope she had always wanted for herself, her son and her mom. This was a prison of memory from which she would never be released.

The baby growing inside her was hope, she knew. It was the only hope she had left.

Forty-seven

ZACKARY'S FUNERAL WAS ATTENDED by all of the birthday party guests, a pastor and the funeral director. It was a small event, but poignant nevertheless. A small bunch of long-stemmed Calla Lilies, tied together with a white bow, graced the coffin. They had been provided by Cleo, Edith and Walter.

Cleo got up in the small chapel located on the cemetery grounds in Glendale not far from a huge water spout falling into a small man-made lagoon. White swans gracefully swam on the water. As she made her way to the podium, her heart swam with sorrow, the sorrow of losing a friend, or the friend she had imagined Zackary could be.

"I only knew Zackary Barnette Hughes for a short time. I believe I knew him deeply as few others have. He was a good man. He loved his wife more than his own life and he loved his family. It was a terrible pain he carried with him that his family, his wife, his children, his brother, his friends had all died leaving him behind. It was a great tragedy of his life to be left behind like that needing to be cared for by strangers."

Her voice caught with the pain in her chest that emanated up to her throat, "I was one of those strangers, but I tried as best I could to understand him and his world view. It wasn't always a positive world view, but it was derived from a young life with an abusive father who loved his older brother more than he loved Zack. He wanted the love and approval of his father more than anything else in his life."

Her tears flowed. "He lived a long time, ninety-five years, and wondered at times if he was being punished by God, being left behind as he was without his beloved wife and family. I believe he thought that his long life and being left behind was God's punishment for the sin of caring more about what his father thought about him than he cared about the lives of four Negroes. He came from the Deep South, from Georgia, and it isn't surprising he thought the way he did.

"I came to care for Zackary in spite of his attitude about black people. He was very old when I got to know him and I came to understand his beliefs were fashioned from his early upbringing in the South and his father's attitudes toward people of color. There was a black nanny in his very early life; he only remembered how she comforted him and that she was fired because his father was jealous of the love he was developing for her. An old, white nanny was hired to take her place; she was a 'very mean woman' as he remembered her.

"He joined the military as soon as he was able to, but it was after World War II and his brother had been heroically killed late in that war. Zackary had left the military before the Korean War, and that didn't sit well with his father either. His father's grief over the loss of his first son overshadowed everything Zackary tried to do to win his father's approval and love.

"I am sorry for his loss. I think we would have become good friends given the chance. We had begun that process. In truth and in spite of his intractable attitude toward black people, I came to love Zackary Hughes. May God bless his soul."

More tears formed in her eyes as she left the podium and joined her mother, Jamal and Wally who was, gratefully, becoming a constant presence in their lives. They were more than grateful to have him. He provided a needed male influence for Jamal.

Only one more joined her in eulogizing Zackary. It was Angus Dunne, the grocery boy. Sauntering and then stumbling up to the podium, he took out a piece of paper on which he had written his speech, unfolded it carefully and began. His hands shook with anxiety.

"Good afternoon. My name is Angus Dunne. I got to know Zackary Hughes when I became the one to deliver his groceries and soon after he asked me to take care of him while he awaited the day nurse when Elsie, the night nurse, left about fifteen minutes ahead of Mrs. Delcroix's arrival. He only needed me to make sure he didn't have any accidents in the meantime. Sometimes, I brought him his breakfast that had been cooked by Elsie the night nurse and left behind in the kitchen.

"He was a nice man and he taught me many things while we waited for his daytime healthcare worker to show up. We had many times together which I came to appreciate like he was a father. I was a believer before, and what he taught me only cemented those beliefs. For that and his friendship, I am very grateful to him. Thank you."

Angus hurried to his seat evidently embarrassed by his performance.

The procession advanced to the gravesite where Zackary's wife and family were buried. They had purchased those graves many years before while they were still available. Now of course, there were no more sites left.

Cleo leaned against Walter for strength and wept for Zackary. Jamal, who was too young to understand, watched perplexed. He was sad for his mom and leaned against her because he knew she was crying.

Edith stood by stoically not knowing how she felt about Zackary Hughes because of all he had done. She couldn't feel anything, truth be told. Though she wanted to, she didn't truly understand Cleo's tears. She had to assume they were meant for the loss of Clarence more than for Mr. Zackary Hughes. She knew her daughter would mourn the loss of her husband for many more months, if not years, to come.

The group paid their respects as the casket was lowered into the burial place.

Angus approached Cleo as they were about to leave. "I believe Mr. Hughes cared about you, Mrs. Delacroix. You were right when you said that you and he would have become good friends given a chance."

She was wary of him because of the lie he told in court, but she said, "Yes, it's too bad he had to come to the end with the discord between us. And, I am sure he cared deeply about you, Angus."

As they walked away, Edith stopped Cleo for a moment. "Honey, I have always been proud of you, but today I am prouder to be your mother than ever before. You didn't have to be kind to that boy and you were."

"Mom." She didn't have more she could say without bursting into tears, so she hugged her mother tightly.

They quickly left, except for Angus who remained there for some time.

Forty-eight

SITTING THERE NEXT TO HIS COFFIN by the grave, Angus had a quiet conversation with Zackary, whom he had come to think of as a good friend. "I miss you, Zack. I never thought I could miss anyone this much. But now I know what it is like to miss someone. I mean, really miss someone.

"I miss Sarah, too. She was my girlfriend for a little while; I told you about her. We had gotten pretty close, close enough to want to make love to each other. But when she saw my chest with the president's face, she freaked out. I mean, she really got mad. She saw the Swastika, too. We never discussed politics, so I guess I shouldn't be surprised. It's just that I figured we were on the same page when it came to stuff like that. She lived in our neighborhood, but when I took her home that night, there he was, her dad, standing on the porch of the house, two palm trees like sentries standing on each side of the driveway, and he was one mean-lookin' dude. He was black, which surprised the hell out'ta me. I mean, Sarah looked tan, but I thought she was just … well, suntanned. She looked more like her mom, but now I can see that she was that light, milk-chocolate color. I guess I was so dazzled by her pretty green eyes that I forgot she could be bi-racial. I assumed a lot because she lives in *our* zone. We have a few nigger kids in school, but I just didn't think she could be colored. I was blinded by her. It hurts, really hurts that she won't speak to me anymore.

"She's made some friends with a couple of the girls at school now. Before, she was pretty much alone except for me. Gosh, I sure do miss her. I wish that hadn't happened. It really sucks to have to do without her. That dad scares me though. He is one tough dude.

"I don't know what to do anymore. I don't have anyone in my life that I really like or love. The kids at school just bully me about my name. My parents are okay, but I mean, they're my parents. I can't really talk to them like me and you used to talk and, well, I love Sarah and we could talk about anything except that one thing. I sure do miss her and you, but I miss her most of all.

"I'm real sorry what happened to you, Zack. I guess it was your time. But I hated hearing how you died like that."

Forty-nine

WALLY TOOK CLEO, Edith and Jamal to spend a few days in nearby mountains where it was snowing, renting a small cabin and returning home after a very short time. Cleo took advantage of the time in the car on the way, and asked Jamal about his experience going to the big theater to see '*It's a Wonderful Life*' with Uncle Wally and Grandma.

"Oh Mom! It was really the bomb!" he declared. "The theater was awesome," he used his hands to show how gigantic it was, "and it had huge chandirs hanging from the ceiling and a long stairway to the balanies."

"I think you mean chandeliers and balconies, Jamal," Cleo corrected.

"Oh yeah, that's what I mean," he said shyly, feeling embarrassed.

"Hey, Buddy, don't be embarrassed," Wally advised, watching him in the rear-view mirror. "Ya know what I'm sayin'? We all make mistakes. You're learnin'."

"Yeah, I guess."

"What about the movie?" Cleo continued.

"It was really good, Mom! Wasn't it, Grandma?"

"Oh, I sure thought so. I've always liked it, even on TV."

"But it was funky the way they acted," Jamal added. "And, it looked weird because there wasn't any color. It was called Black and White. I liked the angel the best."

Cleo, Edith and Wally chuckled.

"He said 'whenever you hear a bell ringing another angel is getting his wings.' Do you think that's true, Mom?"

"Well, I hope that means that girl angels get their wings, too, but yes, I do believe it's true."

Wally added, "I always liked to think it meant that someone was changing the way they think about something really important."

Wally's presence made them a small family and that made Cleo very happy, even though Clarence was gone. This was the family she had always wanted and it made her feel glad in spite of all that had happened. Having her brother back was promising.

Edith was equally delighted to have her son back with them again. She was thrilled he was doing so well in his new job working as a waiter in an upscale restaurant where the tips were plenty enough to help pay the household bills.

Knowing she was pregnant with Clarence's baby gave Cleo a hope she hadn't felt in a long time. Jamal seemed excited about being a big brother. Of course, it was hard to know how that would all turn out. Siblings were often at odds with each other. But Jamal being older—he would be seven years old by the time the baby was born—felt right. He could guide the little one into his or her new life with a more mature hand. She would put Jamal in charge of handling those aspects of the baby's life that would make him feel grown up and accountable. It would be a good experience for him, make him more responsible. If only Clarence could be here.

Once they got home, they sat down to eat some take-out they had gotten on the way. They were all chatting, remembering their time in the mountains and all the fun Jamal had sliding down the snow bank in his makeshift sled. He'd hit a bump and go flying every time. In one instance, he even managed to slide off the trail into a pine tree.

Only one thing took some of the joy out of Cleo's time. She was feeling guilty for Clarence's and Zackary's death. She stopped eating her hamburger and began to weep again as they sat at the dining table for their evening meal. The recent events, losing both men, were still raw and she often fell into a terrible mood.

"Hey, what's the matter, Girl?" Wally and Edith knew what it was, but they both wanted her to voice her feelings of grief.

"Oh, go on, you know what's going down, "she blubbered. "I just can't throw off these dark moods."

"Tell us anyway. We want to hear it from you." They both spoke almost in unison.

"I don't want to talk about it. It hurts too much and voicing it just makes it all the more real and painful."

Jamal left his seat at the table and hugged his mom. He began to cry, too.

"Zackary was due," Walter said. "You know that. His body was wearing down even as he sat there in the courtroom. You could see it."

"That's exactly what I mean. I put him through that and if I hadn't been so easily enraged, I might have left that evening without everything that happened. I should have had more control over myself—I could have spared him that downward spiral."

"Come on. You know that's not true. Zack was old. He was ninety-five and he'd had a stroke the year before which, you know, took a lot out of him. In all likelihood, his heart was pumping too hard and too fast most of the time just trying to get the blood in his system to move while he sat there disabled. That wasn't your fault."

"It was my fault that I wasn't able to tolerate him any longer."

"Yeah, Mom," Jamal piped up. "You told me it was wrong to hit people; that if I felt angry, I should wait and go back later, right?"

"I did, and I so regret that I didn't do that myself, Sweetheart."

"Look at what really happened," Edith added. "He'd acted out his hatred for people of our race, innocent people, and he took that damnable souvenir, for God's sake. That was evil and he did it out of selfishness, only wanting his father's approval."

"I think you may be right about that, Mom. But I am so sorry that Zackary had to die that way, being so desperate for his father's love, having to admit to himself that he'd messed up big time."

"At least, he came to that realization, Honey. What if he hadn't?" Said Edith.

When she finally regained some of her composure Cleo continued, "It is true Zackary's act was selfish and ghoulish, and he seemed to have that realization. But Clarence was in his prime. He didn't deserve to die! He was one of the real good guys in this world, and that cop was wrong."

Everyone grew quiet then except for Jamal's tears which flowed onto her arm and soaked her shirt as Cleo held him tight.

When he finally calmed down a little, he asked, "Mommy. When is Daddy coming to see me?" His lower lip said it all. He needed a dad more now than ever.

"I'll call him again tomorrow and see what he's up to. Maybe I can coax him to put aside his plans to come over."

"Really, Mom?" Jamal seemed almost excited and like his usual self again.

"Sure, it's been a long time and he should come by and see you."

Wally smiled. "I can see all of the love and hope in your heart, Cleo. You never give up, do you? Don't beat yourself up about Zack. He got what was his to have. And, my God, I can't tell you how sorry I am about Clarence. That was wrong, just wrong."

"I know you are Wally. And, we're overjoyed to have you back with us. Please don't ever make yourself so scarce again."

"I'll try. I guess when dad died and you got your divorce, I was sad and disappointed and … well, I can't really describe how I felt, but I was confused. I'd expected you to make all the right choices. You always had and I guess I expected more. I'm sorry."

"It's hard always knowing the right thing to do, Wally. I try. I really do."

"Yeah, I know you do. And, Mom, I miss dad so much. I thought he'd live forever." He took Edith's hand and squeezed it. "I'll try not to disappoint you again."

Fifty

CLEO GOT A NEW JOB taking care of an elderly woman who had emphysema. She lived nearer to downtown LA which made the trip to and from the new job shorter and much easier. The woman was in her early eighties, white, and a lovely person who carried no racial hatred at all. Her name was Janet.

She did have a few slips into prejudicial notions. Cleo was learning all over again that the tendency was pretty common among older white folks who had been reared in an earlier unenlightened environment. Cleo would correct her now and again, but the woman's reaction was always regretful, never angry or insolent. She just didn't know how hurtful those presumptions could be until she was told.

"Oh dear, did I do it again?" She would ask, feeling quite penitent. "I'll have to go to confession now," she would smile ruefully.

"You don't have to feel guilty. It's okay. I'm just trying to make you more aware, that's all."

"Oh, my dear, you make me aware alright. That's why I must go to see the priest."

Cleo often took her to her church on Sundays and sometimes on Fridays when the priest was hearing confession. This was a practice she had heard about often in her young life, but could not relate to. Feeling guilty for such minor infractions seemed excessive to her. Cleo still felt guilty about Zackary. She couldn't help it and she wished she hadn't been so vindictive and insolent. It was possible he could be alive still if she had been better about her emotions. Striking out at him like that was unforgivable.

She later told her mom she couldn't help it. "I even did my own confession. Would you believe it?" She laughed. "Janet wanted to spend some time praying before she went home and there was no one else going to confession, so I thought I'd keep myself and the priest busy. I went into the confessional—can you believe it?"

"Get out'ta here," Edith marveled.

"And, I told him all about Clarence and then, how Zackary had treated me. I told him how my anger had built up over the months just taking it the way I did, and that finally I blew up when I found that box with the finger in it."

"You aren't Catholic, are you?" The kindly voice asked from behind the screen.

"How did you know?" She asked, feeling a little contrite for taking up his time.

"You didn't follow the protocol when you entered. You know, 'Forgive me, Father, for I have sinned...'"

"Oh … I am sorry. I'm not and I won't take up your time." She apologized as she gathered her things to leave.

"No, no. No bother. You obviously have a lot on your mind. What you experienced with the man was dramatic, to say the least, and losing your new husband like that. I am so sorry for your loss."

"Oh yes, thank you. It was horrible. But then, I lashed out and was arrested; I went to jail because Zackary, the old man, hit his head on the coffee table when he fell over in his wheelchair. I was the cause of that injury and, well, I had to go to trial and everything. I was kept in that jail for three months. I thought, at times, I would never see my mom and my son again. And all of this happened as I learned of my pregnancy with my dead husband. It is obvious I deserved everything that happened."

"Well, I must say you are very brave."

"Brave? Oh no, no, no. I wasn't brave at all. I was guilty. I lashed out at him and he went to the hospital. I lost my temper in a way I never thought I could, and did the very thing I thought I would never do." The tears came again; she was unable to stop them. Cleo bent over in pain and wept, the tears searing her face with a hot sting.

"You told that priest the whole story?" Edith was fascinated. "So, what did he say?"

"Well, he said he would have done the same. I don't think he was black. I couldn't see him, of course, because there's a screen between you and the priest. It's really strange. I don't think I could ever be a Catholic. But you know what?" She smiled big. "I felt a whole lot better after that. It was really like a miracle. I felt like if a priest could do what I did, then maybe I wasn't so bad after all."

"Told you so."

"Yes, you did." She laughed. "You told me, but I just couldn't believe it until that priest said it. Weird?"

"Oh, yes, you are so weird." Edith laughed.

"Well, I haven't told you yet what else I did."

"I give up, what?"

"I lit a candle … for Clarence. And, I said a prayer."

"That is a very moving thing to do," Edith said with a smile.

"Oh, and guess what?"

"I give up; I'm terrible at guessing."

"I felt the baby kick for the first time right there at the altar. Isn't that exciting?" She laughed with a light-hearted joy she hadn't felt in a very long time.

"Cleo, that's so thrilling. You know, when the spirit enters, it's the most wonderful time in a pregnancy; because you know that baby is whole and will survive."

"This baby *has* to survive. It's all I have left of Clarence." She held her abdomen like she was already carrying the infant in her arms.

When the spirit enters? Cleo had never thought about it before but that sounded right to her; it was when the baby quickened; that meant something important had happened. It was when life began.

Fifty-one

THERE WAS ONE MORE TRIAL they had to attend. The hearing had been delayed because of 'technical difficulties'—something having to do with the availability of some witnesses. Cleo was called to be a witness in the incident with Etta Stone. She didn't wish to be there; it was such a painful reminder of Clarence and his absence when she needed him so badly, but she was hopeful Etta would come to understand the damage she could do with her rage and resentment.

When she arrived, she was stunned to see Clarence's father. Since she was testifying, she had to remain outside of the courtroom until she was called. She wasn't allowed to hear the other witnesses' testimony. However, Clarence's dad entered the court to sit in the gallery. She was surprised to see him and wondered why he was interested.

Cleo found it hard to let go of Clarence's memory. He should be here with her. She didn't know the details of the event the way he did. He had seen Etta's car and she hadn't.

She was called soon.

Entering the courtroom, Cleo headed through the swinging gateway on the way to the witness stand. Feeling wobbly as before, she took the stand after she was sworn in, and was glad to feel the stable chair beneath her. There was the microphone as before and she acknowledged the judge as she settled into her seat. He was different from what she expected. This man was African-American.

There wasn't a sitting jury, the same as in her case. Cleo assumed this was to be a bench trial too.

The prosecutor, a white man, approached her and asked her to identify herself and her reason for being there.

"I am Cleo Delacroix and I was with my husband and son when he was hit."

"Where were you in relation to the victim, Jamal Henderson?"

"I am his mother and he was standing at the back of the car putting his play things away when the car struck him."

"Where were you in relation to the victim?"

"I was in front putting some of my things in the car, where I was going to sit."

"How old is your son, Mrs. Delacroix?"

"He just turned seven."

"Do you know the person who hit the car, Mrs. Delacroix?"

"Yes, I know who she is, but I don't know her personally. She is the woman sitting at the defense table."

"Thank you. How do you know who she is?"

"She is Etta Stone, my husband's former girlfriend. She had been stalking my husband and me since we began dating. Clarence was furious with her."

"And, what kind of a car was she driving?"

"I saw red but I didn't see the car at the time. But my husband said it was a red Toyota that belonged to Miss Stone."

"Hearsay, Your Honor." The defense stood to make the objection.

"Okay, sorry," the prosecutor accepted the objection.

"Mrs. Delacroix, can you tell me in your own words exactly what happened?"

Cleo told the whole story as she knew it, including the injuries to Jamal and how terrifying it was when he hit the ground in the way of oncoming cars.

The defense attorney then began his cross-examination.

"Mrs. Delacroix, it seems you have had quite a time of it lately. You were on trial in this very courthouse recently, were you not?"

"Yes, I was, and I was acquitted, as I am sure you know," she said curtly.

"You're Honor." The prosecutor stood to object. "I'm not sure why this is pertinent to this case."

"I'll try to forget it," the judge added bluntly.

The defense attorney didn't care the testimony was overruled. He was glad the judge heard it.

"Are you sure it was Etta Stone driving the other car, Mrs. Delacroix?" He knew she hadn't seen the car or the driver.

"I didn't see her—my husband did," she said with disdain. "You know that, sir."

"Thank you, Mrs. Delacroix; I don't have any further questions." She was dismissed.

Etta Stone looked smug and satisfied, her legs crossed sitting back in her seat at the defense table. She was overly made-up as before when Cleo saw her at the bowling alley.

As she left, Cleo heard the prosecuting attorney tell the judge that Clarence Delacroix, the husband, was a suspect in another incident in New Orleans and was shot dead by the police. "That is why he is unable to testify, Your Honor."

Cleo felt the pang of fury at the man. He had described her husband's death as if he was suspect of some crime and the shooting was justified. Clarence was killed, murdered by that foolish policeman for nothing more than wanting to get his new wife out of harm's way.

Clarence's father came out and met her as she headed for the exit.

"'Ello Cleo." He approached with his hand extended. "I hope ya don' min' if I call you by yo first name."

"That would be fine," she forged ahead not sure she should shake his hand. Clarence would have refused.

"Please," he said, kin we talk? I need ya to know somethin' that's very hard for me to confess, but ya need ta know it anyway."

"Of course," Cleo answered. "I need a bite to eat. Will you join me?" She decided to hear him out. He was her baby's grandfather, after all.

They found a nearby café and entered. It wasn't a fancy place, just a deli with a counter where she got a sandwich and fries with coffee. Clarence's dad ordered nothing, just taking a paper cup of water with him to the table. They found a booth and sat down. The place was crowded with attorneys and their clients rushing to get something to eat before going back to court. She felt out-of-place here when some of the customers stared at her and Clarence's dad.

Cleo spoke first. "Mr. Delacroix, I don't know your first name and I suppose you are my father-in-law now, so I should get to know you."

"Ya sure should know," he declared. "It's Benjamin, or Ben as mos' people call me."

She extended her hand. "It's nice to get to know you a little, Ben."

He seemed grateful that she welcomed him.

"What do you have to tell me that's so important?"

"Well, there is no othah way ta put this. I had m' reasons for leavin' Clarence and his mom and I wan' you ta know, though it's too late fo' Clarence. I was into traffickin' drugs and it was no life for a wife and kids. That's why I never came around. Now, I realize tha' was a big mistake."

"It's too bad you couldn't repair your relationship with Clarence. He was very angry and I know he was hurt."

"I got deep inta the drugs. I ended up usin' Meth. Went and married an-othah woman—she was whi'—and I was so strung out, I forgot everythin' that was really important. I'm deeply regretful now. I've since divorced tha woman. She was no good for me. She tha one who introduced me to Meth."

"Hadn't you ever done drugs before, I mean, you know, weed or Cocaine?"

"Oh, sure. I'm not blamin' tha woman for tha *whole* drug thing. Done weed when I was a teen. I stopped when I met Eunice and married her. But tha white woman, while I was with her, it really got bad. She wanned ta party all the time."

"He needed you. Clarence needed you badly and your last rejection, not coming to the wedding, was the last he wanted to hear from you."

"I came ta say I'm real sorry."

"I think if you had tried to apologize before, he may have been able to forgive you, especially if you could have made it to the wedding."

"I was ashamed."

"I'm afraid 'sorry' is very weak now. But I'll try to overcome *my* feelings about this for my son Jamal's sake. And, you may have noticed, I'm pregnant with Clarence's child. My children need a grandfather and you should take that role since Jamal's real father is absent and his birth family has never gotten in touch. So, he will likely never know his other grandfather."

"Tha' would make me righ' happy, Cleo. I didn't know you was pregnant. Tha's real good news. I hope we kin make this work. It'd mean a lot."

"I trust you are done with the drugs for good now?"

"Oh, yeah, I am definitely done. An' my drinkin' has stopped too. I go to AA meetin's all tha time and they help me a lot. So, you needn't worry. I'll be a *good* influence." He said 'good' so resolutely, Cleo had to believe him.

When she got home, she talked it over with Edith.

"I sure don't want drugs around here!" she said adamantly.

"No. I think he means to keep out of that now. He wants to have someone significant in his life and Jamal's the closest he's got now. And the baby," she touched her stomach tenderly, "will need a grandfather, too."

Clarence's dad had been nothing more than a victim of being a black man in a world that had no room for him. Clarence, too, had been victimized by it.

"We try to avoid the pitfalls," Cleo said, "but in the end, there is little that can be done but to live as honestly as possible and allow life to take the turns it has to take."

"Well honey, we can give this Ben Delacroix a try, but it's really up to Jamal. If he likes him and he can stay straight, I'm good with it."

Fifty-two

ANGUS DUNNE, ALWAYS THE SPY, had managed to sneak into the courtroom to watch Cleo as she testified in the Etta Stone case. He also managed to follow her with the man he'd talked to briefly at the hospital, not knowing who he was, but not surprised he seemed familiar with Cleo. Sneaking into the café and up close enough to hear what was going on, he gathered all he needed to know.

And there had been a white woman involved. He had to guess she was jealous of the ex-wife. Angus didn't know the name of Clarence's mother, but she seemed like a nice lady from what he could see at the wedding. She looked well-kept, and quite nice in the gold dress she wore. But Angus was surprised when he heard this man was Cleo's father-in-law. That meant he was Clarence's dad. She had been so forgiving and open to beginning a relationship with him on behalf of her new baby. The new baby was a surprise too.

Interesting. The man had left Clarence's mother for the white woman and some Methamphetamine. Angus heard it was a powerful drug. He'd also heard that black men often left wives and children for the free life of drugs and other women. He wondered if it was the responsibility they couldn't take, or just the call of the wild. Maybe both.

This guy was regretting what he'd done; even promised to do better and to become a part of his grandkid's lives. Interesting.

Fifty-three

ETTA STONE WAS CONVICTED of attempted manslaughter in the case—there had been too many witnesses to her deliberate parking lot rage—and was sentenced to a prison term of five to ten years. The newspaper reported she could be out in three with good behavior.

Cleo grew in size. She couldn't help but be happy. She was eight-months along, not the most comfortable for her, and she was glad the pregnancy was coming to an end.

The fact, that Etta had been convicted was what she needed.

Her job with Janet came to a crashing halt when the woman passed away because of the new COVID-19 virus. Exposed and worried, she had sent Janet off to the hospital never to see her again. Thankfully, Cleo never contracted the bug; she felt *very* lucky. But she was very sad about Janet. The woman had been kind to her and sweet in a way Cleo had never known before with white folk.

In the meantime, Angus continued to spy on Cleo and her family, always, somehow, able to sneak around in a way that made him appear to belong where ever he was, even in their zone. He had the right hair-cut and he'd wear his pants way low on his hips to mirror some of the young kids he saw around. He'd seen the practice before, so it wasn't a real stretch. He rode around in his car most of the time, and when he parked to get out, he always covered his tattoos up while wandering around that neighborhood. He wasn't gon'na get caught looking like a white supremacist by some black dude.

Even so, he was surprised by the area. He'd expected to feel out of place and noticed a lot more than he was. He expected the neighborhood to be crawling with gangs and dangerous black men roaming around canvassing for trouble. He didn't find much of that although there were a couple of dudes who regarded him with some suspicion. But mostly he found a community of folks living normal lives. It wasn't as fancy as his part of town, but people were out mowing their lawns, gossiping over fences, busy shopping in local stores, men doing the barber shop routine, kids playing baseball in the streets, and he noticed the smell of barbeque burning from backyard grills. He felt ashamed that he had assumed the worst.

He saw the black dude from the hospital and the courtroom, Clarence's dad, come around to visit the house where Cleo lived with her son, her mother and her brother. The dude took Jamal out to go to the park and toss the ball around. He was good at teaching the boy how to throw accurately and bat the ball, too. Jamal was becoming a pretty good baseball player with the man's guidance.

The COVID-19 pandemic that had made Angus and his family prisoners in their own home, had taken its toll, especially on him. Even his dad had taken time off from the office. And, Angus was toying with the idea of postponing college work to the following year when in-person classes would resume. He wasn't devoted to the idea of beginning college on-line. He'd had to finish up high school electronically and their graduation was done that way, too. It was very unsatisfying, but Angus hadn't been that involved with other classmates anyway, since they teased him so much about his name, and then about his relationship with Sarah. So, he was only missing out on some in-class schoolwork and the graduation ceremony. He imagined it would be pretty great to walk across the stage to get his diploma from the principal of the school. But that and a whole lot of other things were not to be, not in 2020.

But something was happening to him, with all the time he had to think about things while in his room staying home with his parents. Sarah's rejection had had a powerful effect. He was lonely. Sarah said he would be alone. She was right, he didn't have any real friends. Zackary, his only friend was an old man and now he was dead. Angus had never been able to make easy friendships with kids his own age. As he watched Cleo and her family struggle with life and continually come out on the other side of whatever happened to them, his attitude began to soften.

The events of the summer with the police killings, the protest marches and the riots were all a powerful reminder of what was wrong with his tattoos and how he couldn't be sure he'd been right about race. He began to question the things Zackary taught him. He'd loved the old man, but then, when he heard about his testimony in court, his admiration came to a crashing halt. He still loved Zackary Hughes, but he was learning that the old man's attitudes were based on an earlier time and place. Even Glendale was changing.

His visits with Zackary had ceased with the old man's passing and the continual conversations that had bolstered his beliefs stopped. He tried checking out the Klan on the Internet. But, the more he read, the less he knew. He'd heard of the Proud Boys and some things about Q-anon, and felt he might belong to that group, but wasn't sure just what they stood for. He wasn't sure just what he stood for, either. The covert hatred that permeated the Klan thinking became less and less appealing. And, his observations of a family, Cleo's family, that took care of their own and made the best of whatever was handed them, began to make a deep impression.

There was a new man coming and going at Cleo's home. He didn't recognize him, but he spent time with Jamal and the boy seemed to be close to him. Angus guessed this man was Jamal's dad. Where there had been men missing in the kid's life before, there seemed to be an abundance now. Three men, his uncle, his grandfather through Clarence and his own father seemed to be taking a real interest in the boy and Angus felt jealous of the kid's ample attention. There was a lot to admire about the situation as he was beginning to see it.

Angus had a tense moment with his mother, Kathrine. They were at the dinner table eating their evening meal. His dad, who had taken some time to go to the office, was late because of work. He told his mom about Cleo and about the trial. He told her about her son, Jamal. "He seems like a cool kid." He told her about the husband, Clarence. "He died. I heard it was one of those police things when they shoot because they assume something's wrong. I also heard that her husband was a bad guy who caused the cop trouble. I dun'no, Mom. I liked the guy, Clarence. He seemed okay to me."

"My dear, Angus. You know those people are violent. They are always trouble makers. The police are justified when they kill them."

"Well, I suppose you're right," he said hesitantly, "but Jamal's different. He's young, and his mom seems like the kind of person to do right by him. And, I don't really think his new step-dad was the kind of guy who would cause trouble."

"Well, I suppose it is possible for a Negro kid to do okay. I hope the mother sends her son to college. I hope she can, and *will* do that. It's very important. But I have my doubts."

"Why, Mom? She tried her best to keep Zack alive. I heard about her struggle to keep him going in the midst of his heart attack. The clerk told me that she begged him to stay alive and she worked hard for a long time to make his heart work. And … and, Jamal seems bright enough."

"To be frank, I don't expect him to survive into his teen years without going bad. They all do, you know."

"I don't know, Mom. I was surprised by him and his intelligence. It was something I didn't expect of a kid that young."

"Don't tell me you're going soft on me?"

"What do you mean by that?" He asked stunned.

"It sounds like you're ... Oh, I don't know. Maybe you're going soft on those Negroes. You know, I am not racist. I'm not a bad person, but if those people would only educate their kids. If they would just send those kids to college and make sure they grew up straight and not angry and ready to start fires, getting drugged up and itching to rape young girls and shoot people. Look at the riots they caused this summer."

"Mother, I am ... appalled by ... your words, your attitude!" Angus didn't understand what she was saying. He knew she was racist and her denial was astounding. He didn't know exactly why, but he wanted to see Jamal in a different way. "Please!"

"Actually, I feel sorry for them."

"I think they need your sympathy a lot less than they would appreciate your respect."

"How could I possibly respect them? They are different from us. They don't know what is good for them and their lot. They do all the wrong things!"

He threw down his fork, slamming it onto the table. "You live in this house, in this part of Glendale, you have always had whatever you wanted or needed. How the hell do you know what Jamal's mom should do or not do, what is good or not! And, by the way, we don't know if those riots were caused by blacks. There're a lot of theories about that! There could have been people from the other side, you know, white supremacists who created the trouble."

"You dare to defy me, to call me a liar?"

"You bet!" He shrieked back at her.

His mother reacted badly, throwing her wine glass at him. He ducked and the glass, half-filled with red wine, smashed against the white wall behind him, the wine dripping like blood. With angry words, he fled from the house not knowing what to do.

He walked for miles that night, nearly all night.

The Los Angeles sky was as it usually was with an added layer of smoke from the forest fires that were inundating California's forests and wild lands. It was reported these were the worst fires the state had ever seen. He wasn't exactly a Global Warming denier, but he hadn't taken it very seriously in the past. Now he had to take it seriously just as his classmates did. He couldn't see any stars. The Los Angeles sky was never filled with stars because of the haze and smog on normal nights. The nighttime sky with its billions of stars he'd seen in pictures on the Internet was completely obscured. His mother's thinking was held deeply beneath a fog of obscurity as thick as the expanse that covered the Los Angeles basin.

He began to realize people were pretty much the same, no matter what their skin color. Oh sure, their attitudes diverged dramatically; there were historical and cultural differences and money made a difference in lifestyle, sometimes a big difference. But he was coming to understand that people were people no matter who they were or where they came from, or how rich or poor they were. Culture and other things, like money and lifestyle that kept people apart, were superficial and had nothing to do with what really mattered.

These realizations were slow and hard in coming, but they were seeping into his consciousness. One shining star after another begged to bleed through the thick haze, the attitudes that had dominated his young life. Angus was growing up.

He continued to miss Sarah. He would drive by her house hoping to see her. He had no idea what he would do if he did see her, but he was sure he still loved her. The fact that she was bi-racial began to feel inconsequential. He was as confused as hell, but he wanted to be with her no matter what the circumstances of her life. He thought he would send her a letter and try to win her back. Maybe if he apologized and agreed to have the tattoos removed, she would reconsider their relationship. Angus ached to be near her, to make love to her, to be the person she could love back.

He made a decision, the decision he should have made a long time ago.

Fifty-four

IT WAS AN UNUSUALLY RAINY DAY. The thick haze that en-
gulfed the California skies was being washed away. Angus drove onto
Country Club Drive winding up the road to the house with the two
trees that stood sentry outside the home Sarah lived in. He parked his
car in front and walked up the driveway in the rain allowing the deluge
to wash over him. He nervously arrived at the double front doors of
the Griffith household and knocked loudly, determined to be heard.

It wasn't long before the door opened and there stood Mr. Griffith
looking relaxed in a leisurely shirt and loose-fitting pants. He was mas-
sively large and imposing, but Angus was determined not to be intimi-
dated by him.

"You realize it's rainin' and that you're lookin' like a drowned rat,"
righ' boy?" Griffith said.

"Right, Mr. Griffith. I am Angus Dunne, a friend of your daugh-
ters. At least, I hope she considers me her friend."

"Ah know who you are, young man. Whether she considers y'all a
friend or not is up ta her."

"May I see her?"

The man stepped aside to reveal Sarah, her hair freshly washed
and hanging loosely around her shoulders; a natural curl hugged her
like a warm blanket. She was beautiful and Angus caught his breath.

"'Ello , Angus. What y'all doin' here? Ah thought you knew not to
come here again," she declared.

"I'll leave if you really want me to. But I have something to show you." His shirt dripping wet, he unbuttoned it to reveal a bare chest. The tattoos were gone leaving his torso with red scarring. Both father and daughter stared at him with their mouths agape.

"Mah God, Angus, what did ya do?" She asked alarmed. "That looks like it hurts like hell."

"Yeah, well, it does. But that'll go away over time. That's what they told me."

"Come on in." Sarah grabbed his hand and pulled him inside out of the rain. "You'll freeze out theah."

Her dad provided a towel from the guest bathroom for Angus to dry himself.

"Thanks, Mr. Griffith."

Sarah continued to pull Angus inside to the living room. "Come on in, sit down heah." She offered the couch.

"I don't want to get the couch all wet," he objected.

"Don't be silly. You're cold and, well, Ah want ya to be okay. It's alrigh' if Angus sits down, righ' Dad?"

"Shu'ah son. Please sit down and git dry. Do ya need 'nother towel?" They were being very kind. Angus took note and was grateful.

"No thanks. I'll be okay. I just want to apologize to Sarah about what happened the last time I saw her. I think you know the time I'm talking about."

"Yeah, Ah kin guess when that was. It was quite a while ago."

"Yes sir, it sure was and I've had a lot of time to think things over, being at home with the COVID thing."

"Well, Ah'll leave you two alone then. Sarah, Ah'll be in tha den if ya need me, okay?"

"Shu'ah Dad. Thanks."

"He seems real nice," said Angus.

"Mah dad's a good guy. So, what's up, Angus?"

"Like I said, I want to apologize for that time and, well gosh, Sarah, I've been miserable without you ever since. I knew you hated everything I stood for, but that's different now. You are *all* that's important to me. You're it, Sarah, and I hope you feel the same way. I love you and I can't live without you. You've been all I can think about. I need you, Sarah. Please, do you think we can make it work now that I've gotten rid of these?" He indicated his chest, looking down at the raw remains of his removed tattoos.

She lifted his chin with her cool, long fingers and kissed him lightly on the lips. "Ah've missed ya, too, Angus. What you' done means a lot; it means everythin'. Ah didn't think Ah'd evah see ya again."

A tear appeared on her cheek and he wiped it away.

Fifty-five

ONE DAY, ANGUS AND SARAH arrived on the Delacroix porch, at their door. Angus hesitated because he really didn't know what he was going to say when and if they gained entrance. It was a weekend, so he expected the family to be home. A car stood in the driveway.

He knocked, hesitantly at first, not sure why they were there. Angus felt they had to be, but wasn't sure why. He knocked again, this time a little more loudly. When that didn't work, he rang the doorbell.

"Okay, okay, I'm coming!" Said the voice inside. The door opened suddenly and it was Wally standing there barefoot in his tank shirt and a pair of shorts. It was a hot September day and he was apparently trying to stay cool. The smell of fresh-cut lemons filled the air.

"Oh… Well, I must tell you, you are the last person I ever expected." He laughed heartily. "Angus, isn't it? You testified at Cleo's trial. Not the friendliest witness. You have a mask, don't you, bud?"

"Hey," Angus managed to get out. "Yeah, I have it right here. You want me to put it on?"

"Yeah, why do ya think I asked?"

Angus and Sarah put their masks on. "You're Wally, Cleo's brother, right?

"Yeah, right in both cases. What do you want, Dude? And, who do you have with you?"

"Oh, yeah, this is Sarah, my girlfriend." Sarah waved her hello from behind Angus. "Hi Sarah, welcome," Wally waved back. "So, wha's up?"

"Honestly, I'm not sure. Sorry man, but we were in the neighborhood and thought we'd drop by."

"Don't want to be rude, but what the hell are you doing in our neighborhood? It's not exactly your style, is it?"

"Right, in both cases. What the hell *are* we doin'?" Angus laughed; nervousness clung to him like Mistletoe to a dying tree. "We're interested in how nice the vicinity here is, how friendly people seem to be. I admit I didn't expect that."

"Yeah, well it's pretty early. Just wait until the sun goes down. Jamal, my nephew, isn't allowed to go out after four o'clock and I would suggest you get out'ta here by three. We're real respectable before then, but after, things have gotten real bad since the summer started. Know what I'm sayin'?"

"Thanks for the advice." Angus wasn't sure how to react. "But we're here now and thought we'd come by to see how you folks are doin'," he stammered. "I read in the LA Times about their change in attitude, about how they want to do better reporting about the black community. It seems the whole world is changing and …" He was stammering for a reason to be there.

"Wally, who is it?" It was Cleo coming down the stairway.

Angus could see the house was what he expected. The furnishings that were apparent from his point of view were nice but they were second-hand or hand-me-downs. Porcelain teacups and fancy plates lined a shelf as decoration. Family pictures lined the walls. An old upright piano sat against the staircase.

Cleo was bursting, her belly full of a baby. She ambled down the stairs unable to move fast with her belly full and cumbersome.

"Who's there?" She stopped short when she saw his face. "Angus? What're you doing here?" She took a position next to her brother, pretty much blocking the doorway. "Hi." She waved at Sarah.

"Well, dunno exactly, just wondering how you all are."

"We're fine. I'm going to have a baby, as you can see. What brings you to our neighborhood?"

"Well…"

"I was just asking him the same thing, Cleo, and his answer was the same as you've just heard," Wally interrupted. "Come on, dude. Out with it. What do you want?"

"Wally, let's not be rude. Ask Angus and his friend in and I'll get some lemonade. I made some just a few minutes ago, before I ran up to the bathroom." She laughed, holding her stomach. "I do a lot of that lately."

"Yeah right." Angus answered feebly not sure how he was supposed to react.

"You mean, you aren't afraid, Cleo?" Wally asked. They could be carrying the virus."

"We'd like to come in, if that's okay," Angus said. "We've been holed up with our parents at home and don't think we've been infected."

Sarah was uncomfortable. "Angus, maybe we should just go."

"No, no." Cleo insisted. "Hi," she said to Sarah. "My name's Cleo. These men have no manners," she laughed.

"Yeah. Mah name's Sarah." She smiled and held out her hand to Cleo and they shook their greeting.

"You don't have weapons on you, do you, man?" Wally was suspicious.

"Let them in," Cleo said pointedly. "We'll go into the living room and sit down for a while. Excuse the mess," she said as she led them inside. "We weren't expecting company and it's the weekend, our time to relax and do nothing if at all possible, although Wally has to go to work later."

The room did have some breakfast dishes still sitting around. It wasn't as bad as advertised.

Suddenly, Jamal came storming into the house. He'd been out playing baseball with some friends. He had his mitt and a baseball bat … and a mask. "Hey Mom, Wally!" He stopped cold when he saw Angus. "I know you," he said. "You were at the birthday party at Zack's house and then you came to the hospital." He removed his mask as he stood staring at Angus.

"Yeah, dude. I came there to see you. I'd heard what happened and I thought I could cheer you up."

"Yeah," Jamal said, unsure he was telling the truth. He hadn't felt exactly cheered up by this guy.

"Sorry, I guess maybe we shouldn't've come by. Maybe it was a mistake." Angus suddenly felt on the spot and didn't want to be there anymore. "Uh, Jamal, this is my girlfriend, Sarah." Jamal waved a 'hello' to Sarah.

"Sit down, you two." Cleo said. "I'll get the lemonade. You want some, don't you Jamal?"

"Yeah, Mom. That'd be dope."

"So, wha' sup?" Jamal joined in like he was a grown man as they all sat down.

Wally smiled at the kid. Then, "Yeah, dude, what have you been doin' with yourself?"

"Well, the spring and summer were pretty much cooked, the way things have been goin', you know. We were both stuck at home with our parents just like everybody else. The COVID virus has been a real bummer of a problem. Right now, I'm thinking of starting college. It's a community college, and I'm kind'a stoked."

"Hey, that's rad," said Wally, trying to keep the peace. "So, what's your major, man?"

"I'll probably sign up for a science program. Never was that good at English, if ya know what I mean?"

"Yeah, dude," Wally laughed. "That's cool. I'm pretty hot with science, too. I just finished with a computer class. I thought I'd follow in my brother-in-law's footprints. He was a hell of a guy."

"Yeah, I heard about what happened. It had to be real hard for your sister."

"Oh, it was. She blamed herself for a long time and it took a lot of work for her to finally realize that cop was the only guilty party."

"That's tough. I'm glad she's better though." He struggled to find something else to talk about as the silence lingered in the air. "What kind'a job do you have now?" Angus asked Wally.

"I'm a waiter at an awesome hotel, downtown LA. We're only serving outside on the balcony now, but I make major tips down there. It's real lucrative."

"Wow, that's really bad, man." He was impressed with what he was hearing. "How'd you decide on that?"

"It was pretty much the best I could do without any college. It's great you're gon'na get college in. I'm encouraging Jamal here to study hard so he can go to a good school."

"Yeah, I guess it's important. I never thought I had a choice. My parents have insisted I go ever since I can remember."

Cleo returned with the lemonade in tall glasses with lots of ice. "This should help cool everyone down a bit," she said. She offered Angus and Sarah drinks. They took them gratefully.

"Yeah. Jamal doesn't have a choice either! Do you Jamal?" Wally added as he grabbed a lemonade from the tray.

Jamal, trying to downplay the whole thing said, "Sure Wally."

"Thanks, Cleo." Wally guzzled the icy cold drink. "Wow! That's terrific, woman. Thanks, I'll have some more."

She poured him another big glass while Jamal drank his. "Sarah, what's your plan after high school?"

"Ah'm lookin' into designin' clothes."

"Cool, girl. That sounds really hot. Do I detect a slight accent? What part of the country are you from, Sarah?"

"Ahm from Texas—Dallas." She replied.

"Oh Wow! The Great State of Texas." Cleo hesitated, then … "So, Angus, please tell us why you're here."

"Ma'am. I, I don't really know, except something's changed for me. And, I kind 'a wan'na, you know … apologize."

"Get out'ta here! That's some heck of a reason, Dude," Wally said. "I remember you weren't very friendly to my sister."

"That's true. And, I'm feelin' like I was misled. I dun'no, but it's been eatin' at me a lot."

"That's good Angus," Cleo said. "I think that's really good."

"You mean, all that stuff about white supremacy wasn't really your cup?" Wally added.

"No, it really wasn't. Sarah and I hooked up and well … she made me realize how stupid it all was." He smiled sheepishly at Sarah.

Cleo interrupted, "Angus, uh, I'm having some trouble with what you did though. I mean, you accused me of wielding a knife at Zackary. You knew that wasn't true, but you claimed it, nevertheless. What was that all about?"

"It is one of the biggest regrets I have and the one that eats away at me. I can't be sorrier. It was a stupid thing to do and I think everyone at the trial realized it wasn't true." He hung his head. "I'm real sorry, ma'am. I did it on an impulse and that just said a lot about who I had become."

"Well, thank you for the apology. You sure made my life a living hell with your lies. It was a very tough time."

"I can imagine and if I could do it over again, I wouldn't have been so vindictive. I wasn't so angry with you." Angus grabbed Sarah's hand and drew her closer … "I was really pissed with Sarah here. She broke up with me when she learned my beliefs. I was real mad and I took it out on you, and just because you were a black person."

Jamal, not wanting to be left out, asked, "You have any black friends, Angus?"

"Well, Sarah's bi-racial."

"Yeah, I kind'a thought so," Wally interjected. "Way to go, Angus!" he said smiling at Sarah.

Angus continued. "But there aren't any where I live right now with my family in Glendale. Sarah's family's the only ones brave enough to live where I live. I'm plannin' to move out soon. I got a car—saved up for it—and thought I could, ya know, live independently from my folks. Me and Sarah are talking about getting a place."

"That's cool," Wally interjected. "That's really cool. You could live where ever you like, maybe even in this neighborhood." He laughed jovially at his own joke, hitting his knee.

"Yeah, if my school were down here, we would." Angus' smile was one of relief.

"Where 're you goin'?"

"North Valley."

"Yeah man, that should give you some opportunities. I mean to meet folks who're different from you, know what I mean?"

"That might be really dope, Wally. Actually, I'm pumped about it, bein' out on my own and all, especially with Sarah if she'll come with me."

Just then, Cleo had a pain. "Ooh! That hurts. DAMN."

"Mom, you're not supposed to swear."

Edith entered just then. "Jamal, go on up to your room. I think your mama might be feeling something."

"Well, Gramma, if she's feelin' something, why can't I stay?"

"'Cause she might just swear, Jamal." She smiled. Turning to Cleo, she asked, "Honey, you alright? Was it a contraction?"

"Yeah, I think so."

"That the first?"

"Yeah. I haven't felt anything like that for about seven years," she laughed.

"Well, don't you worry yet. It'll be a while.

Wally turned to mush just then, and a little pale. His stomach turned into knots. "Ya' mean, you're going to have the baby?"

"You know I *am* nine months along, Wally, and I am *supposed* to have a baby. But not this minute; that was definitely a contraction."

"Oh well, we'll let you folks alone then, be on our way." Angus was getting anxious.

"No, no, not yet." Cleo said. "Mom, this is Angus Dunne. You met him at the birthday party at Zacks, and his girlfriend, Sarah."

"Yeah, I recognize you, young man." She held out her hand and he shook it. "I remember seeing you at Cleo's trial."

Edith shook hands with Sarah. "Welcome," she said smiling, and then regarded Angus for a moment. "Take off your masks, you two. You can't drink lemonade with 'em on."

"You sure?" Angus didn't want to take advantage.

"Yeah, I'm sure. Wouldn't say it if I wasn't." She smiled.

"I want to play the piano," Cleo interjected. "It'll keep my mind off the contractions. And, Jamal, you can stay. I'll try not to swear." She held out her hand to him. "Come on to the piano, sweetheart. I want you to sit down next to me so I can play something for you I've been practicing. It's new, or it's new to me and I love it. I think you will, too."

She sat at the old upright, spread the music sheet on the rack and said, "This is a piano piece composed fairly recently by a Canadian. His name is Michael Jones and it's called *I Hear the Earth Singing*. It is a long piece, about nine and half minutes, almost as long as this pregnancy," she laughed.

Angus looked at Jamal and felt a real connection with the kid as he sat on the piano bench next to his mom. Jamal put his arm around his mom's waist.

Suddenly, the doorbell rang. Startled, Cleo looked up at Edith. "You expecting anyone?"

"Nope."

"Walter?" She turned to ask.

"No, not me."

"Me neither, Mom," Jamal chimed in. "But maybe an angel is getting his wings," he smiled, referring to the doorbell.

"Well, someone has to answer the door," she admonished.

"I'll get it." Wally jumped up and grabbed the door handle, opening it to find Jamal's father, Jesse Henderson, standing there. "Jesse?"

"Hello, Walter." Jesse looked contrite, wondering if he should have come. "Sorry, if I'm bothering you."

"Uh, well, you're here. You may as well come in."

Cleo got up from the piano bench when she saw Jesse. Jamal was fast on her heels.

This was Edith's first encounter with him since Cleo was married to him. She knew he'd been by a couple of times to take Jamal for visits, but she'd missed seeing him; thought he was still handsome even though he looked like he'd been through a lot. He still wore his ethnic attire as before.

"Come on in," Edith said. She held out her hand and he took it hesitantly.

"Hello," he said, grateful she was being so welcoming. "Sorry to intrude on your family get-together."

"Daddy," Jamal said. He wanted to jump into his arms but, not sure how to feel, he vacillated.

"Yes, son. I am here to check on you and see your mom."

"What do you want?" He was showing up at a weird hour and hadn't called ahead of time like he should. Cleo was a little piqued about it.

"Well, uh."

She interrupted. "Would you like some lemonade, Jesse? We have some right here." She went to the table to pour him a glass.

"No thanks, Cleo. What I have to say won't take long."

Just then, Cleo had another contraction. "Oh," she doubled over holding herself in pain.

Edith went to her. "You okay, honey?"

"Sure, I'll be fine in a moment."

"I'm having a baby, as you can see, and I've started labor. Maybe what you have to say can wait."

Jamal took his hand and drew him to the couch to sit next to him and Angus. "Hi, I'm Jesse, Jamal's dad." He said to Angus and Sarah.

"Yeah, my name's Angus and this is Sarah." They bumped fists.

"Okay, so why're you here, Daddy?"

"I didn't expect an audience, but here goes. Truth is, I want to apologize for any pain I have caused you, Cleo, Jamal."

"Well, I ..." Cleo stammered.

"No, don't say nothin'. I just feel ashamed that I was so selfish. I didn't see it that way before, but I've had time to think about what has kept me away. I chose a woman over you and your mom, Jamal. I thought I was being real bad to be with her. In fact, I thought I was being hot and super-African. You know, doin' as many women as I could. That was selfish and self-serving. I am deeply sorry for all the pain I caused you." The words caught in his throat and tears ran down his face. "I should never have allowed that and the drugs to interfere with what was most important in my life … you, son."

"Jesse, thank you," Cleo said. "That is a stunning admission."

"Well, I don't care about all that. I just need you, Daddy." Jamal's honestly was all they needed.

"Well, I…" Cleo had to stumble into saying anything. Her mind was numb. "I am surprised and I guess I'm grateful to hear this from you. Have you talked to your mom?"

"Yeah, I spent the evening with her last night. She encouraged me to come see you. She understands, although it was a difficult conversation. I had to tell her about all the women and how I had a hard time resistin' the drug scene. I just ended up feelin' bad the next day and if I had a job interview, it was always a bust because I wasn't up to it."

"Well, I guess we all do stuff we regret later, Daddy."

"That's a very grownup thing to say, son."

"I'm glad to hear Jamal is so accepting. My acceptance may not come that easily," Cleo added.

"Well, I guess we've all had a front seat to some very important life experiences today," Wally commented, laughing trying to ease the tension.

"You know, Jesse," Cleo chimed in, "I was married again and this pregnancy is from my late husband, Clarence Delacroix."

"I heard. I'm very sorry for your loss. That must have been a traumatic experience for you, Cleo. I heard about your legal trouble, too. Jamal and I have had a little time to spend together since you called, and we seem to be getting along just fine. That right, Jamal?"

"Yeah Dad. It's been great! Mom, Daddy's real sorry."

"I can see that, honey," she replied.

Jamal reached up and hugged his dad hard around the neck. "I love you, Daddy."

Jesse returned the affection and hugged him back; then they exchanged dap, laughing excitedly.

Cleo was glad to see the warmth between the two. "A n g u s has come to let us know he has changed his mind about some very important attitudes, too," she said. "And, when you arrived, I was about to play a wonderful piano piece. I'd like to finish it before my new baby comes." Cleo laughed. "It's a very long piece, it may take as long as my labor." She laughed again.

"I'd like to hear you play, Cleo. You were always so good."

She sat down and started the composition.

Edith thought it was beautiful. The notes rose and fell in ways that were sweet and unexpected... She could almost see her new grandchild running and dancing through fields of tall grasses and flowers, arms flung to the sky in joy. And the music was at moments sad, almost desperate, then rising to be filled with love and hope. The notes soared and sank on the music of a world full of song. Optimism grew out of the struggles that Edith herself had endured, and, she knew, grew out of Cleo's hope in spite of the losses she had suffered in her young life—her father, Clarence, Zackary. Edith felt gratified with all of the events that had arisen and thought Cleo was bursting with hope, the hope she would give birth to very soon.

Inside, Cleo was holding back a lot of anguish. She didn't want to spill it all now—the memories she had of Clarence overwhelmed her as she forced herself to concentrate on the composition. Tears spilled from her eyes as the music, which always reminded her of the most important things in life, took over.

Fifty-six

CLARISSA LILAH DELACROIX came kicking and screaming into the world with her father's heart beating wildly in her little chest and her mother's talent filling her head and dancing in her tiny fingers. And, she carried within her teeny body all of the hope her mother had to give.

During the length of her life Clarissa Lilah Delacroix would carry forward all of her mother's hope by adding her own determination, steeped in the genes of a people who never rested in the dream that their lives would grow and thrive.

Postscript

THE LYNCHING OF the Malcombs and the Dorseys by a white mob of twenty-five men is said to be the last "known" lynching in the Southern State of Georgia. It occurred in 1946.

We stand upon ground made up of the bones of our ancestors and their dreams for the future. Let none of us fail to honor them.

Acknowledgments

THERE ARE NEVER ENOUGH WORDS to thank everyone who brought me to this work and those who helped in its accomplishment. I am deeply grateful to all the great writers who took the time and care to pen stories about ethnic peoples, especially about African-Americans. *Caste*, Isabel Wilkerson; *Between the World and Me*, Ta-Nehisi Coates; *White Fragility*, Robin Diangelo; *Why I am No Longer Talking to White People About Race*, Reni Eddo-Lodge, were my most recent sources. Over the years, I have read many works about slavery, Jim Crow, all of the lynchings and other abuses that were heaped upon those who happen to have color in their skin. It is unimaginable to me how awful it must have been and still is to live in a country that values its so-called white-skinned people too highly. However, it would be remiss of me to exclude those who have helped me immeasurably, many people I know personally and some I don't know at all.

Ted Hayes is high on my list of people to thank. Had it not been for my friendship with him over the years, I am not sure I could have been ready to write *The Color of Hope*. Gratitude also to Tyran (Ty) Henderson, now deceased, a dear friend for many years who gave me great insight into the black world. He is dearly missed. I felt like I got permission to write this story from a friend here where I live. Her name is Toni Vaz. She was a stunt person in the motion picture business back when most black people were overlooked. I spoke to her about my plan and told her the plot. She was enthusiastic and told me to call on her for help if I needed it. Her encouragement was and is invaluable. I couldn't end without a special nod to Michelle Obama and her wonderful memoir, *Becoming*. The character and early life of Cleo is fashioned after Mrs. Obama's as told in her book.

Special acknowledgement to John Towey and his beautifully masterful piano playing of the classics for the idea of giving Cleo talent at the classical keyboard.

Enormous thanks also to those who read the manuscript at different levels of its development, always encouraging me to continue and helping enormously with their suggestions and criticisms. Michael Gregg Michaud, Barbara Wagner Joss, Lulu Baskins Leva, Janet McMannis (now deceased) and David Haber, all did a wonderful job of steering me in the right direction.

Thank you also to Charles (Chuck) Alpert, II, who helped immeasurably regarding the legal system and Walter Anthony (Tony) Davison who put me in touch with him.

Many thanks to the Grey Quill Society who patiently listened to the chapters and gave me courage to continue.

And thanks must go to the COVID-19 pandemic which gave me all the time I needed to complete the work.

Last, but certainly not least, my publisher, Ben Ohmart, without whose support my work would never have been seen, and the great editing job of Stone Wallace. My deepest gratitude to all.

www.ingramcontent.com/pod-product-compliance
Lightning Source LLC
Chambersburg PA
CBHW052026020726
47501CB00004B/1274